Dead Man's Switch

Books by Tammy Kaehler
Dead Man's Switch

Dead Man's Switch

A Kate Reilly Racing Mystery

Tammy Kaehler

Poisoned Pen Press

Copyright © 2011 by Tammy Kaehler

First Edition 2011

10 9 8 7 6 5 4 3 2 1

Library of Congress Catalog Card Number: 2011920319

ISBN: 9781590588819   Hardcover
        9781590588833   Trade Paperback

Poisoned Pen Press
6962 E. First Ave., Ste. 103
Scottsdale, AZ 85251
www.poisonedpenpress.com
info@poisonedpenpress.com

Printed in the United States of America

To Pattie and Pam.
For opening doors and inspiring me to step through them.

To Chet.
For everything, always.

Acknowledgments

Begin at the beginning...I was raised to love books, laugh at silly humor, and appreciate an ironic twist. My family (by blood and love) nurtured those traits, and I thank you Gail Vann, Roger and Aggie Kaehler, and Richard and Barbara Fichtel (whom I still miss daily). Thank you to my best friends Chet Johnston, Pam Wheeler, Leticia Buckley, and Lara Kallander, who never doubted I *could* do it, if I only *would*.

I owe a great debt to the racing world for the generosity shown me long before this amounted to anything. Extra special thanks go to Shane Mahoney and Steve Wesoloski for enthusiasm and answers to random queries over the years, as well as to Andrew Davis for teaching me (sort of) what it's like to be a racecar driver and making sure I get it right—any errors are mine, not your doing. For fielding questions and continuing to entertain and inspire me, thank you to Patrick Long, Johnny O'Connell, Doug Fehan, Kevin Buckler and The Racer's Group, Leigh Diffey and Dorsey Schroeder (and the whole SPEED team), Pattie Mayer, Tim Mayer, Lauren Elkins, Drew Bergwall, Ed Triolo, Charlie Cook, Beaux Barfield, Bob Dickinson, and Julie Bentley. Kudos and thanks to Dr. Panoz for conceiving an amazing racing series.

Thank you to Dr. Jason Black, from whom all literary medical information (and ongoing friendship) flows.

Thank yous also to those who started, encouraged, maintained, and cheered my fiction writing: Leslie Keenan and her

Wednesday writing group, as well as Book Passage for doing so much to celebrate books and writers. Special shouts-out to Christine Harvey, Wendy Howard, Tracy Tandy, and Cary Sparks for "being here for me" from 400 miles away. Thank you to Hallie Ephron for timely and critical guidance (whether she knew it or not). To Harley Jane Kozak, Wendy Hornsby, and Simon Wood for inspiring me, cheering me on, and taking me under your wings. And to Joan Hansen for producing amazing literary events that allowed me to meet many wonderful authors.

Finally, many, many thanks to my agent, Lucienne Diver, who kept assuring me she believed in Kate and would find her a home. More bouquets of gratitude to Annette Rogers for taking me in, to the incredible Barbara Peters for showing me how to find the diamond under all the rough, and to Jessica, Rob, and the rest of the Poisoned Pen staff and authors for making me part of the family.

Author's Note

Fans of racing will notice that I have been creative in my descriptions of Lime Rock and the American Le Mans Series. The track surface and configuration, as well as the ALMS class structure, have undergone restructuring in the years since I wrote this, and I chose to preserve the pre-renovated character of both. I have similarly combined real companies, organizations, and locations with entirely fictional characters. I hope readers will forgive those liberties and enjoy the ride.

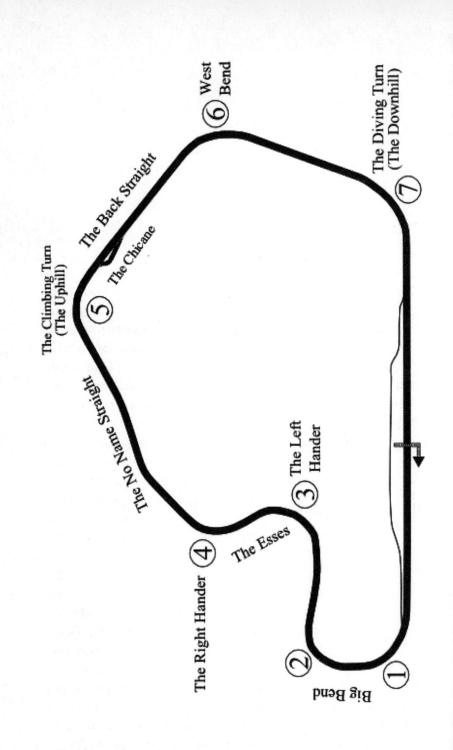

The Climbing Turn (The Uphill)

The Back Straight

West Bend

⑥

The Chicane

⑤

The No Name Straight

The Diving Turn (The Downhill)

⑦

The Right Hander ④

The Esses

The Left Hander

③

Big Bend

②

①

Chapter One

My first big break in auto racing came at the expense of someone's life. But I took it.

You have to have that attitude in racing. Sometimes you lose because your clutch cable breaks or your tire blows, and sometimes you win because disasters strike faster teams. No asterisks get posted next to those wins, no explanations. It's just racing. Sometimes you have it rough, and sometimes you get lucky.

On this day, I got lucky and the driver I replaced…"unlucky" would be an understatement. We're talking about murder.

I knew I'd endure weeks of sideways glances and sneers for a couple reasons. First, I'd be labeled an opportunist. It wouldn't be personal, because any driver hired as a replacement would receive the same treatment. Second, my skills—or lack thereof. "She could only get a ride by someone dropping dead." I'd have the last laugh from the podium at those naysayers.

What I didn't anticipate were the whispers that maybe I'd engineered my predecessor's death to get the ride. I wasn't sure whether to be offended, scared that someone who counted would believe them, or flattered that someone might think of me as ruthless.

I was female. I was twenty-four. I'd been steadily working my way up the auto racing food chain since I was twelve. I knew myself to be tenacious, aggressive, and stubborn. The racing world saw me as reserved and feminine, yet competent—and I worked hard for it. But the bottom line, to the good old boys of the racing world, was that I was too female to be ruthless.

I hadn't heard those whispers yet, and I wasn't thinking beyond the ride being handed to me on a silver platter. I was going to be paid to drive for one race, and maybe for the remainder of the season. Despite what followed, I'd make the same choice again in a heartbeat.

Chapter Two

As usual, I'd gotten to the track early that morning. It was July, and the American Le Mans Series, or ALMS, was running at Lime Rock Park in Lakeville, Connecticut, for the Fourth of July weekend. ALMS cars ran in the finale of four days of racing and celebrations that comprised the New England Grand Prix. Due to a local regulation against engine noise on Sundays, the racing world's standard race day, the main event would be run on Monday, July 5. Sunday would be a rare day off.

I was following the ALMS that year, traveling from race to race like the rest of the participants, though I didn't have a ride or team. I'd given myself a year to break into this series, which featured two classes of recognizable sportscars and two classes of prototypes racing together on "road" courses—tracks with hills and turns of varying sharpness to the left and right. No NASCAR ovals. In past years, I'd driven in some of the other races that accompanied the ALMS race, and now I wanted in on the marquee event.

I hoped my presence would remind everyone I was available as a full-time, occasional, or one-time-only driver. I'd take anything. I daydreamed of being offered a permanent ride for an ALMS team, but never asked myself what would have to happen to the other guy first.

I was more likely to get a ride if I was on the spot than sitting at home, so here I was, pulling my twenty-year-old Jeep

Cherokee into Lime Rock's entrance on Saturday at 7:00 a.m., ready for the day of practice and qualifying.

I waved my Series ID at the sleepy attendant and drove through the main gate.

"Get some coffee!" My words prompted a smile and a wave before he closed his eyes again.

At that hour, he didn't need to be alert. Only a trickle of cars was arriving at the track, most carrying people like me who had passes or tickets and knew where they were going. I drove across the creaky wooden bridge that spanned the racetrack and continued past grass parking lots to my right. I slowed as I veered left and approached another attendant. She saw the parking pass I held up and waved me through.

A golf cart labored up the hill from the paddock as I cruised down, and I recognized the driver who angled toward me.

"Good morning! If it isn't Kate Reilly!"

I stopped in the middle of the road and leaned out the window, pleased to see one of the two main SPEED Channel announcers. "Hey, Benny. I didn't see you yesterday. What's new this weekend?"

"Nothing. Leastways nothing I know about. You gotten into any trouble here yet?" He liked to tease me about my efforts to scrounge up a living from the Series. Benny Stephens was the primary announcer, the journalist by training, of the broadcast team. His partner, Ian McAllister, was the racing expert, having driven and won in every kind of racecar, series, and track that existed. I enjoyed their stories from thirty years of experience in the racing world. In return, they liked my gumption—that was Ian's word.

"Not yet. But I keep trying, Benny."

"You heard anything I should know about?"

"Only that too many teams have forgotten how to race through corners for it to be a coincidence. But I'm sure you know more than I do."

"That one's a puzzler. I've heard rumors, but no answers yet. Let me know what you hear, about that or anything else."

"Sure thing." With a wave, I continued down the hill. Benny and Ian's sources were a hell of a lot better than mine when it came to the Series grapevine, but I'd pass them whatever I heard. They were friends of mine, but I never forgot I was storing their goodwill for the day they'd report on me as a driver here, too.

I reached the bottom of the hill and turned right, heading toward the paddock. On impulse, I pulled over and turned off the engine. I was stopped in a strict no-parking zone, but I hopped out anyway and crossed the road, stopping at the fence that separated it from the pits. I curled my fingers into the chain link and took a deep breath. I loved this time of day at the track. Still some moist-earth smell and coolness from the thunderstorms the night before. Though I could hear noises from paddock garages, the racecars had yet to be fired up, and the birds had yet to be scared away.

A sense of impending action, possibility, and even tension hung in the air. These moments rejuvenated me. In them, I knew one day I'd drive the track as part of a professional team contending for a championship. One day I'd own this race. With a nod, I pushed off from the fence.

Back in my Jeep, I headed for a parking space at the far end of the infield. At Lime Rock, the paddock was located behind the pits along the front straight and in the interior of the one-and-a-half-mile track's first turn, the big, sweeping horseshoe called Big Bend. Each team had a temporary garage setup along the paddock's one-way loop road, where they could do everything from a tire change to an engine rebuild. At this race, the paddock loop wasn't full of team setups, and the end of it was given over to general parking for passenger cars. I drove around until I found an open space on the grass, finally squeezing between an obvious white rental on my left and a black-and-white-checked oil drum turned into a trash barrel on my right. I was pointing at the end of the track's Main Straight, separated from it by only a few yards of grass and another chain link fence.

My attention was half on the track and half on my parking job, and I jerked to a halt as I saw the trash barrel wiggle and felt a bump. I turned off the engine and sat looking at Big Bend. For the two hundred and thirty-seventh time I calculated where

I'd brake from 160 miles an hour and start the turn. I'd ridden around the track with a friend in a rental car last season. I'd also walked every inch of it, but I'd yet to drive that straightaway at speed.

I pulled the keys from the ignition, slung the lanyard with my ID around my neck, and got out of the car. As I twisted the key in the lock, I looked at my reflection in the window, reaching up to smooth stray shoulder-length hairs. My hair was stick-straight and black, two characteristics that took too much time and too many salon products to bother changing. Hair, fine. Face, fine. Same fair skin and blue eyes as always, touched up with a bit of powder and mascara. I looked down at myself. Comfortable dark sneakers, clean jeans, short-sleeve, tan button-down shirt—this one logoed by VP Racing Fuels, a sponsor of the Star Mazda series. My sunglasses were on my head—though the sun had yet to break through the overcast. My black baseball hat from Jean Richard, the official timekeeper of the ALMS, was in the car, as was the weekend's program and my all-important notebook, where I kept notes on drivers, cars, teams, and tracks. At least I look the part of the racing veteran, I thought.

I climbed onto my front bumper to look over the fence at the track, standing sideways, one foot in front of the other, and balancing with my fingers on the car's hood. I twisted to look back at the empty pit row, and followed the Straight down to the turn, seeing more details of the track surface from my perch. I was starting to jump down when I noticed a pile of dark fabric on the ground next to the trash barrel. Under the front of my car. I stared at it longer than it deserved, not understanding why.

Were there feet and shoes attached to the pile of cloth? My insides clutched. Part of a man's body was under my bumper. I lost my balance and scrambled to the ground, knees wobbling. I darted a glance under the car and saw my tire against the guy's leg, but not on it. I hoped.

I swallowed, looked again. I wasn't sure. I reached out a hand to shake his shoulder. No response. I tugged slightly, rolling him onto his back—then recoiled, cringing. Two facts were immediately clear. This was Corvette driver Wade Becker lying there. And Wade was very dead.

I froze. Then I heard my own ragged inhale as I turned and ran for help.

Chapter Three

I stopped on the crossroad that led to pit row on my right, scanning for someone familiar. Ahead: crew working on the M&Ms-logoed prototype car. I didn't know anyone there. To the left: a lone mechanic wrenching under the hood of the Saleen. I didn't know anyone there either. My best friend Holly was probably in her team's paddock, but she was at the farthest point away, over near the ALMS trailer. The Series people, that's who I needed. I took two steps and saw a man in an ALMS shirt writing on a clipboard. I was running toward him before I realized it was Stuart Telarday, the most annoying member of the ALMS staff and the third most annoying person on the planet.

I knew the feeling was mutual from the cranky look he gave me when I reached him.

"Stuart. Someone. The end of the paddock," I gasped, pointing back toward my car. "You'd better come. Look. Help." I was disproportionately out of breath for the brief run I'd had to reach him, and I knew he could see my distress.

"Kate? What's wrong? There shouldn't be any problem." He set off at a fast pace.

"Wade. Becker. By the trash can," I panted, trying to calm down, breathe, and keep up with him. "I hit him. Maybe." My words got jerky, as I spoke my thoughts aloud. "I think. Oh, God. Dead."

I led him to my car and gestured to the front, closing my eyes against what I knew he was seeing: Wade lying on his side, jaw slack, eyes open, skin almost blue. Stuart straightened with a grim expression, pulled out his cell phone, and flipped it open.

"Damn!" He closed it and looked at the Michelin Tower looming above the finish line a few hundred yards away. "No cell phone reception." He clenched his jaw and looked back at Wade.

I tried to think of anything other than the memory of Wade's open, lifeless eyes. "I think my cell works. Hang on." I retrieved my phone from my car. "Stuart? Should I move my car out of the way?"

Stuart took the phone from me. "Absolutely not. Everything needs to stay as-is. You said you hit him?"

"No! I mean, maybe. But only when I parked just now. I thought I bumped the trash barrel. I didn't know...." I leaned my head against the car window.

Stuart raised an eyebrow. "Why didn't you call someone?"

I was blank. Why hadn't I? "I panicked. I didn't want to deal with this alone. It's nothing to do with me."

"Hmmmm." He looked like he didn't know whether to believe me or not, but as that was how he always looked at me, I ignored him. I wrapped my arms around myself and listened to his conversation.

"Yes, I'll send someone to meet the officers at the entrance to the track. Yes, I'll stay—we'll stay here. Thank you." He pushed the button to end the call and looked at me again. Then he got on the radio that the ALMS employees used and called for help.

"Attention ALMS staff: we have an emergency at the end of the paddock near the footbridge. I have already contacted the proper authorities, and they are en route. Allison, meet officers at the front gate. Hamilton, Tony, and Michelle, get here with me, and get four other support staff to block all access to the paddock road past the road to Pit Out. I repeat: stop all but emergency personnel."

I didn't hear responses, but I assumed he received some, from the way he pressed the earpiece of his radio system into his ear. I snorted to myself: like a secret agent—and I bet he enjoys that look. To avoid thinking about Wade, I studied Stuart, wondering why he bothered me so much. It shouldn't be his looks, since he was, as my friend Holly put it, "one gorgeous hunk of a man." He was tall, probably six feet, with sandy hair and green eyes—one of those all-American types, except that he'd come to America early in life by way of German birth and Scottish ancestry. I'd never seen him not dressed in his neat-as-a-pin uniform of black trousers, black dress shoes, pressed white ALMS shirt, secret agent radio, ID, and clipboard. And I'd never seen him smile. The only hints of personality came through in his sunglasses—severe, heavy-rimmed, 1950s-engineer tortoise-shell numbers—and in his wavy hair that by the end of the day flopped onto his forehead. His hair was the only part of him that ever looked disheveled. That alone was intimidating.

Overall, Stuart Telarday stopped just short of being slick. That was the problem. I hated slick, couldn't trust it. But he had to be slick to be the Vice President of Operations and Communications for the American Le Mans Series at only thirty-three. The ALMS wasn't a huge operation, but he'd risen fast and proven himself a capable organizer and salesperson. Holly claimed she wouldn't kick him out of bed for eating crackers—or any other reason—but he still made my lip curl.

He stopped listening to his radio and studied me. "Everyone's on the way. What happened, anyway?"

I extended a hand for my cell phone, and after a moment's hesitation, he returned it. I took a deep breath and the reality of the fact that I'd discovered a dead guy slammed into me again.

"I got to the track, drove down here, and parked." I gulped and went on. "I guess I was focusing on the track. I squeezed in here and bumped the trash barrel—oh God, I hope it was the trash barrel."

"Then you looked and found him?"

I rubbed my arms for warmth. "No. I got out of the car and stood on my bumper to look at the track. Then I saw him."

"So you don't know what happened? To him?"

"Wha—No! Of course not. Why—what—I mean—no!"

Stuart raised a hand. "OK. You didn't look at him? Touch him?"

What was he, the police? Oh no, I was going to have to talk with police about this, too. "Yes. I mean, first I thought it was just a pile of clothes—or a drunk sleeping it off. I touched his shoulder to see. Then I ran for help." I was freezing. I opened my car door again, tossed the cell phone on my seat, and grabbed a sweatshirt.

I was struggling into it when I heard Stuart asking if I'd liked Wade. I shoved my left arm through the sleeve and blinked at him. "I didn't know him. What the hell kind of question is that? And why are you asking me these kinds of questions? Who elected you God?"

He spoke to me with exaggerated patience. "Kate, we have a hell of a situation on our hands. My job is to keep the Series running smoothly, so I want all the information I can get." His face started to flush and his voice to rise. "And I'd say you'd better damn well get used to these questions, because you found Wade's body. Wade, who was a healthy guy."

I didn't understand.

"Come on, Kate! Natural causes, suicide, or—help. It was one of those, and the police are going to figure it out."

I stared at him in shock. I'd not only found a dead guy, maybe I'd found a dead guy who had help getting that way. I felt nauseous. I crossed my arms over my chest and curled my hands into my sleeves, searching for warmth. I turned away from Stuart to see two cop cars and an ambulance pull around the bend.

Chapter Four

An hour and a half later, I was still talking to Detective Jolley, who was anything but, being tall, slim, and stern. The first time he asked a set of questions, I'd been intimidated. Imagine, me, Kate Reilly, being questioned by the police. Stuff like that didn't happen to me. The only time I talked to cops was in line at my hometown burrito joint. I didn't even get speeding tickets. The second time he asked them, I was tired. I was sitting on the asphalt of the paddock road, watching the police push my car away from the fence and the body. By the third time, I was annoyed. I explained again my arrival at the track and my parking job. Jolley seemed to think I'd come to the race that weekend with the sole purpose of finding Wade.

"Now, why did you park here?"

"Because it's a parking place. I could see the track from here." I stood up and started to pace. In spite of the sun and the growing warmth of the day, my butt felt flat and cold from sitting on the ground. I craved movement. I also realized I was not only starving, but dying for caffeine. Ugh. I might have to stop using that expression.

"And you said you drove straight in here?"

"Right—wait. I stopped for a minute down at the far end of pit lane."

"Why?"

"I wanted to look at the track and the pits."

"Why would you do that? You'll be here all day, right? See the track plenty."

I took in his sober khaki trousers, dark brown sports coat, and blue-striped tie. "Look, I'm a racecar driver. I'm looking for a job, and I want to drive this track. I like looking at it, thinking about driving it. It was quiet when I got here." I shrugged. "I wanted a peaceful look at it. My friend Holly tells me I'm trying to commune with the track."

"Who's that?"

"Holly Wilson. She works for the Western Racing Team. Over there." I gestured to the far end of the paddock. "Porsches. Bright orange, you can't miss them."

"Ms. Wilson is a friend of yours?"

"Yeah."

"Would she be able to verify where you were last night?"

This was new. "What? Last night?"

"Yes, Ms. Reilly. Where were you last night?"

"You're kidding."

He didn't look like he was kidding. "Just answer, please."

"Great." I ran a hand through my hair, wondering how the hell I'd gotten involved in this. I'd been minding my own business. Why'd Wade have to be dead under my car?

Detective not-so-Jolley was waiting for me to respond. "I was out to dinner and then I went back to my hotel room. I watched a movie and went to sleep."

"Was Ms. Wilson—"

"Yes, I was out to dinner with Holly."

"And when did you leave her?"

"About 9:30. We each had our own cars."

"Is she staying at the same hotel as you?"

"No. And before you ask, I was alone all night after I left her."

"I see. What movie was it, Ms. Reilly?"

"On TV?" He nodded. "It was Dirty Dancing. I missed the first few minutes, but I've seen it fifteen times."

He made a note. "And when was the last time you saw Mr. Becker?"

"Last night."

"Last night?"

"After dinner. Holly and I ate at The Boathouse. Afterwards, we stayed in the bar chatting with some people from the track—you know, other team members, drivers, a couple sponsors. Wade was there for a minute. That's the last time I saw him until—" I waved a hand toward my car.

A few yards away, a coroner's van had replaced the ambulance, and a gurney was being removed from it. I crossed my arms over my chest. Cold again. I couldn't stop staring at the activity surrounding Wade's body with the same sick fascination I felt driving past a traffic accident or flipping past a beauty pageant on TV.

Jolley had probably seen plenty of dead guy removal, because he didn't turn his attention from me. He cleared his throat. "Did he talk to anyone at the bar?"

"Yeah, Wade chatted with a couple people."

"When did that happen? When did you see him leave the restaurant?"

"About quarter to nine."

"And you left around 9:30?"

"Yes."

He gave a brief nod. "OK, that's it for now, Ms. Reilly. I'll need your contact information and to ask you not to leave the area."

"Not to leave the area? For how long?"

He held up a hand. "We'll be in touch, Ms. Reilly. Just for the next day or two at the moment."

"OK, my plan isn't to leave until Tuesday anyway." I gave him my hotel and cell phone information, wondering what the hell else he might find to talk to me about.

"I can go now?" He nodded. "And my car?"

"We'll find you and give your keys back when we're done with it."

Great. I took one last look at the scene, swallowing hard and turning my back on the sight of a black body bag being loaded into the van. I started down the paddock road, not realizing until I was almost upon it that there was a large crowd assembled at the caution-tape barrier. Any hope I'd pass easily through to some food and coffee faded as I got within ten feet.

"Kate! Kate! What happened? Who is it? What did you do? What did the police want with you?" The words came from a dozen mouths, with dozens more hanging open for my response. I ducked my head and made for an edge, trying to ignore the questions. Just before I had to do physical battle with the crowd, Holly came pushing through it to grab my arm. Petite, flaming-redhead Holly made a tunnel through the throng, yelling at the closest individuals by name and bullying or shaming them into letting us pass. I was never so grateful to see another human being in my life.

"You OK, Kate?" She turned around to hold people off with a snarl and tugged me toward her team's trailer.

I shook my head. "Not really. Food and coffee will help. I didn't eat on the way in and then…."

"You leave that alone, sugar. Just come on, and we'll fix you up."

I looked around as we walked and tried to focus on the normalcy of a race paddock instead of the drama I'd left behind. Teams worked on cars, fans stopped to watch and take photos, and three people stood talking in a small aisle where the back of one paddock garage met the back of another.

I did a double take and stopped walking, because one of the trio looked like a guy I'd known in high school: Sammy Bostich, a shaggy surfer-dude transplanted from California to Albuquerque, New Mexico. I only understood how dazed I was when I realized I'd been staring, mouth open, at a stranger for more than a minute. He wasn't Sammy Bostich, who, last I'd heard, ran his father's gas station at home; this guy worked for the SPEED Channel, judging by the logo on his polo shirt, the cabling gear strapped around his waist, and the laptop under one arm. But one of his friends was Jim Siddons, another driver in the ALMS. The third was an Asian guy I'd never seen before. They were all looking at me in shock.

I was beginning to wonder why they'd picked that out-of-the-way place to talk when Holly appeared in front of me, fists on hips.

"What now, Kate? I was three garages down the road."

"Sorry. I—a guy who looked like...." When I turned to gesture to them, they were gone. "I thought—never mind."

She tugged my arm. "Just keep moving."

Chapter Five

I owed Holly big time, I thought, as I sat on a green plastic deck chair in the Western Racing paddock area. Her team occupied a wide space, bookended by a motorhome on one side and a transport semi-truck on the other. Each vehicle sent out an awning from its side, leaving a four-foot uncovered gap between them. Under the motorhome's sheltering arm was a sitting area, racks of drivers' equipment, and a table and cooler both stocked with food and drink. Under the larger awning of the truck was the garage: enough space for two teams of eight mechanics to work on their cars at the same time.

I sat in the shade nibbling on a banana and waiting for it and the yogurt I'd eaten to hit my bloodstream. Holly had gotten me there without allowing anyone else to talk to me. She'd sat me down with food, water, and coffee, let me talk through the morning's trauma, and then left me alone. As I tried to pull myself together, I was happy to let the activity of the team flow around me.

There was always action in a race team's paddock—careful cleaning and polishing of a racecar, if not substantial rebuilding and assembly—and I sat watching, though I couldn't have described what specifically was taking place. The bustle of the mechanics, and of Holly prepping drivers' suits and helmets, was a blur, and I barely registered the bright, sunny day. With any justice, the skies would have been dark and heavy to match my mood. I kept replaying the sight of Wade's lifeless body, the empty shell. I'd never come face-to-face with death before.

"Reilly!" A voice boomed from my left, and I jumped in my seat. I turned to see Jack Sandham stepping around the rope barrier meant to keep fans out.

I choked down my last mouthful of banana and stood up. "Jack."

He loomed over me, yanking off his aviator sunglasses to reveal angry green eyes. I tried to hide my nerves. Jack Sandham, of Sandham Swift Racing, ran a Corvette team. Wade Becker had driven for Jack for more than ten years—right up until that morning.

"Jack. I'm so sorry about Wade—"

He growled at me. "I'm down a driver."

I winced. "I know. I found—I saw—I'm sorry about your team's loss."

"You."

"Me?" What the hell did he mean? I told myself not to feel guilty. I hadn't done anything to Wade, just found him and run. Well, OK, maybe I'd bumped him a little.

"You."

I was frozen.

He rolled his eyes and mimed turning a steering wheel. "You. Driving? For me." He nodded as he saw comprehension dawn. He still looked angry.

"Oh!" I gasped. "Yes. Thank you, yes!" I tried not to gush.

"For this race, and then we'll see about the rest of the season. Same terms as Sebring." He gave a curt nod and turned to leave.

Jumbled thoughts flashed through my mind: A ride! A Corvette! Wade. Oh God, this wasn't how this was supposed to happen—but I had a car to drive in the race! I spoke and stopped him a few steps away. "I'll work hard for this, Jack—to do you and Wade proud."

His face tightened at the mention of Wade's name. "Just don't turn into him."

Before I could respond, he spoke again, hands fisted on his hips. "What are you doing? Your time's mine now, Reilly. Get your gear and get to our setup. We've got practice in an hour."

He paused. "Shit. More like an hour from whenever they get this circus going again—but you've got to get up to speed." He ducked his head to clear the awning and stalked away.

While his sense of urgency had reached my brain, my limbs refused to respond. I sank back into the chair and looked at Holly, who stood in the open doorway of the motorhome.

"My, my." She exaggerated her Tennessee drawl.

"How about that?"

"That's great, sugar. We knew your time would come. But you watch your back."

My mind was full of the glories of my windfall. "What do you mean?"

"You're going to sit in a dead man's seat." I gaped at her. "I'm sorry, Kate, but you may as well get used to that now. Everyone will be watching. Some folks'll be jealous, and some'll be waiting for you to fail." She shrugged. "On the other hand, maybe they won't. Wade was Mr. Reckless, not Mr. Congeniality."

"Huh." I knew Holly'd been around the Series for about eight years, though she was only two years older than I. She'd told me many stories, but never any about Wade.

"You'd seen his unpredictability on the track. And off...well, he'd turned angry and grasping—acting entitled. Like he was going to take what, or who, he wanted and not care who was in his way. He wasn't sporting about it either. Heck, did his own boss seem broken up?"

I considered Jack's demeanor, and Holly went on. "But let's not speak ill of the departed. Hadn't you better get a move on?"

I jumped up. "Yeah. We'll talk over dinner?" She nodded and I gave her a hug. "Thanks for saving me. I'd better go kick some racing butt now."

She shut the door behind her and slipped her sunglasses on. "Your suit and things are in the car, right? I'll go battle that detective-man with you. Then you make sure you show 'em what you can do."

Chapter Six

I slowed my steps as I approached the Sandham Swift team paddock, taking deep breaths. I'd tried to use the trip to my Jeep to calm and focus my mind. It hadn't worked. My thoughts careened from giddy pleasure at a paying job to terror at the tasks ahead: driving the Corvette and dealing with the fallout of Wade's death. Because Holly was right. I was being handed a plum opportunity with a great team, but I was also stepping into the middle of a lot of emotion. I took another deep breath and started forward.

Aunt Tee caught sight of me first. "Kate!" She hurried to hug me, rising to her toes to throw her arms around my shoulders. "I'm so glad you're here, sweetheart."

I responded with pleasure, my first uncomplicated emotion of the day. Aunt Tee—officially the Hospitality Director—was the team mom for Sandham Swift, doing for them what Holly did for Western Racing: keeping the drivers and crew fed, hydrated, organized, and clean. Aunt Tee had been in racing for most of her adult life, working next to her husband Sam, a mechanic, crew chief, and now the chief engineer for Jack's team. Shorter than me and on the plump side, she was probably in her early sixties, though she had the energy, appearance, and strawberry-blond hair—thanks to Clairol—of a woman ten years younger.

She was no blood relation to anyone at the track, but she was everyone's aunt. And she was, bar none, the nicest person you'd meet in the Series. I relaxed a notch as she took my helmet and led me forward. "You just set your things down here and let me take care of them." She was already pulling my driving suit out of my duffle and shaking out its folds.

I looked around. Sandham Swift's setup was almost identical to that of Holly's team: motorhome and transport truck with respective awnings covering a sitting area and a temporary garage. Everything in the same color scheme as the cars, which for Sandham Swift was black with white and yellow racing stripes. As befitted the team's longevity in, and commitment to, the ALMS, their paddock boasted a few extra feet in width and a better location, only one space away from the access road to the pit. I swallowed hard. Given the events of that morning, I'd have preferred a less prime location, farther away from my car and police activity.

"Thanks, Aunt Tee. How is everyone here?"

She put my suit on a hanger and turned to me. "We're trying to move forward again. It's been a real shock." She gestured to the garage where I saw crew members listlessly working on the racecars. A couple guys cleaned bodywork with spray bottles and rags, others sat with a soda or a cigarette.

"Do they—Does everyone know I'm…."

"Yes. When Jack told everyone about Wade, we talked about it—would we be going racing, and who'd be driving. Everyone agreed we'd carry on and he'd look for you."

"Is everyone really upset? Were they close to Wade?"

Aunt Tee tilted her head. "Upset, yes, about the suddenness and surprise of it. And the passing of a human life. But close to him? Wade wasn't one to get close to people. He did his job well— that boy could be fast on the track. And he could be a charmer, particularly when he wanted something. He knew enough to keep on my good side, but he didn't bother with anyone else." She moved to hang my suit with others on a rolling rack.

"People didn't like him?"

"He'd been with the team since the beginning, before the rest of us. He belonged here in a way no one but Jack does—and Ed Swift, of course, but Ed's never here. Wade was a great driver. He pulled off some wins by sheer guts alone."

"So Wade didn't have to try. He was good, and he had seniority—so it didn't matter to him if the crew liked him."

"No, he never really tried." She glanced at the crew. "And that really hurt them personally and hurt the team's overall performance."

I nodded. I'd learned through mistakes of my own and careful observation that the key to a great car was a relationship with the crew based on mutual respect. Solving problems together would always yield the best results.

She nudged me out of the way and started unpacking my shoes and racing undergarments. "Don't you go behaving like that, Katie."

Though her hands were full, I gave her a quick hug. "Never fear. You'd keep me in line, anyway."

"True. Now you go get used to that car again. I've got your things here."

I studied the cars as I walked toward them. Sandham Swift was a private team that ran two Corvette C6.Rs purchased from General Motors, Numbers 28 and 29. The Corvettes competed in GT1, Grand Touring 1, along with large Ferraris, Vipers, Maseratis, Aston Martins, and Saleens. GT2 featured Porsches, smaller Ferraris, Panoz, BMWs, and Mazdas. The Le Mans Prototype classes, LMP1 for the larger versions and LMP2 for the smaller, were swoopy, unrecognizable cars purpose-built for racing by manufacturers like Audi, Porsche, and Acura. Our GT sportscar classes looked like cars you'd see on the street. More or less.

In all classes, two drivers shared a car in each race, and typically three drivers rotated stints in the longer races. Wade had driven different cars—mostly Corvettes—as the Number 28 for the eleven years of the team's existence. Mike Munroe had been his co-driver for the last three years, and I'd joined them as the third driver for last season's twelve-hour race at Sebring. I knew the car, team, and co-driver a little bit.

The crews from both cars greeted me as I entered the garage area. I introduced myself to everyone, shaking hands and imprinting a dozen names on my brain. Some were new to me, some I'd met last year, and two I had kept up with from Sebring: Bruce Kunze, the car's crew chief, and Sam Nichols, the chief engineer and Aunt Tee's husband. The 29 car's crew drifted back to their side of the garage, and I exchanged small talk with my new crew about the track surface and the car's performance. I tucked away the glory of the words "my new crew" and focused on the technical aspects of the car.

"The setup isn't much different than last year at Sebring, Kate." Bruce pulled a red shop rag out of his back pocket and wiped a microscopic speck of dirt off the car. Bruce was in his fifties with snow white hair cut into a military flattop. He knew everything there was to know about Corvettes and then some, from the first C1 street and race models in the 1950s to the most recent, the C6 and the C6.R.

Sam chipped in. "Just a few regulation changes is all—ride height, rear wing, that sort of thing. But let's get you in there so you can get a feel for it again." He moved toward the car door, and I stopped him with a hand on his arm.

"Sam. Bruce. I'm sorry about Wade. I feel awkward, being here so soon."

Sam gave a sad smile. Bruce nodded and patted my shoulder. "Life goes on. So does racing. Now let's get you in here."

Five minutes later, I was happily ensconced in the seat of the 28. The car's roll cage, made of two-inch-diameter steel tubing, had high sides, and to climb in, I'd slithered feet, hips, shoulders, and head through the narrow opening. It was an easier maneuver that morning because I wasn't also encumbered with a helmet, a head restraint collar, or a door, as I would be during a race. The steering wheel was removed to get in and out, and as soon as I was inside, I'd taken it off its ceiling hook and pushed it down hard on the steering column to lock it into place.

Because the Corvette's seat was in a single fixed position as far back as possible, I was only able to reach the pedals through a conjuring trick of Bruce's. He'd produced the custom-made seat insert I'd used last year at Sebring from the recesses of the transport trailer, so I could reach the steering wheel, throttle, clutch, and brake—and see over the dashboard.

I was refamiliarizing myself with the buttons and switches on the dash and wheel when my stomach lurched. Looking through the Corvette's windscreen—not one piece of glass, but three pieces of heavy-duty plastic held in place by two metal strips running from roof to hood—I'd seen four men emerge from the transport and look my way: Jack Sandham; Tom Albright, Jack's media guy; Stuart Telarday; and Detective Jolley. This wasn't going to be good.

Chapter Seven

Surveying the controls of the machine I was sitting in let me ignore the four men walking toward the car. The interior of the Corvette C6.R was more airplane instrument panel than passenger vehicle. The hard, molded-plastic dashboard was all that remained of the Corvette's origin as a luxury sports car, though it now featured rows of lights, toggle switches, and a digital display screen. The rear-view mirror—useless because of the solid firewall behind the driver's seat—had been replaced with a small video screen fed by a camera mounted in the rear bumper. Everything unessential inside—stereo, climate control, glove box, airbags, passenger seat, and more—had been removed. Everything essential—seat, seatbelts, steering wheel, shifter—was upgraded to tougher, race-ready versions.

Safety was a primary concern, so the driver's seat had high molded sides and a five-point harness seatbelt. With my seat insert in place, I was stuffed like sausage into casing. Legs, back, shoulders—I had no wiggle room anywhere. No room to move meant I wouldn't bang into the sides of the driver's seat lap after lap as I negotiated turns at forces up to three Gs—or go far in a wreck.

Space was at a premium in the rest of the car as well. A large eye bolt stuck out of a louvered vent in the top center of the dash, holding taut a safety net from ceiling to shoulder height through the middle of the cockpit—a net that would keep loose items from hitting me in an impact. Cooling hoses, an on-board computer, and lots of wires filled the remainder of the small interior.

I was touching each button and switch in turn, remembering and rehearsing their positions, when I heard a voice next to my ear.

"Now you're here, Ms. Reilly."

I turned to find Jolley's face close to mine, peering into the car. He straightened, and I leaned left, poking my head out. I nodded at the group without saying anything.

Jack Sandham clapped his hands together and rubbed them back and forth. "Kate's going to fill in for us. Just getting used to the car again. Kate, have you met Tom Albright? Our marketing director and go-to guy for all things nonmechanical. Tommy, Kate Reilly. You'll need to get some background from her so you can do a press release…well, to promote her."

Stuart chimed in. "I'll need some of that information as well."

I scowled at him. "Why?"

"For our own releases. Damage control."

Jolley kept watching me. "Still, it's strange you're here now and you found Mr. Becker this morning."

"Lucky me. I'll be another minute." I pulled my head back in.

I took more time to think and mime my way through accelerating, upshifting, braking, downshifting, pressing communications buttons, making lights blink—a message to slower cars to pull over—and checking all displays. When I'd thought my way around every turn on the racetrack, I sat there for one last minute with my hand on the shifter, wishing I could remain in the car the rest of the weekend, rather than deal with people. But that wasn't going to happen. I hauled myself out.

Jack and Tom Albright were over in the sitting area talking with Aunt Tee, Jack towering over her like a cartoon at nearly twice her height. Stuart and Detective Jolley stood at the front of the 28 car speaking quietly. I approached them, determined to be pleasant.

"Look, Detective Jolley. I apologize if I was flip. If they haven't told you, I'm here because Jack asked me to drive for them.

Remember, I said I drove with them once last year? So I know the car and the team. I'm a logical choice."

"It's just an interesting coincidence."

"An unfortunate one."

Stuart sniffed—the man actually sniffed. "A coincidence I'm going to gloss over, myself."

"How much are you really going to have to talk about this?"

"You think this isn't news, Kate? My office has received a dozen calls already—not counting questions from the media on-site."

"Why?"

Stuart lifted a palm. "The detective here is from the Major Crimes unit."

"That means—you're sure? Not natural causes? Suicide?" I addressed them both.

Jolley shook his head.

"Muh—" I didn't want to believe it, though I'd been chewing on the idea all morning. I blinked, emerging from the shock and numbness I'd wrapped myself in. Voices were louder, colors brighter, and my situation more precarious. I got it. I was a murder suspect, due to coincidence and bad timing.

"Detective, let me be clear. Just because I found him and I'm here—I didn't kill him!"

He stopped me with a wave of his hand. "Don't leave town, Ms. Reilly. Mr. Telarday, I'll be in touch." He nodded at Stuart and left the paddock.

Stuart regarded me without expression, and the normality of that helped me regain my focus. "I'm going to talk with Jack—do you know when we're back to the schedule?"

He pulled a slim notebook out of his shirt pocket and flipped it open. "For ALMS cars: the hour of morning practice was canceled, lunch will run from 1:05 to 2:00, and there are thirty minutes of practice time at 3:00, before your class qualifying starts at 3:30." He closed the notebook. "Plus, I think, we'll have this team skip Monday's autograph session. We'll put up a sign, you're not participating due to Wade's untimely passing...add a note that donations can be made to a charity in his name." He was talking more to himself than to me as he started toward the team's sitting area.

I fell into step with him, worrying over the most important information he'd given me: the team was only going to get thirty minutes of practice time that day. Added to thirty minutes of warm-up before the race itself, that gave us one hour. Even if my new co-driver, Mike, gave me most of that time, I'd still only have forty or forty-five minutes to get used to the car before I had to hang my guts out in a race. No prep time and lots of pressure. I had this shot to race hard and well, to earn my place. And there might be that other matter of proving I didn't kill Wade for the chance.

I reminded myself I was a good driver and I was prepared for this opportunity to perform. I hadn't killed Wade and had nothing to hide. Then I reminded myself not to hyperventilate.

Stuart was explaining the adjusted schedule for the day to Jack and Tom, as well as his plan for the autograph session. I agreed we didn't need a mob scene, and we didn't need to explain the situation to the public. I smirked. That was a job for Stuart's secret agent team.

But there was other business to take care of: I needed to talk to the crew chief, the chief engineer, my co-driver, and anyone else who could tell me how to manage the car on this track. I also needed to convince Detective Jolley I hadn't committed murder, but right now, racing came first.

"Jack? Stuart? I'm sorry to interrupt, but I need to get moving, talking to Bruce, Sam, Mike—anyone seen Mike?"

Tom nodded toward the transport. "I think he's still over there."

"I'm sorry, Tom. We need to talk, too. There's a lot to take care of right now."

"No problem, Kate." His smile lit up his face, and goodness radiated from him. I decided Tom was someone to trust. Plus, he was cute.

"I'll check in with you or Tom later for your background info," put in Stuart.

Jack put a hand on my shoulder. "Tom, shadow Kate for a couple hours. Get her whatever she needs, ask your questions, find Mike, that sort of thing. Then connect with Stuart later. OK, Kate?"

"Sure. Come on, Tom, let's hit it."

Chapter Eight

My life was drama-free for the next thirty minutes. Tom and I found Mike and collected pens and track maps from Aunt Tee. We commandeered a corner of the garage area, taped a map to a small white board, and propped it against the trailer on a storage cabinet. Mike was talking me through his data from yesterday's practice.

"Some oversteer. It got a little loose around Big Bend and the chicane. You'll have to ask Bruce what he did about it—lowered tire pressure, adjusted the wing, I'm not sure. We'll see how it is today. Otherwise the car was solid." He held a heavily marked-up track map in his hands, one of several he'd produce for the crew over the weekend. That was part of the driver's job: give the crew detailed feedback, usually in the form of scrawled notes on a map and plenty of discussion. Since I hadn't yet been in the car, I made notes for myself on tricky corners, the best passing areas, and where to watch for the car getting loose.

"Any tricks with the chicane?" Lime Rock's touchy S-shaped section was called the "chicane," though the word was also used to describe any section of a track with right and left turns in quick succession. I didn't like asking this kind of question of another driver, preferring to answer it for myself. But I wouldn't get much seat time, and an error-free drive was more important than my pride.

Mike shook his head. "It's pretty straightforward. Now, the thing you want to be ready for is that bump in the apex of the

Diving Turn." He referred to the downhill right-hander that led onto the Main Straight.

"Bump?"

"Yeah, you see that great turn, take a normal line through it—and there's a bump in the middle of it. We've got our dampers set so it doesn't affect us, but it'll move you some. So be ready. Also, the Porsches will turn in late to avoid it, so be prepared for that. And don't get too far offline in that corner or you'll head into the tires."

"Bump, check." I made a note on the map on the board. "Has this team run into any of the problems that other cars have been having?"

"You mean losing traction in the corners or something?" At my nod, he went on. "No, hasn't happened to us. Last I heard, they don't even know for sure what's causing it. What've you heard?"

"A lot, but not much worth believing. Just that it's more likely to be the ECU than tires or fuel." The ECU, or engine control unit, was the brain of the racecar and modern street cars. A mini-computer, it controlled the components that made the racecar go, from engine timing to fuel behavior, and monitored most everything else, from engine and oil temperatures to engine, wheel, and vehicle speed. In addition to being preprogrammed to manage the engine, the ECU logged data, sending it to the pits in real time.

"Yeah, from what I've seen around our garage, it seems like ECUs—but only Delray's brand. I don't know any details, but the teams that have had problems all use Delray ECUs."

Tom spoke up. "I know that Victor Delray's been in and out of our place a lot—and his other team garages—looking pretty worried."

We were silent for a minute. Then Mike slapped a hand on his knee. "We're going to hope they figure it out so the gremlin doesn't get us. Now, you'll want to know where to pump the brakes." Mike looked embarrassed.

"What?"

"I'm telling you what you know or will figure out in ten seconds on track. I don't mean to treat you like you don't know how to drive."

I patted his hand. "Let's pretend I have no ego. I'd rather hear it twice than miss something important. Keep talking."

"All right. Number one, at the end of the front straight, before Big Bend."

I made a note. When nearing the end of a long straight and heading into a heavy braking zone, common practice was to tap the brakes with your left foot, even while your right was firmly planted on the throttle—to make sure the brakes were ready when you needed them.

Mike put a finger on the map. "Number two, right before West Bend, tap the brakes to balance the car."

"Weight's all at the back?"

"Yeah. The Back Straight is a slight uphill, then West Bend's a fast enough turn that you'll need it all balanced under you."

"Gotcha." The less weight on the front tires, the less turning them would make the car turn. Tapping the brakes at the end of the straight wouldn't slow the car, but would shift some of its weight forward to help me.

"Good to know. Any other surprises? Anything unusual—"

A wailing voice captured our attention and we turned to see a knot of people—Aunt Tee, Sam, Bruce, and some crew—bending over someone in a chair next to the motorhome. Then another cry and a pair of flailing arms erupted from the middle of the group, pushing the cluster of people apart. It was a woman I didn't recognize, but who I'd noticed arriving a couple minutes before—noticed because her look just screamed money. Obviously Tom and Mike knew her, because they both groaned.

I looked sideways at them. "Yes?"

Tom shook his head, watching the scene, but making no move to join it. Mike grunted and turned his back. The woman had her arms wrapped around her middle and was keening—there was no other word for it—as she rocked back and forth in the chair. It all seemed very dramatic.

Tom sighed. "That's Susanah." He pronounced it with an "ah" in the middle.

"Su-saah-na?" I exaggerated the syllable.

He didn't laugh. "Right."

"Who's that?"

"She's the wife of one of our sponsors. Mrs. Racegear.com—that is, Mrs. Purley, wife of Charles Purley, who owns Racegear.com."

"What's Su-saah-na's deal?"

Mike snorted. Tom hesitated before speaking. "She and Wade were…close."

"Understatement," muttered Mike.

I nodded. "I take it that Mr. Purley didn't know—or care?"

"Ha!" exclaimed Mike. "He'd care. We were waiting for the blowout."

I turned to Tom, who shrugged. "Not the best kept secret, except from Mr. P."

I was appalled. "You had to be worried about messing up the sponsorship. Wade knew better than to bite the hand that feeds you."

Mike leaned close to us. "Let's not forget, the woman is hot. Besides, Wade wasn't the only one. There have been others."

"And no one asked any questions," Tom put in. "Honestly, I can't prove there was anything going on—" He saw the look on Mike's face. "You've got proof?"

"Saw 'em."

Tom grimaced. "It looked suggestive—a strange relationship. But no one said anything."

"Just when you think you've seen it all," I commented. The race circuit could be a soap opera. A small, insular community, engaged in a competitive and high-energy pursuit. Emotions and passions boiled over at the slightest provocation. It was pure melodrama, with plenty of sex and aggression thrown in. There was nothing like racing for entertainment—and I didn't just mean the on-track action.

Aunt Tee managed to guide Susanah into the motorhome.

"That'll stop her. Mrs. Purley does love a good public show."
Mike sounded both amused and disgusted.

I shook my head and returned to the track map, wondering
how else to save precious tenths on the track. Mike put a hand on
my shoulder, and I could see a kind look through his sunglasses.

"Kate, no one expects us to win—no one expected Wade and
me to win. They expect a good effort, which you'll give. You've
got the skill, and you'll get your feet under you fast. I'm glad to
have you here. Hell, you'll be a lot more fun to work with!" He
finished with a heavy pat, and I tried not to stagger from the
impact. Mike reminded me of a bear: unruly hair, big brown
eyes, large in every dimension—and little of it was fat.

The sudden cacophony of thirty buzzing engines stopped
further talk. As the clock struck eleven, practice time was officially on for the open-wheel, Mazda-powered racers, and almost
three dozen of them were laying on the throttle to get out of the
pits fifty yards from where we stood. As always, the first blast of
engine noise from a full complement of racecars was stunning.
Regular communication outdoors was over for the day, except
for the lunch hour and a few minutes between practice sessions.

I gave Mike a thumbs up. We both reached for our custom-
fitted earplugs and poked them into our ears, while Tom pulled
a foam pair out of a plastic bag.

Mike leaned in two inches from my ear. "I'm going to grab
some food and relax. I'll catch up with you around two. We'll
talk strategy."

He left with a wave, and I leaned close to Tom. "I need water
and a break."

I heard his voice through my earplug. "Sure, water in the
coolers. Then the office." He pointed to the front of the transport
trailer. "We'll swap stories."

Tom was the team's media director, which also meant press
guy, computer guy, human relations guy, and Jack's right hand.
I'd give him my background, and he could tell me what I needed
to know about the team.

We headed across the garage area to the coolers next to the motorhome, sidestepping our Michelin tire engineer studying eight tires on a rack. I was taking the first swallow of ice-cold bottled water when a wiry crew member opened the cooler packed with sodas. He grabbed a cola and sat down on the closed lid, the deep, tanned wrinkles of his face creasing into a wide smile. What I found strange in his manner was the cheerfulness of it, the jauntiness of his walk—at odds with the demeanor of everyone else in the team's compound.

I gave him the half smile and nod of the unacquainted. Tom capped his water and turned to us. "Oh, Alex." The guy stood up, and Tom went on, "Kate, Alex Hanley, brake specialist for your car. Alex, Kate Reilly."

Alex and I shook hands, and he beamed at me. "Pleased t'meetcha, Miss Kate."

He was a little man—about my height and weight, but at least thirty years older—and as friendly and engaging a person as I'd ever met.

"Oh yah, sure, you betcha, and I'm pleased t'meetcha. Glad to have you around—replacing the likes of you-know-who." At least I thought that's what he said. He gave my hand a final shake and winked at me before strolling back to the garage.

I turned to Tom, surprised, as he spoke. "Not Wade's biggest fan. Come on, I'll fill you in."

We settled onto the leather banquettes of the small office at the front of the transport trailer. With the door closed, racecar noise was reduced to a dull roar, and we took our earplugs out.

Tom flipped open his leather portfolio. "I'm sorry. Since I'm new this year, I don't know your background."

"No problem. I've got it written down, and I'll walk you through the highlights." I produced my racing bio from my shoulder bag and went through the basics: started out in karting at the age of eight, graduated to open-wheel and sportscars at eighteen, and raced in a variety of cars and series, nationally and internationally.

"So I'm clear, you raced with this team once before?"

"Last year at Sebring." In response to the questioning look on his face, I elaborated. "Jack asked me to join you guys for your two endurance races since then: Petit Le Mans last September and Sebring again this year. I had a commitment to another race for Petit and had a family issue this year for Sebring."

I still felt the disappointment of missing those opportunities, but the "family issue" had been my grandfather in the hospital with double pneumonia. He'd been discharged the day of the race, and we'd watched it together, Gramps chastising me for giving up the chance to race with the team. I'd preferred being there with him all healed and healthy.

"Let's see. Last year Sebring, the 28 car was fourth, right?" He muttered to himself. "Maybe start with that, great performance with the team, kept its eye on her, skills have grown over the years…." His words became unintelligible as he scribbled away on his notepad.

I looked around the room, thinking how different this experience was to when I raced with the team before. That had been a twelve-hour event, the season opener, and stressful. I'd felt like the green rookie I was, and no one besides Aunt Tee had done much to make me feel more comfortable. Jack had been busy with sponsors and the inevitable last-minute problems of a brand new racecar. Mike had been reserved, either shadowing Wade or plugged in to his iPod. And Wade had been the worst, totally ignoring me.

I dropped my head into my hands. For ten whole minutes I'd forgotten why we were here.

Chapter Nine

"You OK, Kate?" Tom asked the top of my head.

"Just still trying to process it all."

I heard him sigh, and I sat up straight. "It must be weird for you, too. You really knew him."

"I didn't really know him. But yeah, he was part of things here. I don't know whether to be sad, angry, or relieved."

"Relieved?"

He bit his lip. "I shouldn't have said that."

"But that's what you meant?"

He got up, made sure the hall outside the office was empty, and sat back down. "OK, relieved. He was a handful. He didn't want to give me quotes for press releases, didn't want to deal with sponsors. He thought I was a complete idiot, and he hated me."

"Why do you think that?"

"He told me so."

I tried to imagine the conversation. "How rotten for you."

"No kidding. I don't know what he was like in the years before this one, but he was a pain in the ass this year. So, yes, relief at not having to deal with that." He looked contrite. "Not that I wished him dead."

"Of course not. Who would? Oh, should I be concerned about Alex, the brake guy?"

"No, he seems to like you, but he and Wade got along like oil and water—like race fuel and oxygen. Instantly combustible.

Wade blamed Alex for any problem on the car, and Alex gave it right back to him."

"Sounds like fun."

"No. Something was going to give soon."

"Move Alex to the other car?"

Tom pursed his lips. "That or let him go. He's a genius with brakes and everything about wheels and suspension. But he's a hothead, and Wade outranked him. Wade was getting more vocal about Alex."

I didn't like asking, "Did Alex know what was coming?"

"Well, he'd almost have to have some idea, which probably explains the attitude today." He paused. "But wait, you don't mean—"

I waved both hands in the air. "I'm just asking. Wade seems to have been killed. Since I'm Detective Jolley's A-number-one suspect, and since I can't prove I was in my hotel room watching a movie, I'd like to suggest some people who aren't me. I guess that's selfish."

"I don't think so. Natural. I guess if it was important to Alex to stay here, that means he has a motive. I hate that I said that."

"I know. I don't like wondering who had a reason for hating Wade."

Tom rubbed his hands over his face. "Not just who had a reason, but if they acted on it."

We sat in silence for a minute, then Tom cleared his throat. "I never thought I'd say this, but I want you to know I didn't do it."

"But—"

"I was with people until one in the morning, and I'd loaned my car out, so I didn't have one. I was stuck at the inn five miles away."

"Jolley's the one you should tell, not me."

"I did tell him. But if you're a suspect—even though you didn't do it—you've got to wonder who's walking around with a big secret. I just want you to know I'm clean."

"Thanks, Tom. I appreciate it." I paused. "Maybe we can figure out some other secrets."

"Huh?"

"I need to give Jolley names, so he'll stop focusing on me. Will you help me figure out a list of people who had a grudge against Wade?"

He looked alarmed. "I don't want to feel like I'm tattling on people to the police."

"I wouldn't tell them unless it's a real possibility. But I've got to do something." I was already thinking I'd regret asking for his help.

He looked at his notebook and fiddled with his pen. "OK. I'll ask around."

A knock on the door startled us. Tom opened it to reveal Stuart Telarday, ALMS VP extraordinaire.

"Sit down, Stuart." Tom was full of guilty welcome. "I, uh, Kate and I were just—I was about to get quotes from Kate."

"I have good timing then." Stuart sat, and they waited for me, Tom's pen poised over paper, Stuart's mini tape recorder running.

I dragged my jumbled thoughts into line. "All right. I'm terribly sorry for Wade, for the team, and for the sport, which has lost one of its stars. I'm grateful for the opportunity to drive with Sandham Swift Racing, and I realize I have some big shoes to fill. If I can be half the driver Wade was, I'll be happy."

Stuart looked at me as Tom finished writing.

"What?"

"Direct, humble, discreet. Not bad."

"Thank you."

He and Tom shared a glance.

"What's that about?"

Tom responded as Stuart put away his recorder. "Just that you're already a lot more than half the driver Wade was."

"Really?" I aimed that at Stuart.

"You'll probably be better. Thanks for this." He opened the door to leave and Tom stopped him.

"Stuart, Kate and I were talking about everything going on here today—"

Fortunately, I was hidden from Stuart by the open door. I made a slashing motion across my throat at Tom.

"Yes?" I heard from Stuart.

"Oh," Tom fumbled. "Nothing really. We're glad we don't have to do the driver autograph session on Monday. Thanks. See you later!"

Tom shut the door and turned to me. "Why didn't you want me to say anything?"

"Why did you?" I berated myself. Why the hell had I trusted Tom so quickly? How did I know he would help and not just blab?

"Look, Tom, I can't tell everyone that I'm wondering who might have had it in for Wade and oh, by the way, ask them how they felt about him. Maybe you should forget asking around."

"Why? Of course we can't say that to everyone. But this is Stuart."

I wrinkled my nose.

"How come you don't like him?"

"I don't know. Oil and water."

"He's a good guy. I've gotten to know him pretty well this year. He may seem rigid and stern, but that's business. He's not like that underneath. He could help us."

I was saved from further discussion by a thumping on the door. This time it was Benny and Ian from SPEED Channel, wanting an on-camera interview—quick in the ten minutes of quiet we had between practice sessions.

As Tom and I followed them outside, I was surprised to see a petite, blonde woman sitting at the countertop of the transporter with three laptops open in front of her. Tom introduced her as Nadia, the Delray ECU engineer assigned to the team, before he hustled me out the door to Benny and Ian. Just before the camera rolled, he whipped the Sandham Swift baseball cap off of his own brown curls and plopped it on my head, saying he'd gather team gear for me later.

I answered the same basic question again: how did I feel about Wade's death and getting to drive for the team as a result? As I was finishing, Zeke Andrews strolled up, cheeky grin and notebook at the ready. He covered races from the pits for SPEED, and I counted him as a friend. I wasn't pleased with him, however, when he threw me a zinger: "Hey Kate, did you do him in to get the ride?"

My jaw dropped. The camera was still running, and I flicked a glance to Benny and Ian, who looked amused.

I scrambled for something broadcast-worthy. "I had nothing to do with Wade's death—"

Zeke didn't allow me to continue. "Except for finding him, yeah?"

Benny went from chuckling to serious in the blink of an eye. "Well, Kate, that must make you the prime suspect. Would you like to address that for our viewers?"

I was speechless.

He stepped closer. "You found him, and you certainly benefit from his death. The police must be looking at you. Are they?"

It hit me: no one would care about my driving or the race when they could talk about Wade. The only question would be, "Did you do it?" until I proved my innocence to the whole world, not just the police.

Everyone was still staring at me. Camera still filming. I told myself to be mercenary about getting more air time. If I couldn't avoid the questions, I'd deliver good answers.

I started again. "The last time I saw Wade was last night at a restaurant—until I found him this morning, I'm sorry to say. I have no idea what happened to him, and I was not involved in any way. It's been a tough day, and on top of it, I've got to get ready to make Wade proud in his car. He'll be in everyone's thoughts."

The second the camera was off, I went to Zeke. "What the hell?" I asked in a low tone. I wanted to yell.

He was more amused than ashamed. "Just pokin' at you, girl!"

Zeke was eleven years older and three inches taller than me, tan, tow-headed, and burly. His accent was South African, and his expressions mostly Australian. His smile could usually charm anyone—male or female—into anything. But I was in no mood.

"On camera, Zeke? You know Wade was killed, right? It's not funny joking with me about that. The police already think I did it!"

He sobered. "They don't. Really?"

"They think I'm a suspect. What with Wade shouting at me last night in the restaurant—" I broke off in horror. "Oh my God, Zeke. I forgot. How could I forget about that?"

"Forget what?"

"Wade, last night, threatening me at the restaurant. I forgot to tell Detective Jolley about it." That was going to look bad.

"It wasn't a big deal. All of us talk a little trash."

"Are you kidding me? Hours before he's killed? He said he'd fix me before I could steal his ride, and I said I'd 'nail his ass' first. Plenty of people heard us. I need to find Jolley, soon." I was jittery with nerves, and I shook a finger in his face. "Back to my point. I need support, not jokes."

He put an arm around my shoulder. "You got it. Anything you need, Katie-Q." He'd started calling me Katie-Q nearly twelve years before, back when he was a professional racing sportscars, I was racing go-karts, and we were both being sponsored by the same glove manufacturers. He and his wife had become the brother and sister I didn't have, and Zeke had alternately been my sounding board and my mentor.

We walked the three paces to where Tom was chatting with a General Motors rep and Ian, who'd stayed behind when Benny and the camera operator headed down the paddock. I needed to find Detective Jolley before someone else relayed the words Wade and I had thrown at each other.

Then I heard a voice behind me. "Kate? There's someone here—"

I turned, expecting another member of the media and finding the last person on earth I wanted to see. He was standing at the edge of the garage space. My father.

Chapter Ten

Fortunately, I was saved by the engines. By the Miatas, to be precise, buzzing onto the track for their miserly fifteen minutes of morning practice time, precluding lengthy interaction.

James Hightower Reilly, III, had never been part of my life—and if I could help it, wasn't ever going to be. After literally going in different directions at the time of my birth—him back to his well-heeled eastern family home, and brand-new me to my maternal grandparents' 1960s tract house in Albuquerque, New Mexico—we'd arrived in the same place: the racing world. Me, because of early talent exhibited at the multitude of kiddie birthday parties held at a local go-kart track, and him through a long career as a bank executive. It was my bad luck that his bank was a major sponsor of the American Le Mans Series. It had taken him the first year of his bank's involvement to figure out who I was, the second year to introduce himself. This was the third year, and he'd grown more intent on prolonged conversation.

Zeke was at my side again, following my gaze and speaking close to my ear to be heard. "Kate, who's that?"

I gave my father a miniscule nod and turned to Zeke. "Nobody important. How about I buy you a Coke and you tell me what you know about the track?" I'd find Detective Jolley after we talked.

Zeke looked at his watch. "Yeah, but it's lunchtime, Kate. Come on, I'll buy. Just give me a sec." He turned to say something to Ian.

I considered. My father hadn't moved, and Zeke was chattering away. Though I'd rather have had a root canal than deal with him, I squared my shoulders and approached my father.

"Hi." I stopped inside the perimeter ropes, far enough away that we had to strain to be heard over the noise of the cars, but not so close that he was in my space.

"It's good to see you, Katherine."

He was one of the few people who called me by my full name. I'd never felt like allowing him the informality of my nickname.

"I wanted to offer my congratulations on securing a role with a team. Though I'm sorry it had to happen the way it did."

"Thank you."

He sighed. "Look, Katherine, could we speak somewhere else for a few minutes? I'd like to—"

I saw Zeke approaching and raised a hand to stop him. "I'm sorry, but I've got to prep. This isn't a good time." I walked away, heading Zeke off and angling toward the concession stand nearby.

"Who's the bloke?" Zeke asked again.

I started to answer, but my attention was caught by a man walking toward me. A man I looked for at every race. I didn't know his name, but he was the most gorgeous specimen I'd ever seen, a classic statue come to life in hip, European clothing. I stared in silent appreciation, only belatedly returning the nod of greeting from the driver he was walking with.

"Kate?"

I blinked at Zeke. "Sorry."

"Who's the bloke?"

"I don't know his name, but I see him at most races." I turned to look at his retreating form.

Zeke punched my arm. "Not him, the bloke at your garage."

"Oh, him. Distant connection. No one I've got time for now." I shook off my daze and tamped down my guilt, reminding myself that walking away from my father at a race was nothing compared to him leaving me as a newborn in a hospital. "Tell me what I need to know about this track."

Twenty minutes later we were polishing off lunch: a cheese-burger and fries for Zeke and a turkey sandwich and some of his fries for me.

"Zeke, what should I know about the ALMS? What are you hearing? You know anything more about the cornering issues cars have been having?"

He rubbed his chin. "Officially? Not a thing. Unofficially, fuel and tires still a possibility. But bets are on Delray ECUs. It's just that no one can figure out what's breaking. I know the Series is working with all the different manufacturers on it."

"Anything else you know about?"

"I heard someone didn't like Wade Becker much."

I grimaced. "You think? Tell me about Wade. You knew him, didn't you?"

"Well, sure. I never did race with him, but against him, plenty."

"And?"

"Wade had charisma. Back in the day, he'd come into a room—or a garage—and he'd fill the place. He had charm—and a personality like a spotlight. When it was focused on you, it was blinding, flattering, all of that."

"And when it wasn't?"

"You didn't really exist. And nothing else in the room did. See, Wade wanted…."

"What?"

He shook his head. "He just wanted. Everything. All the attention. All the success, women, praise. He was larger than life. But he'd developed a sharp edge."

"Because he was slipping?"

Zeke eyed me. "You'd noticed?"

"Come on, you know I've kept track of lap times—you're the one who got me started tracking Series statistics."

"Yeah, he'd started slipping. Noticeable last year, a tick more this year. But really, I think the darkness in him came first."

"That's melodramatic."

He squinted and looked into the distance. "It was a darkness and a bitterness. I can't explain it, but I felt it. His personality changed from one race to the next like someone flipped a switch. I remember at the Mid-Ohio race three years ago, he was angry and aggressive and negative, like he's been ever since. Up to then, he'd been a pleasant, friendly guy."

He shrugged. "It didn't take long for everyone to figure it out either, that the Wade we'd known was gone. Word went round. I tell you, Katie-Q, from that point on, like attracted like."

"Evil is all around us, Zeke?"

He didn't care for the sarcasm in my tone. "Look, Kate, not everyone is nice. Or good. And not everyone—even in your beloved racing world—walks the path of angels. In the last couple years, if you heard about aggressive people, or wrongdoing, or anything shady, you also heard Wade's name. Strange things have been going on in this series recently, some bad doings, and Wade was either involved or knew something about it."

"What do you mean? Like cheating?"

"I don't know. But there's something, and it isn't your run of the mill 'push the boundaries of technical regulations and get a slap on the wrist if you're caught' kind of thing that all teams do. That's the nature of racing. But I'd heard…."

"What?"

"Just whispers here and there of cheating, sabotage, blackmail. Bad stuff. And somehow Wade was wrapped up in it. If he really was killed…I can't say I'm surprised he pissed someone off royally—but murder? I dunno, Kate."

"I dunno either, Zeke."

"Oh, Kate!" Aunt Tee hurried toward me, then stopped and smiled at Zeke's affronted look. "Hello, Zeke, how are you today?"

"Fine and dandy, Tee, and yourself?"

She put her hands on her hips. "Run off my feet like always. In fact, Kate, that's why I'm here. Jack's decided he wants a quick drivers' meeting in the motorhome. Er," she hesitated, "probably in the trailer office. The motorhome is still occupied."

"Mrs. Purley?"

Aunt Tee nodded, and Zeke raised his eyebrows.

"Never mind," I said to him, as we stood up and he gave me another hug.

"Go get 'em," he commanded.

Aunt Tee ticked items off on her fingers as we walked. "Now, I've got your kit all ready for you, all laid out. A Ziploc bag for your jewelry."

"Thanks for remembering that." Unlike many drivers who wore watches and wedding rings while driving, I was superstitious about removing everything extraneous. I took to the track with every possible inch covered in fire-retardant material and not a speck else on myself but cotton cloth. I didn't want to learn the hard way how quickly metal could burn and melt in a fire. Last year when I'd driven with the team, Aunt Tee and I had worked out a routine of her holding the sealed bag with my most precious possessions: the tiny diamond earrings and necklace that had been my mother's.

She patted my shoulder as we walked. "Of course, sweetheart. I remember what every one of my drivers needs."

"Mostly you know it before we do."

She beamed and waved me toward the office I'd been in before with Tom. "Here we are then. You go on. I'll be ready for you to suit up when you're done."

Jack was bent over the open engine compartment of the 29 car, the sister to my Number 28. He caught sight of me and straightened, clapping a hand to the back of the crew member who'd been peering at machinery with him.

"Kate, are you settling in OK?"

"Yes, thanks, Jack."

"You're not too nervous about jumping back into this without much practice?"

"I'd be lying if I said not nervous. But I can handle it."

"Remember, I'm not expecting an Andretti. Today, anyway."

He was smiling, so I decided he wouldn't fire me if we didn't win the race.

"I see you gave Tom the slip."

I assumed he was still joking. "I was giving Tom a break—and picking Zeke's brain about the track."

I opened the office door to find Tom, Mike, and the two drivers of the 29 car already inside. I sat in an open chair next to Mike, and Jack quickly got down to business and strategy.

Contrary to what the uninitiated might think, there was more to this sport than sitting in the car and stomping on the throttle. No matter the preparation—and luck—there was always an incident to bring out the yellow caution flag: an accident, a car off-course, debris, or any number of other occurrences. There was plenty of strategy needed to deal with the yellows.

Jack was seated, leaning forward and looking cramped even in the large office chair. He had his elbows on his knees and gestured a lot to make his points. "Like usual, any yellow we get about a third of the way through the race and then two-thirds of the way through, we'll pit for tires and fuel. With this track being short and tight, we should get plenty of cautions. We'll slip Kate into the car during one of the early ones, then put Mike back in to close. If we don't get those yellows, we'll go with the two-stop strategy with driver changes at both."

"We'll hope for yellows," put in Mike. A stop under green, while everyone else was on track at race speed, put you farther behind than a stop under yellow, when everyone else was cruising slowly and you could catch up to the back of the pack.

Jack nodded. "There should be plenty of caution periods, and we're not pushing for the win anyway."

I felt myself flush, and Jack noticed or heard what he'd just said. "We'll take it if we get near it, and Kate's capable of helping us win. But we don't need to kill ourselves—uh." He stopped as we all remembered why I was there.

Jack cleared his throat. "Let's push, but finish. Deliver good lap times, and let placement take care of itself."

He stared at his hands for a moment, then looked up, his gruff demeanor reasserting itself. "But don't get used to this! No slacking!" He almost barked the last, though it was softened by a twisted, wry smile.

"No worries, Jack," chirped Lars Pierson, a slight, easygoing Dane who drove the 29 car with Seth Donohue, a Canadian. Lars and Seth were considered gentlemen drivers: skilled amateurs who paid for the privilege of driving—which helped pay the team's bills. Gentlemen drivers didn't usually compete for the win or deliver the speed of the pros, but good ones, like Lars and Seth, were solid, mid-pack racers.

Jack spent a few more minutes on adjustments made to the cars for handling and balance, contingency plans for radio breakage or other problems, and race-day protocols and procedures, such as who spoke on the radios—the driver in the car, the crew chief, and the team manager only. When he asked if we had any questions, I spoke up.

"I'm curious if there are any new tech requirements. I assume we passed tech inspection? Did anyone not?"

"Cars passed, no problem. Why?"

"I'm wondering about the cornering issues other teams have been having. I heard something about teams pushing boundaries more, and I wondered if there was a new regulation." Jack frowned, and I added, "I'm not saying it's related. There are just so many rumors…." I glanced at my co-drivers, who seemed interested, not disbelieving.

Jack's expression cleared. "I forgot you weren't here for yesterday's briefing. Let me recap." He waved off my protests. "No problem. There are no new requirements or regulations, but there certainly are unexplained issues going on with some teams. We've got every manufacturer here checking processes, equipment, and materials. Fuel, tires, drivetrain, ECU, and so on. It's been pretty well narrowed-down to Delray ECUs, which we also carry, of course. Victor Delray is personally checking everything, and his best engineer is in our pits, triple-checking code, processes, simulations, whatever it is. We're doing everything we can to make sure the problems don't happen to us."

"Thanks, Jack."

He was silent for another moment before speaking again. "I'm trying to tell myself we've caught whatever glitch is causing the problems, but it's hard to know—and it's too damn late to change ECUs. If I knew the car was unsafe...well, we wouldn't run."

He saw the surprise on our faces. "Seriously. We'd pull out until we knew it was fixed. But we don't know what 'it' really is, and if it'll affect us. Odds are, I'm giving you solid equipment. And I guess we're always playing the odds around here, aren't we?"

Mike shook his head. "Not gonna happen, boss. Let's go racing."

I chuckled. That was a typical racecar driver for you: convinced the next guy would suffer the mishap. We knew accidents happened, and we planned how to handle them if they did. But we never, ever expected them to.

Jack smiled. "That's the plan. Just be alert out there—don't screw up, and we should be fine."

That statement didn't help my nerves.

Chapter Eleven

Jack wrapped up our meeting with directions for the day's on-track time. "Kate, you'll take twenty of the thirty minutes of practice. Then we'll pull you in, change tires, get Mike in, and send him out for a couple warm up and adjustment laps. Mike, can you handle that?"

"You bet."

"Then qualifying. They're trying the one-at-a-time qualifying again."

I was surprised and doubly glad it would be Mike's job. I was used to the typical free-for-all qualifying sessions—every car in your class on track, all trying to set the fastest lap time while avoiding traffic. But I'd heard of test-runs of the three-lap scheme. In the first lap, coming out of the pits, you got up to speed, to be flying past the start/finish line for the second, timed lap when you'd have the track to yourself. The third lap was for slowing down and coming back in, while the next car did its out lap for its own attempt.

"Well, guys—and Kate." Jack studied all of us. "Do your best. Exceed everyone's expectations." I responded with more conviction than anyone else in the room. Jack stood and checked his watch. "1:20 now. Practice at 3:00. Car into pit at 2:50, after the Star Mazda race is over. So be back here in an hour to suit up. Thanks."

As I rose with everyone else to leave the office, a fresh wave of butterflies hit my stomach. I waved the guys on to the sandwiches Aunt Tee had set out. It was time to look for Jolley.

But I moved instead to the 28 car. My car. One of the crew was sitting cross-legged on the ground at the front left wheel—at least, what remained of it, as it was stripped down to the brake assembly. Alex, the brake whiz, flashed a grin at me and at the fans aiming cameras at us from the edge of the garage.

"I'm going to hop in for a minute, Alex. That won't bother you, right?" I paused with my hand on the Corvette's roof.

"Nah. Just don't start 'er up and roll out of here."

"Little chance of that." I climbed into the car and immediately stuck my head back out. "Alex, can I put the wheel on?"

"Oh, yah, sure. They're blocked."

"Thanks." I'd wanted to be sure that the spindles were blocked—that the front suspension was held in place and wouldn't turn in response to me touching the steering column and interfere with his work. I lifted the steering wheel from the hook in the middle of the ceiling, slipped it on the column, and clicked it into place. Then I closed my eyes and breathed deeply three times, mentally shedding everything but the car. I visualized the cockpit, thinking through every switch. I opened my eyes, and my mental vision matched reality.

Once again I thought my way around the Lime Rock track, imagining every upshift, downshift, and braking maneuver. I was in a zone where I no longer heard the clank of tools in the garage, noticed the tripping shutters of passing fans, or cared what was happening outside of my bubble. A calm settled over me. I hadn't yet driven the car, but I felt familiar with it, a part of it. Finally. The word rippled through my mind as my keyed-up nerves relaxed.

I scooted out of the car a different person than I'd been going in. My feet were under me now. I knew there'd be plenty to adapt to—the grip of the brakes, the downforce in the turns, the slickness of the track—but at last I knew the tool I'd use to crush the competition. I felt a satisfied smile develop as I gave the car a final pat and moved away. "Thanks, Alex. See you."

"You betcha, Kate." He waggled a wrench at me.

Instead of walking across to the motorhome and my team-mates, I left the garage, stepping around the pole holding the rope barrier. Careful not to meet the gaze of anyone walking by or standing in front of our setup, I turned and walked quickly toward the track, stopping at the end of the pits where I could see the straight and Big Bend. I crossed my arms and thought through my approach, acceleration, braking, and turning in the Corvette. I was as ready as I was going to get.

I exited the pits and saw Detective Jolley standing at the rear of my Jeep behind the police tape. I got his attention, and a minute later, he was standing in front of me.

"Ms. Reilly."

I squared my shoulders. "Detective. I remembered something."

He raised his eyebrows.

"Last night, at the restaurant—The Boathouse. Wade and I had words."

"Words?"

"Yes. He made a rude comment, and I said something equally impolite."

"You'd forgotten this?"

I ran a hand through my hair. "I know it sounds ridiculous. But I did—until about an hour ago."

He pulled a notebook and pen out of his jacket pocket. "Give me the details."

"Out of the blue he came up to me and said something like, 'You think you're such hot shit, but you're not going to steal my ride. I'll fix you good first.'"

"Out of the blue? You didn't say anything to provoke him?"

"No! Nothing. I didn't even know he was at the restaurant—"

Jolley held up a hand. "He threatened you. And what did you say to him?"

I swallowed, remembering the shock of Wade's threat and the embarrassment of other people hearing it. "He immediately walked away. I turned to Holly and Perry and Zeke—Perry's with one of the sponsors and Zeke, the SPEED Channel guy—and said, 'Yeah, but he'd have to catch me. And besides, I might just nail his ass first.'" The detective's expression never budged, but I felt his increased interest.

"Come on, I meant on the track—racing. That I'd beat him if we raced together. You know, it was just talk." What a cliché. Is that what Jolley heard every time? Hmm…how much murder did he encounter in the northwest corner of Connecticut?

"Had he threatened you before?"

"No. I never exchanged any words with him at all. Well, I raced with his team last year, so we talked then, and I knew him to say hi to, but nothing more."

"Do you have any idea why he threatened you?"

I shook my head.

"Do you know what he meant?"

"He implied I was trying to replace him, but that's absurd."

"Why?"

"He's driven with that team for years and years. He's their senior driver—he practically is that team. They're not going to get rid of him—weren't."

"But he wasn't fast lately?"

"What do you mean?"

"If he'd have to catch you, you imply he's slower. Is that true?"

Jolley was quick. "He's—he was a great driver. But recently he wasn't running—er, driving—as fast. I wondered if he was slipping for some reason."

"Did you discuss that with anyone else?"

"No! No one." He looked skeptical, and I kept explaining. "I keep track of a lot of data about different courses and different drivers. But I don't share it—or volunteer my opinion."

He nodded and made another note.

A thought struck me, and I blurted out, "Oh God, Wade was right."

Jolley came alive. "About what, Ms. Reilly?"

"Well, not right, exactly. What he said last night. I wasn't trying to, but I've ended up in his place."

"Yes, it occurred to me. Anything else you've suddenly remembered, Ms. Reilly?"

"That's it."

He flipped his notebook closed, nodded, and walked back behind the caution tape.

I was on my way back to the Sandham Swift paddock, feeling less burdened, when I passed Stuart, no doubt heading to check up on his minions who were taking VIP guests on laps around the track. He held up a hand, whether to greet me or order a halt, I wasn't sure. I thought of Tom's belief in Stuart's good intentions and gave him the benefit of the doubt.

"Hi, Stuart. How's it going?"

He raised an eyebrow. "Fine, thank you, Kate. Are you settled in?"

"I'm as ready as I'm going to get before practice, yes. Thanks for asking."

"Tom sent me a press release, and I've returned it with some modifications for your approval. I'd appreciate your input before your practice session. I have a long list of media to send it to."

"I'll take a look. But that's all about Wade, right? I mean, they're not that interested in me."

He tipped his head to the side and gave a small shrug. "Most. Most are about Wade. And you as a byproduct of that story." He saw me wince. "Just you replacing him as a driver. I didn't go into…the rest."

"Good."

"But there are a couple of media outlets who want your story for you. Since you're a woman driver."

I had to stifle a snort. I'd noticed.

"And maybe you'll be full-time this season."

"With any luck."

"I wish you that luck." I could have sworn I heard his heels click together.

"Thanks, Stuart. See you later. I'll review the release with Tom." I walked on in shock. Détente. Who'd have thought?

Chapter Twelve

I approached the team motorhome with trepidation. Susanah Purley, drama queen, could still be in there. However, so was my gear. In I went.

Aunt Tee was at the far end of the main room, wiping down the kitchenette's counters. Mrs. Purley was draped across one of the two tan leather couches that lined the walls. She lifted her hand from her brow and said a weak hello.

Aunt Tee bobbed her head at each of us. "Kate, please meet Mrs. Susanah Purley. Susanah, this is Kate Reilly. She'll be… filling in for Wade."

Susanah sat up with a burst of energy. "A female racecar driver?"

"You got it. Nice to meet you." I moved past her to sit at the mini kitchen table.

Her voice grew faint again. "A female racecar driver. How Wade would have liked that." She blinked back tears. "He was so supportive of an individual's talent, in any arena. He was so kind, so nurturing."

Aunt Tee and I exchanged glances as Susanah leaned her head back and closed her eyes. I saw tears trickling down her face.

"Just so sad." Susanah gave a delicate sniff. "Such a waste of life and talent."

I made a polite noise of agreement and caught Aunt Tee rolling her eyes. But Susanah wanted more. "You knew him, didn't you? Wouldn't you agree?"

I replied with care. "I only knew him slightly. I raced with the team once last year. Anyone who follows sportscar racing knows of Wade. But I didn't know him. He was extremely talented." Once, I thought.

Aunt Tee handed me a bottle of water with a smile. "A snack, Kate?" She gestured toward a bunch of grapes.

"Sure, thanks." I watched her add some cheese slices to a plate with the fruit.

Susanah allowed this small diversion before returning to her topic. "Well, then, you wouldn't really know the extent of how interesting Wade was. How diverse his interests, how multi-dimensional he was."

"No, I guess not." My reluctant response was all the invitation she needed.

Susanah sat up straighter, tucking her feet under her and leaning her elbows on the wide arm of the sofa. "Just think about where he came from. His mother grew up on a cotton farm in Alabama. His father was from New York City. 'The farm girl and the city boy,' he used to call them. By the time he was ten, Wade was spending half the year with each remarried parent—in radically different environments. Small wonder he was so adept socially."

I nodded thanks to Aunt Tee as she handed me a napkin. Susanah was going on about Wade's equal comfort with the executive sponsor types—those with the money and power, I translated—and with the crew—those at the bottom. During an anecdote, Aunt Tee managed to ask silently if I wanted Mrs. Purley out of there. I shook my head. It was entertainment while I ate—and the distraction was probably good, to clear my head of race anxiety.

"And of course, you know that Wade went to college too," Susanah continued.

"Mmm."

"Here and there, while he was racing. But he did get a degree—in literature and philosophy, if you can imagine that." I couldn't imagine it. "Really?"

Susanah had an "I told you so" look on her face. "Oh, yes. Every once in a while he'd explain something about Aristotle and race strategy—I mean, philosophy? I didn't understand a thing."

I wasn't sure if that made Wade smart or Susanah dumb.

"I guess there was family pressure to go into law or finance, or even the academic world. But he loved racing. And of course, there was his skill on the track."

"Mmm, hmmm." I was finishing a bottle of water, on my way to another. I always tried to over-hydrate before getting into the car, since I could lose as much as five pounds in a race stint, primarily through sweat. I was also thinking about getting into my race suit.

"You'd know about that."

"Uh, yeah." I focused on her. "Wade's skill. Championships in three or four different series. Won the 24 Hours of Le Mans, the 12 Hours of Sebring, ran a couple NASCAR races, tested for Formula One at one point. He was all over the racing world."

I'd gotten Susanah misty again. "'One of the sportscar greats'—that's what the TV announcers said about him at the last race."

"Excuse me, but I've got to change."

"Oh, sure." But she kept talking to Aunt Tee as I walked to the back of the motorhome, stopped in the bathroom, then shut the door of the small bedroom where Aunt Tee had spread my gear out on the bed. I tucked my street clothes and shoes into my now-empty duffle bag, putting on cotton underwear and a cotton sports bra, then a layer of Nomex fire-retardant long-underwear. Once I added the Nomex socks, I was covered from neck to wrist to toe in fire-retardant fibers.

In any other racecar, I'd have put on a "cool suit," a Nomex shirt with a tiny hose sewn to it in a looping pattern through which cold water would be pumped. But the C6.R had a better and lighter system: an air conditioner that plugged directly into my helmet and kept my head—and the air I breathed—cooled.

The last step in the process was the race suit itself: a thick, quilted, fire-retardant jumpsuit, black on the bottom with a white top littered with sponsor logos. I was sweating already, from the close air in the motorhome, air conditioned though it was, and the layers of Nomex. By the end of the day—by the end of only twenty minutes of practice—I'd have sweated through every stitch I had on. That was the norm. I unzipped my suit and climbed in, poking my feet through the elasticized cuffs and shimmying the suit up over my hips. I zipped from mid-thigh halfway up. I wouldn't put the top half on until I left the motorhome.

I could still hear Susanah talking. I slung my earplugs—custom fitted, on a long set of audio wires that would plug into the car's radio system—around my neck again. Then I took a deep breath, grabbed my race shoes, and went back out front.

Aunt Tee gave me another bottle of water and a long-suffering look. I dropped my shoes near the sofa and pulled a couple items out of my bag under the kitchen table. A pen, a small spiral-bound notebook, and some chapstick. I set them all on a sofa cushion and sat down opposite Susanah.

She'd been quiet, watching me. "You're starting to get in the zone, aren't you?"

I nodded, surprised.

"That's what Wade used to say, that putting on all the gear, pulling out the special tools—that was part of getting mentally ready."

"He was right."

She cocked her head to the side. "He was so smart. And yet—he could be so funny."

"Funny?" I repeated, then cursed myself for encouraging her.

"So insecure. Needy. Wanting reassurance."

"Well, we all sometimes—"

"Like he'd call me because he thought he was being passed over by the top teams at the big races—the 24 Hours of Daytona or Le Mans. I'd reassure him that he wasn't being disrespected, he'd find another team to race for. Or he called me to rant about how he wasn't sent to some ALMS press conference. You know, when the Series needs drivers to talk to the press? For years, he was always the one to go. He was angry. He kept saying, 'They're idiots. I'm one of the best drivers in the ALMS. You know that.' He'd wait for me to agree. What else could I do but agree?"

The question was obviously rhetorical, because Susanah pressed on. Aunt Tee handed me a plastic bag with a deliberately blank expression.

"And really, he was right. So I'd tell him he was right, he was a champion, the Series wasn't smart about who they had as representatives—I mean, Wade was a natural salesman. I used to laugh about how he'd answer a question on camera with every sponsor's name, series name, track name, and his own upbeat response." She raised a hand to her mouth as her giggles turned to sniffles.

I stowed my earrings, necklace, and watch in the bag and handed it back to Aunt Tee, nodding at Susanah. "He was really good at that." I didn't add that self- and sponsor-promotion were skills as necessary to racecar drivers as the ability to turn a wheel. I'd always thought Wade's sales job overdone. But there was no doubt he'd been popular with the Series and sponsors. Or had he been, at the end?

"Mrs. Purley, when was that conversation? When he wasn't sent to the press conference?"

"I think it was back in March, or maybe it was the end of last season. I'm not sure—wait, last October, but he brought it up again in March. Or maybe it happened again in March?" She wrinkled her forehead.

"I see." I paused. "Is your husband going to be here today? I'd like to meet him."

"Not today. Charlie's coming in late tonight, so he'll be here for the race on Monday. I spoke with him this morning, and he's terribly upset too."

"Did he know Wade well?"

"Oh yes, he liked Wade a lot. Thought he was a great guy."

I didn't know how to ask the question I really wanted answered—didn't he mind that you and Wade were such good "friends?"

The knock and shout came together. "Kate! You in there? You suited up?" Mike opened the door and popped his head in. "Let's talk for a couple minutes."

"Just give me a second, Mike. I'll be right out." He was in his suit too, and I figured the other three drivers had changed in the trailer office. Usually the four of us would hang out together in the motorhome, but they were avoiding Mrs. Purley.

"Got to go," I announced to Susanah and Aunt Tee, and tried to stay calm as I pulled up the top half of my race suit, put my shoes on, and tied the laces firmly.

"Breathe, Kate," Aunt Tee advised.

"Right." I took my standard three deep breaths and felt better. Then I looked for my notepad and pen, which had disappeared into the cracks between the sofa cushions. I rummaged around for them, trying to inventory what I was wearing and carrying for missing items. I felt the pen and notebook and drew my hand out. Except it wasn't my notebook, but a small, black, leather-bound version. I frowned at it as Mike shouted a second time. "Kate! Come on!" I stuffed it into my suit pocket and plunged my hand back in the sofa, this time coming up with my blue spiral-bound.

"Coming!" I turned to Aunt Tee. "Thank you. My helmet—"

"Outside, with your gloves and everything. Good practice, Kate."

"Thanks." I dashed out.

Chapter Thirteen

I was following Mike, Lars, and Seth down pit row to our team's setup when I was jostled by a driver I recognized brushing past me.

"Hey, Jim."

He turned and shot us a glare.

"Nice guy." Mike's tone was sarcastic.

"You know him? Jim Siddons?"

"Sure, I've driven with him a couple times. He drove with us at Sebring this year, since you couldn't make it. He's been around a while."

"We've both been in the same boat—looking for a permanent ride. I guess he got one if he's driving for someone here."

We'd reached the Sandham Swift pit setup, and Mike nodded a greeting at the Michelin rep standing next to our racks of tires on the other side of the walkway. We stopped in front of a pit box, a large, white metal storage cabinet with eight lockers on each side, and Mike pulled a locker open, gesturing to the door on its right. "That's Wa—it's yours now."

I pulled it open gingerly, not sure what artifacts I'd discover, but it was empty. I let out the breath I'd been holding, set my gear inside, and closed the door again.

Mike had done the same. "I think I heard Siddons was driving one of the Porsches—but he was paying to drive it."

I was surprised. I didn't know Jim Siddons' history, but he'd struck me as a thoughtful, intelligent, experienced driver—someone temporarily between paying teams, not permanently so. "Did he ever have a long-term gig with an ALMS team?"

"Nope. He was always the guy hanging around for emergencies or when someone needed a third driver in the longer races. He was paid for a couple races each season. Until you came along, anyway."

"Me?"

"Yeah, you." Mike smiled. "You've got two drivers looking for a chance: one's young, fresh, talented, and on the way up; one's older, hasn't ever broken through, and on the way down. Who do you pick?"

"I had no idea. He looked pissed just now."

We both saw Jack waving a long arm at us from pit lane.

Mike led the way. "Come on, let's go."

The pit space was crowded with supplies and people. Jack stood at the 29 car, parked behind ours, talking with Seth. Lars was gearing up to drive. Bruce, Walt, and Sam, our car chiefs and chief engineer sat on top of the pit box with Nadia, the ECU engineer. We walked forward, skirting the looped fuel hose and stepping over air hoses and tools.

Jack stopped me before I sat on the pit wall next to Mike. "May as well get ready, Kate."

I returned to my locker. First, I secured my earplugs with pieces of green masking tape that covered each ear. Then I emptied my suit pockets into the locker, stuffed my gloves into them, and headed back with everything else in my arms. Jack finished with Seth and checked the time. "Fifteen minutes left. Kate, let's have you get in and out a couple times to practice."

"Sure."

Mike held out his hands, and I set my helmet in them. I pulled the balaclava over my head, arranging the fire-retardant hood so the three openings left my mouth and eyes unencumbered. I slipped the HANS or Head And Neck Support device, which reduced how much my head could move in an impact, onto my shoulders, and then put my helmet on, fastening the chinstrap while Mike attached the HANS tethers to it. By now, fully suited up, I was blind in my peripheral vision because of my helmet, unable to turn my head without swiveling my entire body because of the HANS, and nearly deaf because of my earplugs. I was pumped. This was it!

Jack was holding the 28's door open. He pointed in the car, then at himself. I pulled on my gloves, took one last breath, and stepped up to the car. Peered in. Someone had put my seat insert inside, ready for me. I took another deep breath. In and out of the car.

I grabbed the top bar of the rollcage and slid my right leg in the opening. Half-sitting on the ledge of the lower rollcage bar, I lifted my left foot and slid that leg in. I held the top bar with both hands and lowered my body into the seat, twisting my torso as my helmet cleared the doorframe to end up sitting squarely. Almost without thinking, I grabbed the steering wheel from its hook on the ceiling and snapped it into place. Doing so would be my major responsibility as I got in the car, in addition to making sure the shoulder belts sat on top of my HANS shoulder braces and putting the right-side lap belt into the hands of the driver's assistant, the crew member allowed over the wall to help us make our driver change. He'd fasten my belts and connect cables to and from my helmet, partly because his light gloves made the job easier, but also because I couldn't bend over or turn enough to see the connections.

Jack assisted me this time, first fastening my belts—the five-point harness that had straps over each shoulder, one from each side of my waist, and one coming from under the seat between my legs. I tightened the belts as he plugged in my earplug cable for the radio, and poked the air conditioning tube into the left side of my helmet. I couldn't see him doing the last tasks, but I felt the tugs and bumps as he worked and felt a final pat on the helmet that signified he was finished. I was set. Wait—I'd forgotten the drink tube. I found it on my right and plugged it in to the front of my helmet where it fit into the tube that terminated close to my mouth. I looked up at Jack fastening my window net. He gave me a thumbs up and mouthed, "Hang on."

I spent the two minutes he was gone looking at all the buttons and taking deep breaths. My panic hadn't risen far by the time he was back wearing a radio and a big headset.

"Radio check. You comfortable, Kate?" I heard Jack's voice in my ears.

I pushed the button to activate the two-way radio. "Check. Yes, I'm good."

"Great. Let me talk you through everything, and you do it all to get out again."

I gave him a thumbs up.

"OK. You approach pit lane from the track. About ten yards before the entry line, hit the speed limiter button." I tapped the button on the steering wheel. When I was driving the car, keeping my foot on the throttle and hitting that button would limit me to the pit lane maximum of thirty-seven miles an hour.

Jack continued: "Loosen your belts on the way in, unhook your cables—but not this time, so you can still hear me—and remove your drink tube." I pulled the drink tube out of my helmet and pulled up on the metal slides on my shoulder straps to loosen them, making room for Mike to put them on after me. I also reached to my left and unhooked the cooling tube.

"Pull in, stop, and release the harness." I imagined stopping and turning off the car, and then I removed and hung the steering wheel. With a twist of the central round lever, I released the seatbelts, and the shoulder straps snapped back on bungee cords toward the ceiling, out of the way but accessible. By this time, Jack had opened the car door, unfastened the window net, and unhooked my radio cable. I scooted sideways, aimed my head at the doorway, grabbed the top bar of the rollcage, and heaved myself out, reminding myself why I did pull-ups in my regular workouts. Left foot out, then the right, and I was standing on the ground next to the car again. Oops. I bent back into the car and yanked out my seat insert. Jack nodded and smiled. I looked at Mike, who mimed applause at me.

Jack looked at his watch again and held up one hand, fingers splayed. Five minutes left. The bottom fell out of my stomach at the same time as adrenaline and excitement fizzed into my blood. I nodded to Jack and Mike. Then I got back in the car.

Jack buckled me in and plugged in my cables a second time. I heard Mike in my ears and saw him through the windscreen as he spoke to me. "Take it easy at first, Kate, just get used to her. Ask any questions you want. I'll be on the radio until you come back in." He smiled. "And have some fun!"

He couldn't see me, but I grinned at him in return. I gave him a thumbs up, resettled, and sat there in silence, waiting, both hands on the steering wheel. I concentrated on my breathing and on calming my speeding heart rate.

Jack over the radio: "It's time. Let 'er rip."

I pushed the ignition button, and the Corvette's V-8 engine roared to life.

Chapter Fourteen

I was the fifth car out of the pits. All four classes were practicing together, so two Porsches, a Viper, and one of the smaller prototypes were in front of me as we exited. They all got away quickly as I took the first lap at maybe seven-tenths of my ultimate speed. I was going as fast as I dared in an unfamiliar car with cold tires on an unknown track, and I was barely fast enough to be out there with the others.

My first thought as I maneuvered through Big Bend was that Mike hadn't told me how bumpy this turn was. Speed: 71. I touched the first apex, drifted to the outside of the track in the middle of the turn, then touched the second. An apex was the point in a corner where the car touched the inside curbing, and it represented the optimum line through a corner. You could drive faster through a wide, sweeping turn than you could through a narrow, sharp turn. Hitting the apex—touching the inside curb of the track—meant taking the straightest line through the turn and maintaining maximum speed. Most corners were only single-apex, but since Big Bend was almost 180 degrees, drivers touched the inside of the turn twice while taking the fastest line through it.

I saw some of the concrete patches he'd referred to on my driving line for the Esses—and then I was making a high speed slide on them through the left-hander. I kept my hands still, ready to correct when my wheels touched asphalt and found grip again. I glanced at the run off: a narrow swath of slippery grass and a metal guard rail. Nothing there to scrub energy and speed or provide a soft landing. Make sure not to get off track in this turn, I thought. Make sure not to get off track anywhere. I hit concrete patches again on the No Name Straight—wondering as I reached 115 through the slight S-shaped curves why they called it a "straight" when it wasn't.

Then I was braking and downshifting at the end of No Name, looking to my right at the track disappearing over a rise. A blind hill and turn. Also bumpy. I turned right and quickly topped the hill, swerving right again into the chicane—damn! Carrying too much speed into the turn. Brake as much as I dare, but not so much that I lock up the tires or put the car into a spin. Shit! Missed the corner and punted a cone. Up on the curbing—thump, down hard onto the track. Please God, no damage. Swerve left in the chicane and right again as I pop out. Damn again—wheels on grass and dirt at the right edge of the exit.

I checked my mirror: one of the corner workers was waving a yellow flag and watching the track anxiously while the other edged out to replace the cone I'd sent flying. Next time, less speed, snappier turning. And inside the chicane, more room to the left. Turn harder to clear the exit. Speed: 50 coming out. Decent.

I accelerated and upshifted as fast as possible into fourth gear going down the Back Straight. Bumps, bumps, bumps. Narrow track. I remembered Mike's advice and tapped the brakes at the end of the straight, shifting weight to the front for turning into West Bend. The track was wider here, which wasn't saying much. Glad I didn't have anyone trying to pass me at the moment. Mike had told me this was a high speed corner—stay in fourth gear, he'd said. I glanced at my speedometer: almost 100 miles per hour. He'd said we'd get 110 to 115 out of it, and that it took confidence. He was right. I'd push harder next time.

Out of West Bend and onto the sloping downhill. I went under the bridge—the same one I'd driven over that morning—and upshifted into fifth gear. My eyes flicked to the speed again. 130 this time. Getting closer to Mike's estimates. Then I took the final turn—shit! The car wiggled as I hit the bump Mike had warned me about. I didn't react fast enough and the car swung to the left. Left wheels running on the dirt and grass. Tire barrier on my left, angling in as the grass verge narrowed. Closer. I eased right with the wheel, trying not to brake too hard, let off the throttle too suddenly, or jerk to the right. Easy. More throttle, ease right. Wheels back on track. Shift to sixth. Main straight. Speed: 148. Flying now. Bumpy. Breathe, Kate.

Back into Big Bend, and I was better prepared this time. I'd been blissfully alone for the first lap, but just into my second lap, I was surrounded. Cars pelted past me one after the other, in the bends, on the straight, everywhere. It took everything I had to cope with shifting, steering, remembering to avoid the problem areas I'd noted, watching the corner workers with the flags, and risking occasional glances in my mirrors. This time I made it through the chicane with no cone casualties and ignored the corner workers watching me carefully. I balanced the urge to be a gracious competitor and stay out of the way of faster cars with my need to learn the track—and with my innate competitive instincts, which weren't about to give way to anyone I could run with. Under the deluge of drivers and cars whizzing past, I was precariously slow. But I hung in there and tried not to imagine the frustration of other drivers.

The driver of one car in particular didn't make it easy. I came down the hill at the end of my second lap, into the Diving Turn, and I remembered the problem bump at the last moment. Braced the wheel so I didn't drift left. A bright, neon-yellow Porsche just tapped me from behind. Was it intentional contact? This wasn't purposeful bump-drafting in NASCAR. We didn't do that here. Maybe I'd caused it by turning earlier or harder than the overtaking car expected. But it felt more aggressive than accidental.

I had no time to think about it in the moment, however, because I was focused on keeping my car on the pavement. The Porsche rocketed away to my right, and I fought the wiggling back end of my car—turning the steering wheel left, then right, letting off the throttle gently. It didn't take much disturbance to get sideways at the speeds we ran through turns and over hills. But that yellow Porsche got my dander up, as my grandfather would have said, and I laid into the throttle completely for the first time. By the end of the next lap, my third, I finally felt comfortable. I'd picked up speed and found my rhythm, which had to do with my line around the track; with braking, accelerating, upshifting, and downshifting points; and with the sound of the car throughout: throaty here with full throttle, whiny and protesting there with heavy braking and downshifting.

The Corvette felt like a second skin by the fourth lap. By then, I adjusted to the flood of sensory input I was receiving, and I could process it all. I even stopped noticing the constant bumps or how narrow the track was. I'd always thought of racing and chess as similar pursuits, minus the physical exertion, because you needed to be able to visualize and anticipate every possible move on the board or the track and plan your path accordingly. I started to read the traffic around me, to look ahead and behind my current position and plan not only my own moves, but everyone else's.

Other tasks had also become automatic, like watching for flags at corners, and watching my gauges for speed, the RPMs that told me when to upshift, and engine temperature readings. More than any gauge or sensor measurement, the car communicated its health through its sound, vibrations, and feel. I felt it through my arms from the steering wheel, and I felt it from the seat and floor through my butt and feet. Through the hum of the vehicle, you could often feel an engine problem or the first signs of a tire giving way—if you were lucky enough to get a slow tearing-apart rather than a sudden blow-out. We literally drove by the seat of our pants—and a lot of other body parts.

Sometime in my fifth lap, I started to enjoy myself.

"Kate." Jack's voice crackled over my radio. "You doing OK?"

The radio. I shifted my left hand to press the button. "Doing fine now."

"You remembering to breathe?"

I smiled under my helmet. "Yes, sir."

"Kate?" A new voice, my crew chief. "Bruce here. Don't forget to take a drink."

"Will do," I transmitted, and I pressed the drink button to take a sip. Like many drivers, I had to be reminded to drink water while driving. Non-racing people often asked if it was tough to sit in one place for an hour or two at a time and not need to use the bathroom, but the reality was that I concentrated on driving so intensely that I rarely thought about my body's needs. It never occurred to me that I was hungry, thirsty, had to go to the bathroom, or had a headache. A cramp might force its way into my consciousness, but only because it affected my driving. I was typically grateful for the reminders to sip water, and I could already tell I needed it, as my mouth was dry and my body was soaked in sweat—after only six minutes of practice.

About twelve minutes later, I'd done fifteen laps, and Bruce got back on the radio. "Take two more after this one, Kate, then come in."

"You got it." My tension returned. I'd used half of my total practice time, and it had felt more like the blink of an eye than twenty minutes. But I'd found my groove in that time. I was shifting and braking smoothly and no longer learning my line around the track. I took another breath and concentrated on making my second-to-last lap as fast as possible—using my nerves to push myself.

That flying lap felt good, and I kept up the push until I was two turns from pit entry, exiting West Bend and approaching the Diving Turn. I slowed through the last curve and hugged the right side of the track, allowing cars that weren't pitting to pass on my left. Jack's voice came through my headset as I reached Pit In and pushed the speed limiter button. "Good job, Kate. That last one was your quickest. A 55.12-second lap. A good start."

I felt deflated as I stopped the car, turned it off, and released the seatbelt harness. The Porsches could go faster than I'd gone in the more powerful Corvette. And undoubtedly Mike would qualify us with a sub–53-second lap. I was bitterly disappointed in myself.

A crew member opened the door and let down the net. I pulled myself out of the car and climbed over the inner pit wall. After Aunt Tee helped me remove my helmet, HANS, and balaclava, she handed me an ice-cold, wet washcloth to drape over my head and an open bottle of cold water. I watched Mike climb into the seat I'd just vacated and felt my shoulders slump. Disappointment became anger at my poor performance. I'd have to be a hell of a lot faster in the race to support Mike and do right by the team.

Jack descended from his perch on top of the pit box we called the control panel. It was another big cart, like the one that held our lockers, but this one was outfitted with a bench seat, a desk wide enough for four notebook computers, and eight flat-screen monitors suspended from the metal frame of the canvas roof—monitors that carried live feeds from the television cameras around the track. From the control panel, Jack, Bruce, and the 29 car's crew chief could watch us almost continuously around the track and keep an eye on current lap times for every car in the field.

I was gulping down water when Jack's big hand thudded onto my shoulder. I managed to swallow, not breathe, the liquid—but it was a near thing.

I felt my clammy undergarments sticking to my skin as he patted. "It was OK, Kate."

I jerked a shoulder in a shrug and scowled into my water bottle.

"Hey." His voice cracked like a whip, and I looked up at him. "Remember, Kate, I won't bullshit you. If you drive crappy, I'll tell you so. And I'm telling you: you did good. Not fast enough yet, but you'll get there. You're right where you should be for only fifteen laps on the track."

"Seventeen."

He rolled his eyes and put his hands on his hips. "Don't pull that crap. No sulking. It's not your fault you haven't had much practice time. Hell, think of it this way: you're nearly as fast already as Wade was. Yesterday." He ran a hand over his face, looking tired. "That was only yesterday…. Anyway, he only did a 54.03. And besides, you beat the GT2 class."

"Not all of them." I needed to be honest, but already felt better.

"You beat enough of them." Jack clapped his hands and rubbed them together. "Come on, let's see if Mike can put us on the pole."

I made myself toss my worries in the trash with my empty water bottle. Jack was right. I'd get faster in a hurry in the race. I climbed onto the bench of the control panel after him, only then realizing how physically tired I was. I willed my arms to stop shaking as I sat on a dry towel Aunt Tee handed me.

"Just to be sure, Kate, when the car got squirrelly at the end of lap two—was there a reason?" Jack looked worried. "It's fine, but was it you or one of our mystery problems?"

"It was me."

"You're sure? Because the Viper had the same kind of problem at the same place yesterday, and he ended up in the tires."

I hoped I was still red from heat and exertion, to mask my embarrassment. "I'm sure. My problem was the yellow Porsche getting too aggressive and me not being settled yet. It was driver error, not the car."

"That's a relief." He turned back to his monitor.

"Jack? Who is the yellow Porsche, anyway?"

Mike started the car, and Jack pointed to a line on the screen in front of him listing cars in the current session. Ours was there with my last name and my fastest lap time. Jack was pointing to the Number 83 car. Last name: Siddons.

Jack spoke into my ear. "Siddons won't back down. He was aggressive with us after Wade spun him off track last year. Don't you dare get into it with him too."

As the 28 car tore out of the pits for qualifying, I sighed, afraid Jack's warning came too late.

Chapter Fifteen

Mike qualified well, ending up third in our class after one of the Saleen drivers turned in a blistering lap to bump us from second. Third suited us fine, being about where the Sandham Swift Corvette usually finished in the field, as "the best of the rest" after the factory-backed Corvettes ran off with the first two places. They were the same C6.Rs we drove, with the addition of the finest-available General Motors engineering and support. But one of their cars had sprung an oil leak at the end of the practice session, and their crew hadn't been able to fix it in time to qualify.

I'd watched and cheered Mike's run from the pits, eating a granola bar, drinking water, and feeling my strength return. I knew the race would also be hard on me, not because I wasn't fit, but because I hadn't been in a racecar in a few weeks. For all of the C6.R's beastly sounds and aggressive looks, for all that it was powerful and heavy, it was an easy and comfortable car to drive. It was more taxing than driving a street car, but it had such good balance and setup that steering it around the track—even one as constantly demanding as this one—didn't leave the driver feeling like the loser in a wrestling match. Unless she hadn't been in a car for weeks. But the best way to be fit for racing was to go racing, and even today's twenty-minute stint would prep me for the hour-plus I might do in the race. I'd make it through on adrenaline alone, if necessary.

I perched on the edge of the bed in the motorhome, having returned early and alone to the team's paddock and tiptoed past the sleeping Mrs. Purley. Car noise had stopped for the ten-minute break between qualifying sessions, and I sat still, relishing the quiet, private space. Then the door of the motorhome opened and slammed shut. Heavy footsteps shook the vehicle. I started to stand, but sank back down when I heard the voice.

"Wake up, Suz," it growled.

Mrs. Purley sounded sleepy. "Ch-Charlie?"

"Yes, my dear, your loving husband."

"Charlie? What are you doing here?"

"I've come to save you, dearest."

"Wh-what?"

I heard a rustling of movement, and I considered announcing myself and getting out of there. But I was frozen, hearing the next words from Mr. Purley.

"I decided it was time to see what you, as Director of Sports Marketing, did for the company. What occupied you at these races. I haven't cared for what I've heard and seen."

"But, Charlie, I—"

"But that's resolved now, isn't it? The problem has taken care of itself, and I don't think you're likely to get as...distracted as you've been. Are you?" The last words were both command and question.

"No. No, Charlie!"

"I didn't think so. I'm fixing things here for you, so there'll be no more distractions and no comment on the past."

"Charlie." Susanah was gasping, crying perhaps. "I don't want you to think—I mean, I'm sorry you...."

"It's done. You're my wife. And I'm not letting you go." The hard-edged possession in his tone softened. "We're a team, remember, Suz? You and me, building a great company, building our life?"

I heard more rustling sounds, and I imagined an embrace.

"But Suz," Mr. Purley's voice was hard again. "This won't happen again. I'm not going to do this—go through this—again."

"No, Charlie. I love you."

"You do, don't you? And I'll let you prove it this weekend. Now, we're going to our hotel and to dinner tonight. Let's go." The motorhome wiggled again, and a few seconds later I heard the door open and slam closed. I stood and peeked out. Empty.

What the hell had he meant, he'd "fixed things" for her? I didn't like the sound of that—or of Mr. Purley—at all. I changed out of my driving suit, still shaken. I was tying my shoelaces when I felt the motorhome move again.

"Kate? You in here?"

I relaxed the shoulders I'd tensed. "Yeah, Aunt Tee. Just a sec." I scooped up my suit and other gear and went forward.

She smiled at me. "Great. I'll take those and hang them up for you." I handed over my sopping-wet suit and Nomex undergarments. Aunt Tee would turn them inside out and hang them to dry in the breeze outside the motorhome, with all the rest. I'd yet to decide if teams didn't care how unattractive inside-out suits were, flapping in the breeze, or if they considered them a flag of honor, testament to the work ethic of their pilots.

"Kate, are you OK?"

"Just disturbed by something."

"By what?"

Before I could pull my wits together, Tom climbed the steps into the motorhome. "Kate, there you are. We've got a press conference to go to."

"What? We didn't take pole." Only the top qualifier in each class, the driver who would start the race from pole position, was required to attend a press conference after qualifying.

"Yeah, I know, but the Series is asking all drivers in the top three teams of each class to go."

"Why?"

"The press wants to talk to Jack, Mike, and you. No one wants it to become a free-for-all about Wade, and so the Series is compromising by sending a bunch of drivers and limiting questions." He grinned. "Plus they were good GT2 and LMP1 qualifying battles. Big Porsche grudge match going on in GT2 between Turner Racing Group and the Johnson team. Most of the media don't care much, but we'll feed it to them anyway."

Facing the press wasn't appealing. It was great that my appearance in the ALMS was garnering some attention. On the other hand, I knew the media interest had nothing to do with me. Nothing to do with Wade. It had to do with murder.

"Kate?" Tom sat down opposite me. "Are you ready to deal with this? You'll have to sometime."

He was right. More crucially, it was my job to do anything my team needed. If that meant more scrutiny about Wade, I'd deal with it. "Of course, Tom. Whatever you need."

"Great! Here's a bunch of team gear—shirts, a hat." He picked up a stack of clothing he'd brought in with him. "Could you wear one of the shirts to the press conference?"

"Sure. How much time have we got?"

"Fifteen minutes."

I nodded as the door to the motorhome slammed open.

"Aw, shit. I always forget how this thing springs open." Jack stomped into the cabin, pulling the door after him. "Anyone seen my...."

"Keys, Jack?" Aunt Tee was holding out a set of rental car keys she'd picked up.

"Thanks. Now, Kate. Tom told you about the press conference?"

"I'll be there. Just have to change."

"Good. Also, dinner."

"Dinner?"

"Tonight with sponsors. At the White Hart Inn. Know it?"

"Yeah, I do."

"Good. Seven o'clock."

I looked at my watch. It was about four.

"Oh, and I've got you a room at the White Hart." Jack picked up a cookie from a plate on the counter and took a bite.

"What?"

"The team's all staying there, and you're part of the team. I got you a room."

"It's not—I mean, Wade was—it's not his—"

Jack swallowed another mouthful. "It's not Wade's room. I think the police have that one occupied. The hotel found another one for you."

Tom grimaced. "That would be creepy."

"No kidding," I replied. "But I've still got a room where I've been staying."

"So go check out. You need to be with the team—and you need to be at that dinner. OK?" Without waiting for an answer, Jack left the motorhome.

"OK?" Tom repeated Jack's question.

"Sure. I've just got to run up, collect my stuff, and check out. I'll have to do that before dinner. Oh, and I was supposed to meet Holly for dinner—I'll have to change that to a drink." I looked up at Tom and Aunt Tee. "Sorry, just thinking out loud."

"Well, first you've got to get to this press conference." Aunt Tee plucked the stack of clothing from my lap. She pulled a shirt out, a black polo with the Sandham Swift name stitched in yellow and white, to match our car. "Wear this one to the conference. I'll iron the rest for you." She eyed my hair. "And wear the hat, dear."

I laughed and ran a hand over my still-sweaty head. "Thanks, Aunt Tee."

Chapter Sixteen

The press conference was a zoo. A twenty-five year old trailer-turned-media center that normally held four drivers and a handful of media representatives now overflowed with twenty-four drivers, twelve team owners or managers, and thirty journalists. I had to hand it to the ALMS staff, Stuart in particular, for carefully orchestrating the proceedings.

As Stuart began by asking for quiet, a reporter in the front called out a question about the traction problems cars had been having.

Stuart's face could have been carved from granite. "We are here for another topic. We'll address your question if and when we have something to report." Then, ignoring the murmur that swept through the room, he presented drivers and team reps by class and qualifying position. In turn, the press dutifully asked questions they didn't care about the answers to.

First, the LMP1 class. Then LMP2. Next: GT1. My class. I shuffled to the front of the small dais with Mike and the other drivers, and the energy in the room ramped up a notch.

Stuart turned a stern eye on the room and pointed to the factory Corvette drivers who'd taken the pole. "Pole position, the LinkTime Chevy Corvette team. Questions?" There were a few, one concerning the fate of the sister car that hadn't managed to qualify.

"Second in class: the Vance Racing Saleen. Questions?" My mind wandered to the feel of the Corvette in different corners of the track, as I replayed my practice laps in my head.

"Third in class: Sandham Swift Corvette. Questions?" I snapped back to attention. Showtime, Kate.

"Kate. Mitch Fletcher from *Racer* magazine. How did you feel when you found Wade Becker's body, and how do you feel now that you've taken his place in the Sandham Swift car?"

I took a deep breath—while it seemed everyone else was holding theirs. "Hi, Mitch. Everyone. This morning, I was shocked, stunned, and very, very saddened. Sorry for the loss of life and talent. Since then, of course, I've joined the Sandham Swift team for this race, as I've joined them in the past. I'm not a stranger or an unknown to the team, and I'm happy to say we're all coming together to do the best we can under the circumstances."

I paused, then held up a hand at the swell of audience noise. "Personally, yes, I'm happy and eager to prove myself as a valuable, contributing member of the team. And though I'm going to make the most of my chance, I'd trade it away again for Wade to still be here." Boy, was I glad for the speech classes my grandmother had forced me to take in high school.

The buzz started again. Stuart deflected questions to Mike and Jack, who rattled on about the change in team dynamics—"we're humming along smoothly"—and thoughts on how the new driver would affect their finishes—"we expect to be as competitive as ever, and we're aiming to see you on the podium."

I thought about what I'd said. I meant it.

The rest of the press conference went quickly once the main attraction was over. But as the event broke up, a few reporters tossed out questions, one of which I couldn't ignore.

"Kate! Can you live up to the hype?"

I was walking out the door, following Jack, with Mike behind me, and I stopped. I poked my head around Mike. Everyone in the room was quiet, even Stuart, and given the expectant expressions on more than one face, I couldn't tell who'd asked the question. I lifted my eyebrows and smiled. "Hype? Hell, yeah. Haven't you heard? Girls kick ass." I exited to laughter and applause.

"Subtle." Jack eyed me as we walked out of the media center with the rest of the drivers and team owners.

"If I don't believe in myself, no one else will." I might worry later about bragging to a room of reporters or be concerned about adjusting to the car and the track, but deep down, I was confident I'd turn in a good performance.

I tilted my head to look Jack in the eye. "I'll deliver."

"I'm looking forward to that. It'll be a change for us."

I hesitated, wondering if I had the nerve to ask him to elaborate, but he thumped me on the shoulder, said he'd see me at dinner, and strode off in the direction of the parking lots, taking Mike with him.

They'd no sooner left than a Porsche driver named Eddie waved a hand at the group of drivers around us and started an interesting discussion. "Well, respect to the dead and all that, but I think we'll not be missing Wade. Glad to have you with us, Kate."

I heard chuckles and murmurs of agreement. "Thanks, Eddie."

"Even if some people think it's a mite convenient, you finding him and getting his ride and all." His lopsided smile and lilting Scottish accent made it a joke—at least to him. "We don't believe any of that, do we lads?"

I glanced around, registering amusement, doubt, and disinterest on the dozen faces within range of Eddie's voice. Doubt? I reexamined faces, not sure where I'd seen it and not finding it again.

"Thanks. And who thinks that?"

Eddie laughed. "Now, and I meant that well!" He saw my face and sobered. "It's just one of the whispers around, you know? Like so many other ridiculous rumors. No one thinks it's true."

I wasn't sure. "OK. But why won't you miss Wade?"

"Well, and I'll tell you. He'd as soon run you over as look at you on the track."

"Odd," drawled Heinrich, a dry, laconic German who drove one of the fastest cars in the ALMS. "I never had that problem."

"No, you wouldn't, would you?" Eddie rolled his eyes. "But try being in his way sometime. Marco knows what I mean, don't you? He punted you off on more than one occasion."

Marco, a dark-haired, expressive Italian driver of the Saleen in our own class, wasn't saying much. Just scowling.

"Everyone bumps each other now and then," I said. "Did Wade do more than anyone else?"

"The problem was with his attitude after the race." This was from Dave, a short, slight Indiana-boy with white-blond hair and a serious demeanor. "Sure, we all bang wheels, but we laugh it off afterwards. Even when we get pissed at each other—" He nodded to Eddie, with whom he'd had a running argument over three or four races last season. "We get over it. But not Wade. That man held a grudge."

Eddie jumped back in. "And not even for something reasonable, like you bumping him. He'd hate you forever if he bumped you. Right, it was my fault I was in his way! Mad."

"He confused fear with respect," noted Heinrich.

Eddie nodded. "Exactly. He changed—it's like he thought he could intimidate us so no one pushed him around on the track."

Marco suddenly burst out, "He—he was not right in the head."

I turned to look at Marco walking behind me. "Really?"

Torsten, a Swedish driver of one of the factory Corvettes, put a hand on Marco's shoulder. "Now, Marco. You're just angry because Wade told everyone about your wife and your girlfriend. And your other girlfriend. And your—how many is it, three?— children that aren't your wife's." His broad face creased into his habitual smile, revealing large white teeth.

Marco glowered at him. "And I should pay him? Not Marco!"

"Blackmail?" I couldn't tell if he was serious.

Marco didn't respond and the other drivers either shrugged or looked blank.

Torsten chuckled as he patted Marco's shoulder again. "I guess that's why he told everyone your secrets then. It's a good thing you can prove where you were last night and this morning. No, Wade wasn't crazy. But he had his own way of looking at the world. I think there was only one thing important to him: winning. Winning the race and maybe everything else too. Just that one thing." His smile disappeared. "And he'd do whatever it took to get it."

"Reckless." Eddie dropped the word. "That's what he was, reckless. And the public may think we're all nutters, but reckless, we're not."

I'd known, of course, that Wade had been aggressive, but I'd never heard of behavior outside the norm. "Reckless," I repeated, remembering Holly saying the same. "You mean on the track?"

I saw nods. Torsten looked thoughtful. "Yes, unpredictable, especially lately. Maybe Wade realized he was starting to lose his speed."

"Was he?"

No one was going to point the finger. "Maybe," Eddie finally admitted. "Maybe he wanted to make sure we all paid attention to him, even if he was no longer the fastest guy on track. I mean, we all slow down sometime. I just hope to do it gracefully."

"Not Wade, though," piped up Dave, the Indianan. "He'd have fought it tooth and nail."

"Maybe he did," I mused. Then I remembered something Zeke said. "Guys? Have you heard of something weird going on in the Series?"

"Like cars that can't maintain grip?" Dave Hacker frowned. He'd been at the wheel of the Racing Systems Panoz at a previous race when it broke loose in a turn and spun into the tires, ending his day.

"I still say it is the tires!" Marco took every opportunity to disparage tires that weren't Pirellis.

"No." Torsten shook his head. "I've heard it's the Delray ECU customers who should be worried. But what do you mean, 'something weird,' Kate?"

"I'm not sure. Just a rumor that Wade had been involved in something…dark. Maybe he knew something about the current problems."

The group was silent. I couldn't tell if no one knew anything or no one wanted to say.

Heinrich had the last word as the group split up in the paddock crossroads. "Anything is possible. Of course, based on the evidence, it might be dangerous to know anything at all."

Was that why Wade died, because he knew too much about something bad going on? I wondered, as I drove north to my cheap motel just over the Massachusetts state line. Deeds so terrible that murder would be done to cover them up seemed unbelievable. But Wade had been killed for some reason.

I thought of other questions I should have asked the drivers, questions about Wade, who—besides Marco—didn't like him, and the whispers floating around about me. I also thought about what Dave Hacker had doubled back to tell me, after everyone else walked away: that Wade had threatened him with "fixing it so he couldn't race again" if Dave didn't stay out of his way. I'd been too stunned to ask questions before he ran off to his team.

You must get better at investigating, Kate. Think faster. At least Holly always had her ear to the ground. She'd tell me what she'd heard when we met for a drink at six.

I stopped the car in front of my motel and slumped in the seat. The day had been busy enough for five lifetimes. Oops, just not Wade's lifetime. My cell phone rang.

"Kate Reilly."

"Ms. Reilly, Detective Jolley here."

I was glad I was sitting down. "Yes?"

"Ms. Reilly, I'd like to talk with you again tomorrow. Could you meet me at the track at nine in the morning?"

"I've told you everything I can think of."

"I'd like to walk with you through your actions of this morning, to see what else you might remember."

"Certainly, Detective. I'd be happy to help. Does this mean you have other suspects?"

The line was quiet. "You're not at the top of the list, Ms. Reilly, but you're still on it."

"You have a list? Who—how—I mean, wha—"

"I'm not going to talk about this with you. Please meet me at the Series trailer at nine tomorrow. You'll be at your hotel in Massachusetts tonight?"

"Oh, no. Jack—Mr. Sandham booked me into the White Hart Inn with the rest of the team. I'll be there. But you can reach me at this number anywhere."

"Thank you, Ms. Reilly. See you tomorrow morning."

I disconnected and leaned my head against the steering wheel. I'd yearned for the day I got a full-paying gig so hard it had been a physical ache…but I'd never expected anything quite like this.

I was back in the car, headed south to the White Hart, when my cell phone rang again. I fumbled to answer it.

"Katie!" My grandfather's voice boomed out.

"Gramps!" I smiled down the phone line.

"What's this I've been hearing? Are you in a bit of a pickle?"

My grandfather, who'd started out as a small-town mechanic, had developed the best network of informants I'd ever heard of within the racing world. He often knew the news at home in New Mexico before I knew it at the track. "What have you heard, Gramps?"

"Well, now, I've been told my girl found two things today: a ride and a dead man. Only not in that order. Either of those true?"

I sighed. "Both, Gramps. Both."

"Well." He paused. "I won't waste your money talking about something you can't fix—since I know you didn't kill the man."

"No, but he did happen to be the guy whose ride I'm taking. So I've been talking with the police. They think that's quite a coincidence."

"Tricky. You just remember what I always told you."

I nodded, though he couldn't see me, and repeated his mantra with him. "'Concentrate on your driving, and everything else will take care of itself.' I will, Gramps. And how's Grandmother?"

"Fine. She's cooking dinner."

"Saturday. That must mean it's roast chicken."

"Likely to be." We both knew few things in life were as predictable as my Grandmother's menus.

"You hiding out in your shop?" I could picture him there, sitting in his favorite chair of worn, cracked, brown leather, hitched up close to his workbench, dozens of multicolored spools of wire within easy reach. As he'd built a chain of car repair shops in Albuquerque, my grandfather had discovered an affinity for the electrical systems of racecars—and at seventy-nine, racing teams from across the country still came to him for handcrafted wiring harnesses. In his small workshop in the backyard he put together assemblies of the highest quality and best luck—teams he supplied won more often than not, and his customers called him their good luck charm.

"Yessiree," he crowed. "Putting together a harness for a sweet little car out in Charlotte, North Carolina." The sweet little car was as likely to be a snarling NASCAR creation as it was a low-power club racer. No snobbery there—Gramps would make gear for everyone.

"Give my best to Grandmother—oh! Gramps, something else today. I forgot."

I paused long enough that he prompted me. "Yes, Katie?"

"My father. My father showed up. He's involved with the ALMS. He's here."

He was quiet, and then he started muttering. I made out a few phrases: "…think he is…won't be telling your grandmother that…what the hell he wants." He raised the volume. "Katie, what did you think?"

"I don't know. Not interested, mostly. He said he wanted to talk to me. I told him I didn't have time."

"Well, Katie, love, I can't say as I blame you. And you'll do as you need to. Ignore the man if that's what feels right to you."

"For the moment. I've got too much else to think about."

"That you do. Drive the wheels off that car now, you hear? I'll be watching!"

"Great. I love you, Gramps."

Chapter Seventeen

I'd admired the White Hart Inn in the tiny town of Salisbury, Connecticut, on past visits to the Lime Rock track, but hadn't ever stayed there. The best feature of the main building, a two-story, white clapboard structure built in the early 1800s, was the deep porch that ran the width of the inn. I hefted my bags up onto it, eyeing the padded wicker chairs covetously, and swung open the door, headed for the reception desk. What I found first was my father.

He was standing at the small desk tucked into the right front corner of the lobby—its origins as a living room were obvious—talking with the one and only desk clerk. I veered left and set my bags down next to a dark, floral-patterned easy chair. I tried to be inconspicuous, staring at a painting with my back to the desk, noting the entrance to the tap room and restaurant on the right and a doorway to a lounge on the left. He finished his conversation a minute later, and my childish efforts at avoidance didn't work.

"Katherine." I heard surprise in his voice.

I turned, nodded, and started to move to the desk to check in.

"Katherine." He stood his ground and reached out as if to touch my arm. I stopped and regarded him with what I hoped was a lack of interest.

He cleared his throat. "I'd like a few minutes to talk with you. Please."

"I'm currently late, I'm afraid."

"Just a couple minutes. Tomorrow maybe? I have something for you from your grandfather."

Gramps? I thought. What could he mean?

He must have seen my confusion. "My father, that is. He passed away a few months ago."

Another family member I hadn't known. I couldn't feel grief for his death or sorrow for the absence of him in my life. My day had been too long, too overwhelming—too already filled with death—to take this on as well. "I'm sorry for your loss. But you'll have to excuse me now." I moved away.

"Another time," he murmured behind me.

I found my room—around the back, in a one-story wing added in the 1950s—and had just enough time to shower and drop into a chair on the front porch before Holly arrived.

"Hello, sugar, what're you drinkin'?" She looked fresh and clean, clad for once in non-team wear: loose, slinky black pants and a blush-pink linen blouse that didn't even clash with her red hair.

"Holly, how on God's green earth do you manage linen with all this traveling?" She was someone whose clothes never wrinkled, whose hair never wilted, and whose shoes never scuffed. I didn't get it.

She winked. "That's one of life's great mysteries. No racing tomorrow, so you'll have wine with me tonight, yes?" At my nod, she patted me on the shoulder and went inside, reappearing shortly with two generous glasses of something red.

"So." Holly crossed one knee over the other and bobbed her foot up and down in its low-heeled black sandal.

"So."

"How was your day, Miss Kate?"

I looked at her blankly. "This stuff doesn't happen to normal people."

"What does that make you?"

"Lucky? Unlucky? I don't even know."

She eyed me over the rim of her wineglass. "Does that cute little Tom Albright tickle your fancy?"

"Where did that come from?"

"I'm just sayin'. He's cute."

"And the original nice guy." I spoke without thinking.

"Ha!"

"Oh, please."

"The grapevine tells me you two spent a lot of time together today."

"The grapevine?! That's all I need. Besides, hello? We both work for the team. At least for this race."

"Hmmm. You also saw a lot of Stuart today."

I almost choked on my wine. "Stop. That man thinks I'm an idiot."

She narrowed her eyes at me. "I wouldn't be so sure. I've seen him watching you…in a way that made my heart flutter." She flapped a hand at her chest.

"Now you're hallucinating. I promise you: he thinks I'm an idiot. End of story. Pigs would fly first."

She shook her head, a smile on her lips. "We'll just see. Besides, I wouldn't be a girlfriend if I didn't rib you about a man now and then, would I?"

"I guess not." I drank more wine. "What else is the grapevine saying? And who is it?"

"Sugar, I never reveal my sources. And really, you don't want to know the details."

"Holly."

She put her glass down and leaned forward. She was more serious than I'd seen her all day. "Kate, trust me on this one. They're the same stupid—and untrue—rumors we hear every week. You know, someone's bangin' someone else's someone. Driver X is about to quit or be run out of town. Can you believe driver Y is so down on his luck that he's paying for a ride? And so on. Plus a few about Wade and you."

"Together?"

"No, nothing like that—unless I haven't heard it yet. Just your…connections."

"Well, the police—and even Benny Stephens—think it's pretty convenient that I got his ride, so why should I be surprised the rumor mill's saying the same thing? That's it, right?"

She nodded.

"Unbelievable. The best and the worst day of my life, all in one."

"It's memorable."

"I know I need to put my head down and drive. But I'm also starting to think I need to clear my name."

"Isn't that what these Yankee police are for?"

"Sure. But they don't have the vested interest I do in putting the grapevine's rumors to rest. Or the contacts."

Holly lifted her glass in a toast. "Here's to Miss Marple in a race helmet."

Chapter Eighteen

Fifteen minutes later, Tom himself showed up. "Hey, Kate. How're you doing, Holly?"

"Good. What are you doing this fine evening?" Holly's drawl was thick.

"Ah, the sounds of the South."

"Sugar, you a Southern boy?"

"Nope, a poor kid from a Colorado ranch—the wild West, ma'am."

As they chatted and flirted, I thought about Holly's question. I tilted my head, narrowed my eyes, and tried to envision Tom romantically. A nice guy. Cute.

"Kate?" Holly's voice was sharp. "You thinking about your last root canal?"

I opened my eyes wide. Tom was looking at me strangely. Oops. No romantic vibe there. "Sorry."

"Tom, join us, would you?" Holly gestured to a chair.

"Sure, if I'm not interrupting."

I leaned forward as he sat down. "No. In fact, I have to tell you both something. Mr. Purley is in town."

"What?" Tom shook his head. "That can't be right. He was clear he was coming in tomorrow."

"It was definitely Mrs. Purley's husband." I described the scene I'd overheard in the motorhome, complete with undercurrents of manipulation and violence. "That's one messed up relationship."

"Disturbing." Holly tapped her lips with her index finger.

Tom agreed. "I wonder what's really going on—what you heard, I mean. Aunt Tee didn't see him at the paddock today. Heck, Susanah was adamant that he wasn't going to be here. You didn't see him, right? It could be someone else." He saw my raised eyebrows. "No, I guess not. But it doesn't sound like who I've met. 'Fixed things?' I don't like the sound of that."

"Me either." I recalled the menace I'd heard and shivered. "But Tom, maybe you can ask around. See if Jack or the crew knows anything about Mr. Purley."

"Sure, I'll see what I can find out."

Holly looked at me. I could read her silent message. Be careful.

I ignored her. "And another thing. Some of the other drivers had interesting things to say. Apparently Wade held on to his mad and nursed it between races. One of the drivers told me Wade threatened him at a race last year."

"It makes no sense!" Tom burst out. "I mean, if a driver had died, I might think Wade had killed him. But the reverse?"

"Kate." Holly was atypically serious. "Who?"

I'd been told in confidence, but I couldn't get myself out from under suspicion, or the rumor mill, if I didn't share what I knew. "Dave Hacker. One of the drivers of the Panoz cars—the little guy from Indiana? But he also told me that Wade let it go at the beginning of this season."

Tom groaned. "Geez, maybe it isn't such a surprise it's Wade that's dead. I had no idea."

"That Wade was sure a peach." Holly raised her glass in a mock toast and drained the last of her wine.

Tom ran his hands over his face. "Do you know who the others were?"

"No. I don't think Dave did either. And don't say anything to Dave. I wasn't supposed to tell."

"But you're going to tell the police." Holly issued a command, not a question.

"I guess I've got to. I'll tell Detective Jolley in the morning—I'm meeting him at the track at nine."

I answered Holly's look. "A reenactment."

Her lips curved. "Delightful."

"Stuart!" Tom waved at the man climbing the steps to the porch.

Doubly delightful. Stuart was shaking Tom's hand and smiling—that was new—at Holly before leaning down to kiss her cheek. He turned to me, and I planted a pleasant expression on my face. "Hi, Stuart."

"Kate." Maybe I only imagined the hesitation before he extended his hand, but I preferred the collegial handshake to the decorative female treatment Holly'd gotten.

"Sit down, Stuart." Tom waved a hand to an empty chair.

Holly shot me a glance. I could read that one too. Behave, it said. And be nice. I sighed again. It was time for that. Time to start playing the race-weekend game for the sponsors, media, and team members.

"Stuart," I began. "Are you staying at the Inn, or are you here for the restaurant?"

"I'm staying just down the road."

"He's here for our dinner, Kate," Tom noted.

I aimed for no inflection at all. "That's nice."

Tom turned to Stuart. "Kate was just telling us she's meeting Detective Jolley tomorrow morning at the track for a reenactment."

Stuart looked at me without saying anything.

"'Reenactment' might be stretching it," I amended. "He said he wanted me to walk through my actions again."

"Maybe you should have someone there with you," put in Holly.

Stuart nodded. "When are you meeting him?"

"Nine, at the Series trailer."

"Then I'll see you there at that time."

"But...OK. Thank you." Holly hid her amusement behind her wineglass as I cleared my throat. "All Jolley would tell me is I wasn't at the top of his list."

Tom leaned forward. "I wonder why?"

Stuart spoke. "Probably because Wade had been dead some eight to ten hours before Kate found him."

We were all silent, absorbing that news. I shook my head. "Why am I so relieved to hear something definite? Have you heard anything else, Stuart?"

"Yes. The cause of death was subdural hematoma. Bleeding inside the lining of the brain."

I tried to reconcile the verdict with the glimpse of the body I'd had. "But there was no blood or obvious injury."

"No, there's often no visible sign. It's what the coroner found."

"But, how?" Tom asked.

Stuart shrugged. "They're not sure, exactly. He was hit on the side of the head, from above. With what object, they don't know, though it was heavy, but smooth, as there was no skin broken."

"Heavy and smooth," I repeated. "What could that have been?"

"Plenty of stuff around a racetrack," Holly commented.

"A mallet?" Tom suggested.

I shook my head. "Wouldn't a mallet break skin? How about one of those sandbags they hold equipment down with?"

"Ooh, yeah!" Tom was getting into this. "Or a helmet? Or a fire extinguisher?"

Holly was thinking about her kind of tools. "Or a serving bowl—even a bag of ice."

I looked at her. "Ice?"

"It's heavy."

Stuart listened, but didn't participate. I turned to him. "You have any ideas?"

He shook his head with a frown. "I haven't had the urge to speculate."

I wanted desperately to roll my eyes.

He unbent a little. "However, based on what the detective told me, any of those objects are possible. But, as you know, Kate, they didn't find anything near Wade's body to tell them for sure."

"So," Holly mused, "someone actually hit Wade upside the head."

"More like over the head," Stuart corrected.

I eyed him. "Should you really be telling us this?"

He raised tented fingers to his lips. "Perhaps not. But I'm confident you didn't kill Wade. And I understand you're determined to prove it."

I swiveled my eyes to Tom, who looked sheepish. I nodded to Stuart. "That's right."

"I'd like to help clear this up as well, for the sake of the Series, Jack's team, and even you."

"Gee, thanks."

Holly kicked my foot under the coffee table.

"I'm sorry," I went on. "I'm grateful for the help—and the belief."

Holly turned to Stuart. "I guess you're working on more than one mystery now."

Stuart raised an eyebrow at her.

Holly laughed. "Come on, the whole paddock knows you're working on 'The Case of the Spinning Racecar.'"

"Yeah, how's that going?" I asked. "Rumors are flying. Any idea what's really happening?"

Stuart turned to me with the same look. "No comment."

At that moment, the main door to the inn swung open and Jack Sandham exited, radiating geniality and power. He and Tom both wore black versions of the white team shirt I had on, and Jack's, combined with black trousers, accentuated his lean height. I looked a long way up to see his face.

"Good evening." He gestured to all of us with his cocktail.

"We're not late, are we?" Tom sounded anxious.

Jack took a sip of what looked like Scotch on the rocks. "Not at all. How is everyone this evening? How're things in your neck of the woods, Holly?"

She held out a tiny hand to be enveloped in his and twinkled at him. "Fine and dandy, sugar. Nothing eventful."

"Ha," Jack barked, sipping again. "Wouldn't uneventful be nice."

"Do what you can with what you've got, right?"

"Indeed." He spoke with feeling.

With a nod to me, Holly broke the burgeoning somber mood. "But Jack, are you sure you ought to take this one on? She'll be trouble, you know."

Another sip. "I'll take my chances. Nowhere to go but up from where we were. And it's not like she was a snap decision either. I'd been thinking along those lines. I'll take my chances."

He delivered the welcome endorsement offhand, while scanning passing cars. He must have seen the arrival he was waiting for, because he took his leave. "See you inside in five—Holly, join us if you'd like." Then he took off in the direction of the parking lot.

Tom smiled. "What do you think, Holly, want to stay?"

"Thanks, but I've got a date with some bubble bath and a romance novel."

"But, sugar," I mimicked her, "how can you stand to miss all the fun?"

She stood up and brushed nonexistent wrinkles out of her pants. "I'll live with the disappointment. You behave." She directed that to me, then nodded at Stuart and Tom. "Boys. I'll see y'all tomorrow or Monday."

"Have a good evening, Holly." Stuart stood when she did and kissed her cheek again.

"Bye, Holly. Thanks." I jumped up to give her a hug and walked her partway to her car.

She had two more parting instructions for me: be good, and go kick some butt.

Chapter Nineteen

Tom, Stuart, and I walked into the back room of the White Hart's restaurant to find a large square table set for twelve and a handful of people standing around. Mike was across the room talking with the SPEED Channel announcers. He lifted a hand in greeting, prompting Benny and Ian to turn around and do the same. All three held cocktails, which explained their expressions of delight. Benny and Ian lived life with gusto, whether that was scouting for gossip—"color"—to add to their broadcasts, telling tall tales of races past, or consuming free drinks and gourmet food provided by a team owner looking for air time. They'd be in their element tonight, doing all three at once while being flattered for the kind of coverage they'd probably give us on-air anyway. It was part of the game we all played.

I wasn't ready to take the plunge of sucking up to sponsors I'd never met before, so I joined Mike. Tom and Stuart had abandoned me the instant we entered the room, Tom heading for Jack, and Stuart talking to a slightly pudgy, balding guy wearing glasses and a rumpled navy suit.

"Good evening, gentlemen." Mike, Benny, Ian, and I were all dressed alike, in the racing fraternity's second uniform: jeans or khakis and a button-down shirt embroidered with logos of the team and sponsor—or television network, in Benny and Ian's case.

"So, Kate." Ian's Scottish burr was softened by years of living in the States. "You can tell us...." He paused, and I braced myself. "Your day was a wee bit boring, wasn't it? Tell us the truth, now." Ian kept a straight face, but Benny was hooting with laughter.

I pretended to think the question over carefully, pursing my lips and nodding. "Just ho-hum." I caught Mike smirking into his glass.

Ian put an arm across my shoulders. "At least you haven't lost your sense of humor."

"Having you two around keeps it in fine shape."

"Seriously, Kate." Benny looked somber. "Has anyone figured out what happened?"

"I don't know anything, except that I'm still a suspect."

Ian was shaking his head. "It's so strange. I wouldn't have put it past Wade to be mixed up in a murder, but I wouldn't have pegged him for the corpse."

"You seriously thought he could have killed someone? People just don't do that sort of thing."

"He had a streak of mean in him. I sometimes watched him driving and dealing with people and thought if he ever lost control, who knew what would happen."

"But, Ian," Benny put in, "he was nothing compared to old Devin Carroll—remember twenty-some years ago? He was a terror."

I lost track of their conversation about racing maniacs of days gone by because I was watching two people who'd just entered the room: a big, beefy, forty-something man who looked like a former NFL player—the classic ex-jock—and Susanah Purley. The happy couple.

I turned back to the three men. "So, who would get Wade close to the edge?"

They just looked at each other.

"Who?" Benny repeated. "Everybody."

"Come on, guys, names."

Ian looked thoughtful. "Marco in the Saleen. Sean—that Canadian guy who drove a Porsche last year, remember? Dave

Hacker, our farm boy. Vincent Bradley. Paul Yaeger. John Newton. The list goes on. Jack. Mike, here. That's not even mentioning the sponsors, Series people, media."

"Wait. Mike?" I looked at him with concern.

Mike, my brawny co-driver—who, if I didn't trust with my life, I trusted with the same machinery I trusted my life to— held up a hand. "Wait now. They'll tell you: Wade fought with everyone. He'd get pissed at me, saying I threw away a race or did something else he thought I shouldn't have done." He looked embarrassed and rubbed his neck with his hand. "I didn't always manage to keep my cool, that's all. I tried, I know what he's like. But get into the heat of the race—or have him get in my face yelling that I'd done something wrong when I hadn't? Once in a while I'd shout back. Who doesn't?"

Benny's laugh boomed out. "Kate, don't you see? He argued with everyone. All the sponsors—heck, everyone in this room!" He waved a hand.

Ian shook his index finger. "Except us, Ben."

"That's right. He knew better than to mess with us."

I wasn't sure I saw the distinction between messing with the television commentators and messing with the wife of a sponsor who paid your bills. Granted, Benny and Ian could give your career a hand up or a slap down by talking about you or ignoring you. For that reason, they were courted by teams, sponsors, and drivers—though it was clear they could see through the crap and fakery in a heartbeat. I liked that about them.

Tom and Stuart joined us at that point, bringing with them the guy Stuart had been talking to, the one who looked like an accountant. As our small group nodded at the newcomers and ended our conversation, I kept an eye on Susanah and her husband across the room. I still had to face that intro.

"Kate," Tom spoke, his hand on the accountant's shoulder. "I'd like to introduce you to one of our sponsors—our best sponsor. Charles, this is Kate Reilly, our new driver. Kate, Mr. Charles Purley."

Chapter Twenty

Tom was looking at me with concern. I swallowed hard and got a grip. "Mr. Purley." I shook his hand.

"Call me Charles, please." His voice lacked menace.

"Charles, then. I met your wife earlier today."

He smiled, a cozy smile that went with his thinning hair and desk-sitter's physique. I began to think I'd hallucinated the afternoon's episode.

Mike started the conversation, asking questions about the Purley business—Racegear.com, an online store for all things race-related—and I tried to behave as if I didn't suspect this unlikely looking man of murder. I was relieved when Jack waved us to the table.

I made sure I didn't sit next to Mr. Purley, ending up in the middle of one side with Tom on my right and the jock on my left. The jock turned out to be a former professional hockey player from near Montreal, Canada. He'd grown up going to the racetrack at Mont Tremblant, and though he'd acquired only modest fame in the NHL, he'd accrued a bank account large enough to start a sportswear company called Active-Fit, which in turn made a lot more money and funded our race team. Canadian Mr. Active-Fit was big, beefy, and as polite as they come. His wife was with him, looking like a mid-thirties, fit, and wealthy former cheerleader—which she probably was. She was nice, too.

On the other side of Tom was a young, short, tan guy—and I mean everything about him was a light, golden brown: his skin, his clothes, his shoes, his hair—everything. He must have rented a champagne-colored car. He was a marketing rep for another sponsor, Leninger's Enduro Shine, a car wax manufacturer looking to go national. Sponsoring our car was a means of getting its name out to car and race fans. We shook hands across Tom's water glass.

Our group of mostly men in casual dress, talking about cars and engines, struck an incongruous note against the décor of the room: English-cottage floral, complete with fake ivy winding up white lattice attached to two of the walls. The wall I faced was entirely windows, and while everyone else tasted the wine on the table and read the menu, I watched the fading daylight cast a pinkish glow on the 19th-century buildings across the road.

"Kate." Jack's irritated voice cut through my daydreaming. I'd been staring out the window over his head, directly opposite me. "Stay with us."

Just then the waiter intervened. "Wine, miss?"

I responded to him instead of Jack and threw myself into conversation with Mr. and Mrs. Active-Fit, determined to make a good showing of schmoozing with the sponsors. We'd all placed orders, and I was chatting with them about starting their business when Benny's voice broke through the multiple conversations taking place around the table. He and Ian were laughing at Mike, who was seated on the left side of the table, next to Mr. Purley.

Benny shook a finger at Mike. "You were wound up that time!"

Mike flushed. "It was the heat of the moment—a misunderstanding."

"The best part was you went after him with your helmet still on, and we had it all on tape!" Benny chuckled. He referred to an incident during a race last year when an inexperienced Porsche driver had spun off-track, collecting Mike and sending him into a wall, hard. Mike had pulled himself from the Corvette, stormed over to the Porsche, and pounded on its roof at the driver, while still in full helmet and gear. Keeping the helmet on had made it an aggressive move—with it, he, or any other driver, was armed against trouble or retaliation. And SPEED Channel had broadcast it all live.

Mike looked more ashamed. "I just hadn't pulled the helmet off yet. I wasn't going to hit him—I was only wishing his car'd been as badly damaged as mine. I backed off immediately when I realized he was afraid to get out." Mike noticed the whole table listening to him. He shrugged. "Kate'll back me up. We drivers hate to lose. Hell, we hate to not finish a race. And watch out if it's someone else's fault that we can't finish or win. Then we'll get in their face about it."

Ten pairs of eyes swiveled to me.

"Kate?" Ian invited.

"He's right. I wouldn't be out there if I didn't know I could win. Call it ego, confidence, arrogance—whatever. That's what I'm working with. There are things we can control: driving, pit strategy, tire wear. The things out of our control? They're infuriating. Tire blowout. A yellow just after you've made a green-flag stop. But someone else ending your day? That's the worst, because it's not an act of God like a tire, but an act of someone's stupidity that's killed the win."

"Speaking of which," Mr. Active-Fit said to Jack. "You're sure you won't have the same problems the Viper had? And the other cars the last couple of races?"

Jack acted quickly to reassure the people who paid lots of money to see his cars finish the race. "We're doing everything possible. Everything's being checked three, four, five times by experts. I won't lie to you and say we know exactly what it is and how to fix it, but everyone in the ALMS is working on it."

Mr. Purley leaned forward to look at me. "You really think you can win the race on Monday, Kate?"

"Sure. The entire team's good enough. And anything can happen."

"Just look at what happened today." Benny's expression was devilish.

Mrs. Active-Fit had a question. "But, Kate, won't it be strange being the only woman?"

I smiled, used to this one. "Not really. It matters less in this sport than any other."

She and the car wax guy looked confused, so I elaborated. "In football or hockey," I nodded to Mr. Active-Fit, "the athlete's size is everything. You wear sized equipment and your mass helps you advance or defend. In racing, Mike and I wear the same size car. Once you get into that car, we're all the same in bulk and power. Racing is about concentration. About always driving the correct line through a corner, driving the car at the edge of its capabilities, more than it's about sheer muscle mass. Sure, the C6.R is heavy—heavier than most cars—and you can feel that, but it's really well-balanced—besides, I have to manipulate it, not carry it. It's more about concentration, hand-eye coordination, and general fitness than the ability to bench press your own body weight."

"What can you bench, Katie?" Ian smirked.

"My body weight," I shot back, making everyone laugh.

"You're a pistol," Ian said to me, then turned to the rest of the group. "And she's right. Aside from Mike here, you notice how most drivers are short and small? Kate's size? Hell, my size, since I'm only a couple inches taller. You've got to be smart more than you've got to have brawn or mass. And don't go thinking this isn't a 'real' sport either, I'm fed up with that attitude."

Confusion was apparent on the face of the tan-themed car wax guy. "I'm not sure I understand. But I'm sorry, I'm new to this."

Ian was off and running, gesturing with his arms around the server distributing our soups and salads. "See, as a former driver, I know whereof I speak. Here's where you have to start. Imagine holding something—your salad plate there—at arm's length in front of you. Not so hard, right? For one, two, three hours at a time? In an enclosed space that's 120 degrees? At 150 miles per hour? Then, the G-forces. Your head and helmet weigh twelve or thirteen pounds. You're going around a corner at speed—hell, in the Climbing Turn here you can pull three Gs in these cars. Suddenly your neck has to hold thirty-six to thirty-nine pounds upright. And your torso has to keep three times its normal weight from flopping around."

He took a bite of salad and poked his fork in the innocent questioner's direction. "I've seen the toughest, fittest driver climbing out of the car bruised and battered after a two-hour stint—and exhausted. It's hard work."

The tan guy was cowed. "I didn't mean to—"

Jack took pity on him. "No, of course you didn't. It's just Ian's favorite soapbox." Jack lifted his glass in Ian's direction.

"No lad, hell, I wasn't yelling at you." Ian shook his head. "But I can't tell you how many times we get comments about 'the drivers aren't really athletes.' Just because it's a sport where the short and lean ones aren't at a disadvantage."

"They mostly have the advantage." Jack topped off the wine-glasses he could reach and passed the bottle to the rest of us. "It's almost harder for the really big guys, right, Mike?" Mike was taller than both me and Ian—close to six feet. But anything taller than my own five-foot-three seemed way up there.

Mike poured more wine. "It's like airplane seats. Kate's got more room in them than I do. My knees are about in my armpits. Easier for her to get to things in the car than for me. Easier for her to get in and out of that small window opening." He flashed lots of teeth, his hair flopping around his face. "Wouldn't trade it though."

"What about you, Jack," asked Mr. Purley. "Did you ever drive?"

"Tried. Couldn't ever get comfortable, just didn't fit. So I started running things instead."

"You didn't ever race?" Mrs. Purley spoke for the first time all evening.

"Go-karts, when I was little. But I grew pretty quickly."

"And you come from a racing family," Ian commented. "Your dad raced?"

"Dad, three uncles, and my grandfather. All in local series, local circuits in the south. Growing up twenty minutes from Daytona Beach, what else would you expect?"

I captured Jack's attention. "Did you think you'd end up a driver?"

"Of course. That's what my family did, hobby and work. My granddad ran a car repair shop, and dad and his brothers grew up banging on cars, racing them on the local dirt tracks, and fixing them again when they wrecked. My generation of kids is also all in racing. It's what we know—but I'm the only one running a team."

I heard the pride in the last statement and saw that Mike, Benny, and Ian recognized it too.

"Yes, this team is everything I ever wanted." Jack raised a glass to everyone. "And I want to thank each and every one of you for being part of it, for supporting us, for driving for us, for mentioning us on-air. In spite of what we're dealing with. I can't thank you enough for your support, and I'm very proud of each and every member of the team."

We all toasted him and drank.

Jack put his glass down with a thump. "Enough of that! Eat up, people! Drink more. We've got a day off tomorrow, then it's back to the grindstone." Our entrees arrived, and Jack issued commands. "Benny, Ian, time to earn your keep. Charles, tell them what's new with Racegear.com, so they know what to say about us when our car's in the lead." He said the last with a wink at me and Mike. I cut into my steak.

Chapter Twenty-one

It wasn't until dessert that the discussion became valuable for me. Ian, with scores of races here in his past and numerous glasses of wine under his belt, became animated describing the effect the track could have on the field and racing strategy.

"The thing is, this track's a rectangle." Ian plunked his elbows on the table, chopping his hands through the air, outlining the shape. Benny rescued his water glass from the onslaught. "It's a big equalizer, because there's not much straightaway. Those factory-backed Corvettes have more power than you, but they don't have the straight line to use it and build speed—a little, but not a lot. And you'll all corner about the same, so it'll even things out. Not like Road America or Salt Lake City where the faster cars can really get away from you on the long straights. Lime Rock's a narrow track and short in length. It's going to be crowded. And you know what? Those short sides aren't for passing.

"You two," he waved a finger at first me, then Mike. "Don't try to pass unless you're on the long sides of the rectangle. It's a momentum track—you don't want to get caught behind slower cars and have them break your momentum. Keep your heads. You ought to be in good shape here."

The car wax guy found his voice. "How much have you driven at Lime Rock, Kate?"

"About twenty minutes today." He and the other sponsors waited for me to go on. "That's it. I've been around the track in a street car, but in the racecar, just today."

Jack swooped in. "Now, don't worry. We're in good hands. Our Kate here is one of the quickest studies I've ever seen. I remember a couple years ago in the Star Mazda series, at—where was it, Kate? Portland?" I nodded, recognizing which story he was going to tell.

"It was her first race at that track. First race in a Star Mazda car—one of the little open-wheel guys. She qualifies eighth out of fifteen—not so bad for her first time. At the start she gets pushed out of line and drops back five places. But damn if she didn't come through the field to win the race!"

The Purleys and the Active-Fits turned to me with wide eyes. I smiled. "My first win in Star Mazda. First race. A great day."

"I saw that, and I thought to myself, watch her." Jack thumped his fist on the table. "Watch that girl, she's going to be good. And hell, by the end of twenty minutes today, she was lapping at race speeds. We're going to do just fine."

With that, Jack pushed back from the table and stood, the rest of us slowly following suit. As the group migrated to the porch of the hotel, settling into the wicker sofa and chairs I'd occupied earlier with Holly, Mr. Purley spoke next to me. "A ringing endorsement."

"It was nice of him to say."

"Doesn't it make you more nervous? The pressure?"

"I get nervous, sure. But I thrive on that kind of pressure. It's part of my job."

Mike and I dragged over four more chairs from the other end of the porch, though I perched on the railing, leaning against a post and facing the day's last light.

Jack emerged from the hotel bar with two more bottles of wine and a waitress behind him carrying glasses. We kept chatting about the local area, the race, the sponsors' companies, and the team.

Sandham Swift had at least a dozen sponsors. Car title privileges—"the Number 28 Sandham Swift Racegear.com Corvette"—cost about a million dollars for the season, and other sponsor contributions ranged from the low to high six figures.

Racing is expensive, and it's fueled by sponsor dollars. Kids racing go-karts have sponsors. Fourteen-year-old drivers sell raffle tickets door-to-door to raise money. And for their money, sponsors get various sizes and placement of their logos on the car, team wear, and advertising. Plus lots of entertaining, before, during, and after the race. Driving the car was almost the least that a racecar driver had to do. The dinner wasn't how I'd have chosen to spend my evening, but it paid my salary. I kept chatting.

A half-hour later, Benny and Ian were the first to leave, promising to see us the next day—at the track or in a bar somewhere, noted Ian—and instructing us to put on a good show for the cameras on Monday, as they'd be talking about us. The Active-Fits left shortly thereafter, thanking everyone. The car wax guy faded away after them, and the Purleys were the next to make their excuses. Jack walked a few feet to the stairs and spoke quietly with them.

Mike, Tom, Stuart, and I sat in silence for a couple minutes. The sky was dark, and even with the low lights on the patio and the lamps on the village green in front of the inn, we could see stars. The warm air smelled of plants and dampness. I was surprised that Stuart was still there and that he'd been a pleasant dinner companion. It had to be the marketing background.

Three drivers swung open the doors of the inn and walked out onto the porch. I didn't know two of them, but the third was Jim Siddons, the Porsche driver who'd glared at me before practice and bumped me with his car. They paused just outside the door, the other two nodding to our group and Jim sneering, then they moved to the empty chairs at the other end of the porch and sat down.

I turned to Mike. "Talk about an attitude problem. Did Wade get into it with him, too?"

"Yep."

"Figures."

I moved to a chair next to Tom and leaned forward, resting my elbows on my knees. "Let me ask you guys something. It's hard to believe everything I've heard—to reconcile it. I mean,

I met Wade, drove with him once. He wasn't all that bad—" I remembered his unexpected attack the previous night. "Until yesterday he wasn't. But if he was so awful and evil, how did everyone put up with him?"

"He wasn't always awful. And he wasn't evil. That's extreme." Tom sounded shocked.

"I was exaggerating. But you also haven't heard the stories of on-track bumping and threats of revenge."

"I think I'm glad I haven't."

Stuart set his glass on the coffee table. "I believe the short answer is he wasn't always a negative personality—he could be charming. He'd been at this level of professional racing for more than a dozen years. In fact, I think that became a problem for him. It was all routine—boring, perhaps."

"How could racing ever be boring?" Tom's sentiment echoed my thoughts, but I smiled at how naïve it sounded spoken aloud.

Stuart shook his head. "Not the activity on-track. But every-thing else? Entertain the sponsors, make nice to the fans, give diplomatic quotes. He'd learned the ropes over the years."

"Done it all, paid his dues," I murmured. "Maybe that was the problem. He expected more success than he had?"

Mike wrinkled his nose. "I've only been with the team a couple years, but if you said to me Wade thought the world owed him a favor, I'd say you're right. He'd gotten more demanding and cranky, that's for darn sure. He was always prickly, but it got to where I'd leave every race feeling guilty or responsible for something my co-driver had done."

"No one held his behavior against you, Mike," Stuart commented.

Mike looked like he'd eaten a lemon. "I know. I was still associated with him. What always freaked me out though, was how he'd talk about keeping score."

He saw our blank looks. "That's what he called it. 'Keeping score.' He'd make notes about different races and other driv-ers. His own personal timing and scoring, he told me when I asked. He was hostile and creepy, hunched over that little black notebook in the pits, scribbling away about vendettas, I guess. I wonder where that notebook went."

I sat up straight. "A black notebook?"

Mike nodded.

"I saw it today."

"Where?"

"I'm not sure. I'll try to find it again."

Stuart wore his familiar severe, dictatorial expression. "If you do, Kate, give it to Detective Jolley."

"What does she need to give to the cops?" Jack was standing next to us again, and the Purleys were on the other side of the porch railing, walking down the ramp to their car.

Tom forgot to use his quiet voice. "The notebook of Wade's that she found."

I detected a hitch in Mrs. Purley's stride, and she started to turn to us, but Mr. Purley spoke to her quietly and they continued on their way. I also noticed a stillness at the other end of the porch, and I glanced over to see Jim and the other two drivers watching us.

Jack frowned. "Notebook? I didn't know he had one. But sure, Kate. If you find anything of Wade's, give it to Jolley—unless it's proprietary team info."

Stuart stood and shook Jack's hand. "Thank you for the meal and the company. I enjoyed both." He nodded to the rest of us. "Kate, I'll see you tomorrow morning."

I'd forgotten my appointment with Jolley. My nerves sprang to life again. "See you then."

The rest of us stood also and dispersed to our rooms: Tom, Mike, and Jack back inside the main doors, and me down the steps to reach my room at the back of the Inn. I circled to the west, through the parking lot. There wasn't much light to see where I was going, and I watched the ground to be sure I didn't trip on anything.

"Kate."

I jumped, my heart thudding. "Stuart. You scared me."

"Sorry. I just wanted to say be careful."

"What? Driving? OK." My eyes adjusted to the darkness, and I could see him shake his head. Locks of hair curled onto his forehead.

"No, in general. Be careful. Stop asking about Wade. Think about driving and leave him alone."

"I'm not asking a lot of questions."

"Yes, you are. It's the talk of the paddock. Everyone knows you're asking who didn't like Wade."

"Well, but I have to—"

His voice was knife-sharp. "No, the police have to, not you. And don't you think someone would find it a threat? Like Wade was a threat? I know I would."

I was stunned. I had to admit I hadn't given much thought to discretion, just to getting myself clear. I felt a twinge of fear.

I took a deep breath, heart again thumping hard. "What the hell do you mean, 'you know you would?' You would what? Find me a threat?"

"I'm just giving an example. A friendly warning."

"That's great. Helpful. And I'm supposed to sit back and have the police and the paddock think I'm guilty?"

Stuart sighed. "Just leave the questions to the police. I'll see you in the morning." He walked to his car.

I muttered about the nerve he had telling me what to do as I rounded the back corner of the hotel and reached my door. Number 16, it was the second in a row of five doors that opened onto a small lawn between our rooms at the back of the inn's main building and the carriage house, now renovated into a half-dozen more guest rooms.

"Deserted and dark, great." There were lights above each room, mostly spotlighting a welcome mat, and not illuminating much else. I blinked heavily in the transition to bright light and raised my key to the lock.

I had an impression of movement to my left, and I turned my head. "Hold on," a voice said.

I wasn't startled this time, just angry, and my fingers shook as I belatedly positioned my key between them to use as a weapon.

"Who's there?"

My father stepped forward into the light. I let out the breath I was holding.

"I'm sorry, Katherine. I wanted to give you something." His voice was smooth, collected. I felt like a frazzled idiot—a frazzled idiot who blabbed too much, according to Stuart.

"Thank you, but—"

This time he spoke harshly. "Katherine. Stop it. You'd do a stranger the courtesy of hearing him out. Have the decency to do the same for me."

I bit my lip to keep from telling him that (a) he didn't know what I'd have the courtesy to do, (b) he was a stranger, and (c) like he had the decency to stick around and be a father to me for any amount of time in the last twenty-four years? I let all that go. "Fine. Go ahead."

"As I mentioned, my father passed away a few months ago. I'm truly sorry that you were never able to know him. He was...a great man." He spoke the last words quietly, with a bowed head. When he lifted it to continue, his eyes were shiny and sad. "He would have liked you, I think. He wanted to like you. He wanted to meet you."

"What?"

"He wanted to get to know you."

"He knew about me?"

My father sounded tired. "Of course. He knew and urged me to find you, long ago, and then to reach out to you once we knew where you were. But I...."

"I don't think I want to hear this."

"Perhaps not. In any case, this isn't the time or place. But my father wanted you to have this. Something he treasured." He held out a medium-sized, dull silver gift box with no insignia. "Please," he said, when I made no move. "For him, if not for me."

I took it from him and nodded.

"Thank you." He walked away into the darkness.

I stood there another minute, holding the box and wondering what kind of family ties I'd just bound myself with. Then I shivered and looked around. The air was warm and somehow expectant, but whether that was because of the humidity I had little experience with or because there was evil lurking around the bend, I couldn't tell. I got into my room fast and locked the door.

Chapter Twenty-two

Sunday morning I went from sleeping to wide awake in seconds.

First thought: race tomorrow!

Next thoughts: Wade. Detective Jolley. Murder.

An afterthought, as I got out of bed rubbing my eyes: my father.

I lifted a corner of the curtain covering the room's single window, set in the wall next to the door. Gray and overcast. I looked harder. Raining. Unheard of on July Fourth where I grew up in the Southwest, but typical here. If we were lucky, we'd have no rain for the race the next day.

My nerves started to hum at the thought of the race and my big chance. Before I could change my mind, I brushed my teeth, got into water-resistant gear, and launched myself through the door to run some of my anxiety out.

I jogged down the main road through town admiring the red, white, and blue streamers and bunting, and the profusion of American flags. I turned left onto Salmon Kill Road and found the trail the desk clerk had recommended about a quarter-mile down. I jogged up the slight incline, feeling springy scrub grass underfoot. Left to its own devices, the land in this part of the country turned into a jungle of trees, shrubs, vines, grass, and weeds, but I was on a twenty-foot-wide swath through wilderness that was carefully maintained.

My muscles finally traded stiffness and fatigue for a smooth flow, and I began to feel more alert. The anxiety and excitement that wanted to jump around in my stomach went quiet as my body dealt with the exertion of running. Over the steady thump of my shoes and my panting breaths, I heard birds and the occasional car on the road behind me. I felt strong, and I pushed the tempo up a notch.

The ground was damp underfoot, but not muddy. I glared at the sky. I wasn't excited about rain for the race. Everything would get more complicated. Rain meant slipping, extra pit stops for different tires, and lots of strategy. On a dry track, our cars ran slicks: tires with a smooth surface, which meant maximum rubber in contact with the road for maximum grip and handling. But slicks couldn't channel water out from under themselves, like grooved tires could, and to be on slicks, or "dries," in the rain was to invite disaster.

Each type of tire worked well for its intended purpose, terribly in other conditions. Slicks on a wet surface tended to imitate ice skates. Grooved wet-weather tires, or "wets," on a dry surface offered minimal grip and wore away at an alarming rate, from excess friction and heat. The issue was when to change from dries to wets and back. I let out a long breath. It was enough to be thinking about managing a new track in the dry. I couldn't worry about rain and strategy also. I'd have to leave that to Jack.

Of course, what no amount of strategy or quick decision-making could control was if our car would be affected by ECU problems—or tire problems or whatever the mystery ailment was. Cars were complex machines, and teams dealt with equipment defects from time to time—a tire blew, an axle or half-shaft broke, screws sheared off, and so on. But usually it was easy to pinpoint the problem. The recent issues were confusing because no one could determine the cause.

Then again, maybe it wasn't a mechanical defect to blame. I'd heard the words blackmail, sabotage, and darkness—even if I hadn't heard them in reference to car problems, they made me wonder.

I chewed over those words. The concept of sabotage was unfathomable. Even cheating, I could accept, but active damage of another team? That was as unbelievable to me as…murder. I stopped, lungs heaving, in the middle of the path. Time to readjust my thinking. Maybe anything was possible.

I jogged forward again, turning my mind to the portrait of Wade that had emerged yesterday. To me, he'd always been the epitome of a racer—and I meant a *racer*. Someone who could drive and win in anything with wheels, even if he'd never made it into the national consciousness as a NASCAR star. Plenty of us were racecar drivers. But a *racer* was something else, someone who loved driving and competing above all else and who'd drive anything anywhere anytime, just to be strapped into a five-point harness. The payoff and the prize money were great, but what mattered was a car, a track, and someone to race with. I'd give my eyeteeth, as Gramps would say, to be respected by my peers as a racer.

Coming up through the racing ranks, I'd followed his career, admired him. He wasn't an idol of mine, but a role model. Someone whose skill and career I'd be happy to emulate. But when I'd driven with Wade and Mike at the twelve-hour Sebring race the previous year, my mental image of him had been tarnished.

He'd been aloof. I thought about that as I turned around on the trail and headed back. Used to it all, even rude. Uninterested in what was going on and unwilling to exert himself, except on the track. It must have been routine, down to the overeager rookie driving with him.

The picture of him emerging now was more detailed and disturbing. His skills—and his magnetic personality—had started to slip. The façade started to crack. He got slower. Less charming, more grasping. As Ian said, as angry as Wade had become, it wasn't surprising he'd been involved in a murder—but it was surprising he'd ended up the one dead.

I swung wide around two women walking fluffy Golden Retrievers. Murder. Murder! What the hell was I doing mixed up in something like that? I didn't think Detective Jolley was pursuing the idea that Wade had been killed by a stranger. And I didn't want to think about rubbing shoulders with a killer.

Instead, as I showered, dressed, and drove to the track, I focused on the Corvette, the racing surface, and my twenty-minute wild ride the day before.

Chapter Twenty-three

Detective Jolley was waiting for me at the entrance to the track, leaning against his unmarked, white Ford Crown Victoria and wearing a carbon copy of his outfit from the day before, plus a patriotic American flag tie. There'd been little traffic on the way to the track, which was holding a Lime Rock Open House in honor of the holiday and the race weekend. There would be no engines running, but there'd be activities for fans, including a Corvette car show, tech talks given by team members, and the usual ALMS open paddock opportunities: to walk around, watch cars being worked on, and talk to teams and drivers. Plus a fireworks show that night. For the race teams, the fact that it was the Fourth of July was irrelevant—we'd continue prepping for the race and entertaining sponsors. And I would go to bed early.

Jolley held up a hand as I approached, and I stopped, brushing the crumbs of the muffin I'd eaten for breakfast off my lap. He pointed at my passenger door and raised his eyebrows. I nodded, and he got in.

"You're serious about recreating my movements?"

"Good morning, Ms. Reilly."

"Good morning, Detective."

"I am serious. Do whatever you did yesterday, only slowly, and talk me through what you saw."

"Sure." I took a sip from my coffee cup, setting it back in the cup holder in the center console. "Only, I didn't have coffee with me yesterday, so that's different."

"I'll keep that in mind, thank you."

I glanced at him. He might have a sense of humor.

"Ms. Reilly?" Jolley gestured forward.

I moved ahead. "Let's see. Yesterday, like today, there were few people around. Yesterday I saw the guy at the gate here." We passed through the checkpoint and waved badges at the attendant. Mine was the ALMS badge, Jolley's was his police badge.

"Same guy," I resumed. "I told him to wake up, because he was yawning. I didn't pass any cars until I got to the turnoff to go down the hill, but there were a few parked on the right." I pointed as we passed the grassy parking areas just across the bridge in the interior of the track.

I indicated where I'd seen cars or people in the lower paddock and the midway, where the vendors set up tents. And then I paused partway down the hill where I'd stopped the day before to chat with Benny.

Jolley's eyes lit up. "He was here at that hour?"

"Yes—but I'm sure he wouldn't have gone down to the other end of the paddock. Their trailer is right here and—"

"Easy, Ms. Reilly."

"For Pete's sake, call me Kate."

He actually smiled. "Kate, then. Don't worry, I just want to know from Mister…."

"Benny Stephens, SPEED Channel."

"Mr. Stephens. I only want to ask him who else he might have seen that morning and the night before. He's not a suspect, Ms.—Kate."

"Good, because he and Ian wouldn't hurt a fly." OK, I didn't literally know that.

Jolley just stared at me, making me uncomfortable.

"What?"

"Murderers are never who you expect. You may not like the answer here." He turned and looked out the front window. I drove on.

Chapter Twenty-four

I took him through my stop at the fence at Pit In and crept slowly through the paddock, trying hard to remember where I'd seen any signs of life. Bad phrase—where I'd seen team activity. I didn't speak as I looped around the parking area and edged up to where I'd parked so fatefully.

Jolley looked behind us. "Were there as few cars yesterday?"

"Just about. Maybe a few less today."

"Why did you park here?"

"If I could only change that…." I shrugged. "I liked the idea of facing the Main Straight and this turn. I wanted to climb up and see the track and later see the racecars from my front bumper. It put me nearer the action, somehow."

Jolley frowned. "It certainly did."

"Too near."

We got out of the car as Stuart walked up, looking agitated. He greeted Jolley, then looked at me. "You couldn't wait for me, Kate?"

"Oops. Detective Jolley flagged me down at the entrance, and we kept going."

Stuart clasped his hands in front of him and sounded cranky. "I've been waiting for you at the Series trailer."

Jolley stepped away from us, toward the fence in front of the car, looking at the ground where I'd found Wade the day before. I didn't want to see that.

"Kate." I jumped when Stuart hissed in my ear. "I'm trying to help you out. The least you can do is make it a little easier on me."

"Help me out? I don't understand."

"Give you backup. Be around if you have problems. Since you don't have a lawyer or anything."

"Because you think I need one? You think I'm going to say something to incriminate myself? What makes you think I need or want your help?"

"Of course I don't think you need a lawyer—or I'd have gotten you one already. But it can only help you to have a witness when you're talking to the police. Besides, this is what I do. I make the ALMS run smoothly, which includes being around to support a driver who's under suspicion of committing murder!" His voice had risen to a shout by the end, and Jolley was watching us from twenty-five feet away.

Was Stuart losing his cool? I looked at Jolley, who was studying the ground and the fence again, and spoke quietly. "I'm sorry I didn't stop for you. To be honest, he freaked me out, popping up at the gate. I wasn't prepared."

Stuart rolled his shoulders. "Fine. I just hope you didn't say anything stu—" He saw my expression, and finished, "that could be misinterpreted."

"What am I? Twelve?" Shoot, I'd said that out loud. I raised a hand to stop him. "Scratch that. I told Jolley what I'd done in the morning, who I spoke to, and why I chose to park here. That's all. You didn't miss much."

We both turned at Jolley's approach.

"Everything worked out?"

I started to speak, but Stuart beat me to it. "Yes, Detective. Kate just forgot that I was going to meet and accompany you both this morning. To give her support and answer any questions you might have about the operation of the track and race."

Jolley looked from Stuart to me to Stuart. I didn't know what that look was trying to say, but I didn't think I liked it.

"You're here now, Mr. Telarday. Anything you've heard about that I should know?"

"Stuart, please. Nothing, except for the notebook, which I'm sure Kate's already mentioned."

"Notebook?" Jolley turned to me. "I haven't heard about a notebook."

"Kate, you haven't told him yet?"

"Would the two of you slow down? No, I hadn't gotten to the notebook yet." They wore matching expressions of disapproval, and I lost it. "Look, I'm dealing with a lot this weekend. So call me birdbrain. I forgot."

No one spoke for a minute, until Jolley prompted, "The notebook?"

"Right." I ran my hands through my hair, gathering my thoughts. "Mike—Munroe, my co-driver—mentioned last night that Wade kept a notebook with…we're not sure what. He says Wade referred to it as 'keeping score.'"

"What do you think that meant?" Jolley raised an eyebrow.

"Well, Mike also said Wade called it his own personal timing and scoring, which is what we call lap times and data on the cars in the race, so it might have been notes on other drivers. Or vendettas."

"What do you think?"

"I have no idea. I haven't seen inside it. It could be his grudges—I've been told he'd hold them. But plenty of drivers and teams keep notes on times—their own and their competitors. Maybe it was only that."

"Who was there for this conversation? And does Mike or anyone else know where the notebook is?"

"It was Mike, me, Tom, and Stuart talking about it. And the thing is, I saw the notebook yesterday. I just can't remember where."

Stuart waved a finger in the air. "Mr. and Mrs. Purley could have heard Kate say she'd seen it too. They were walking past us at the time. Jack was there, and a couple drivers were at the other end of the porch."

Jolley nodded at him, then turned to me. "Where did you see it and what did it look like?"

I put my hands on my hips. "If I remembered where I saw it, I'd remember where it is now. I'm working on it. It'll come to me."

Jolley made a note in his own notebook. "Let me know as soon as you remember—the second you remember. What did it look like?"

When I didn't respond immediately, Stuart did. "Mike said it was a little black book."

"Leather, about so big." I made a rectangle with my fingers about two by three inches. I concentrated for another minute, then let out a sharp breath. "I keep trying to remember where it was. I have a mental picture of it in my hand, and then nothing."

Jolley tapped his pen against his notes. "You said something about Wade holding grudges. Did you know that from personal experience?"

"No. His outburst at me the other night was the only negative interaction I had with him. Some of the other drivers told me he held a grudge."

"Other drivers—is this something else you should tell me?"

"What's that supposed to mean?"

"This sounds like more important information I don't know about yet."

I started to defend myself, and Stuart cleared his throat. Jolley and I turned to him. "Might I suggest we continue this in our trailer? It would be more comfortable and private."

"That's a good idea. Kate?"

"Sure. I'd like some water and a chance to pee. Then you can finish with the third degree." That earned me an impatient look from Stuart.

I moved my car to a different parking space, and the three of us trooped down to the ALMS trailer. I stopped at the public women's bathroom nearby, but quickly regretted it. I was about to exit my stall when I heard two women enter and click-click on high-heeled shoes to the sinks. They spoke loudly to be heard over the running water. About me.

"I can't believe they're actually letting her drive," said a whiny, high-pitched, nasal tone.

"Whyever on earth not?" asked the second voice, in a bayou accent.

"Well, she was Miss on-the-spot, wasn't she?" the first voice complained. "I mean, she found his body, now she's taking his seat. Taking it over more qualified drivers, you know. She's only successful because of the publicity she gets—and that's not fair."

The southern drawl sounded skeptical. "Your boyfriend's got a ride this season. It's not like she beat him out. What do you have against her?"

I heard water turn off and paper towels being grabbed.

"It's not just me," shrilled the first voice. "Ask anybody. Everyone thinks she did Wade in to get his ride. I think she's got no talent. She's only gotten where she is because she's kissed ass, slept with someone, or—who knows?—killed Wade."

"That's a serious thing to say," commented the drawl.

"Plenty of other people are saying it, it's not just me."

With that parting shot, they click-clacked out. I was still frozen, my hand on the stall door latch. I knew—theoretically—that successful women in any field were magnets for jealous and spiteful rumors. But I'd never heard it directed at me. Nor had I ever imagined hearing it from a woman. That shook me, almost as badly as the idea that "everyone" thought I'd killed Wade. The idea that one person thought I'd killed him was too much. I ducked my head and scurried toward the comparative safety of Stuart, Jolley, and the Series trailer.

Chapter Twenty-five

When I entered the private office, Stuart immediately saw how rattled I was.

"What happened, Kate?"

I was shaken to the core. Until hearing that conversation, I'd felt safe in the fraternity of the racing world. Jolley was the interloper, the one to be afraid of, and Stuart was the annoyance. I wasn't yet comfortable with either one, but I finally understood they were the only people trying to help me. Stuart had forced support down my throat, not gossiped behind my back. Jolley might still suspect me, but he sought the truth.

"Kate?"

I shuddered and crossed my arms over my chest. "I overheard a nasty conversation—a nasty woman, really—in the bathroom. She and her friend didn't know I was there."

"About what?" Jolley nudged me to sit on a couch and settled across from me.

"About how I've got no talent, so I sleep with people to get ahead. How I killed Wade to take his place." I swallowed hard and looked at Stuart. "How everyone in the paddock is saying so."

Stuart shook his head. "Kate, you know you're an extremely talented—"

"I know. Wait." I took a couple deep breaths. "I'm not asking for sympathy. I knew, or was warned, this would happen. I'm a damn good driver, and to hell with what other people think.

It just shook me to hear it—that people think I would kill to get ahead."

Jolley looked me in the eye. "There are people who would, without a second thought. For what it's worth, I don't think you're one of them."

"Does that mean I'm not a suspect?"

"Mostly not. No one's off the list until we know who killed Wade Becker. Besides, I think you've got a lot of information you can give me, since you're part of this community and will hear things that I don't or can't hear—or won't understand."

I murmured agreement, staring blankly at the opposite wall, still shocked by how much disdain a stranger had for me. Shocked to realize I might never amount to more than "the murdering racecar driver." The racing community was going to require more than a convincing alibi. For the sake of my career, I needed to find Wade's killer.

I didn't know how to investigate a murder, but I'd never shied away from a challenge. I also hadn't achieved anything by accepting others' opinions about what I should be doing. I'd keep looking for answers, because I wasn't going to let Wade's murder ruin everything I'd worked for. If I could drive racecars, I could handle this, too.

Jolley leaned forward, pulling out a pen and his flip-top notebook. "OK, Kate. What have you heard?"

"You want everything? Important or not—even gossip? Is that police procedure?"

"Everything. I'll take whatever works."

I hesitated, feeling like a tattle-tale. Except that old Chuckles Purley was a scary dude. "The worst came from Mr. Charles Purley, one of our sponsors."

"Whose sponsors?" Jolley looked from me to Stuart.

Stuart fielded the question. "Kate's—and Wade's—team sponsors. Mr. Purley owns Racegear.com, which is the primary sponsor of Sandham Swift's cars."

"What did you hear?"

"Susanah Purley—that's the Mrs., and you have to say it with a long 'ah' in the middle." Jolley raised his eyebrows and made a note. "Susanah Purley was hysterical yesterday morning when she found out about Wade."

"Why's she here?"

"Marketing for Racegear.com. She's at all the races. She and Wade were having an affair." Jolley whistled in amazement. Was this guy a typical cop, or what? "It wasn't her first affair either, from what I've been told."

"Who else?"

"I don't know for sure, but I can find out. Mike mentioned it, so it wasn't a secret from him, at least. I'm not sure about the others, but Mr. Purley knew about Wade."

That produced a reaction from Stuart. "What?"

"Yeah, and here's where it gets creepy." I recapped Susanah's behavior before practice and what I'd heard after, including her husband's threats. I grimaced. "I wouldn't have left with him, but she did."

Jolley looked thoughtful and made more notes.

"No wonder you acted strangely when you met him at dinner," Stuart commented.

"Yeah. It was a surprise to put his face with the voice I'd heard."

Jolley stopped in the middle of writing. "You didn't see him when he threatened Mrs. Purley? Can you be sure it was him?"

"No, I didn't see him until dinner. But it was the same voice."

Jolley turned to Stuart. "Can you add anything? You were at that dinner too, right?"

Stuart spoke slowly, considering. "Yes, I was there as well. His behavior toward his wife could have been possessive or just attentive. Mrs. Purley didn't contribute much, which is unusual, in my experience. She's typically more outgoing, vivacious. Other than what I observed, I know the team expected Charles to arrive a day later. I can tell you that Racegear.com has been a loyal sponsor to the Sandham Swift team for years. We appreciate their support of the Series."

"No odd behavior or rumors before now?"

"None."

"OK. Kate, what else?"

"Alex Hanley, the brake specialist for the Number 28 car—for my car. I met him yesterday morning. He was the happiest guy at the track."

"Because of Mr. Becker's death?"

"I assume so. Downright chipper. Tom told me Alex and Wade had hated each other—Alex might have been fired because they couldn't get along."

"Anything more specific?"

"No, I—" I saw Tom Albright outside the trailer, talking with a Series official. "Tom may know more—he was going to do some asking around, too. Should I go get him?"

Stuart turned to look out the window as Jolley said, "He was…yes, let's get him in here."

"I'll go." Stuart was gone before I could move. He ushered Tom inside and closed the door.

"Good morning, Detective. Kate." Tom sat down next to me on the leather couch. Stuart returned to an office chair.

"Tom, I explained to Kate that neither of you should be asking questions. I mean it. That said, I'd like background on Wade's relationships with people on the team and in the Series."

Tom swallowed audibly. His left leg bounced up and down. "Sure. I asked Jack if Wade had been mad at anyone lately, but he didn't know of anyone."

He looked at me, then went on in a rush. "I'm sorry, Kate. I was going to ask around, but I got caught up writing press releases—we've had a lot of requests for your information—and then I had to do a bunch of computer stuff for Jack. Besides, I wasn't sure what to say to people."

Some help he was.

Jolley addressed Tom again. "Can you tell me who Mr. Becker's friends were in the Series or on the team?"

"Friends? I don't know if he had any good friends. He was a loner. He had some acquaintances and some people he spent time with on race weekends. But no one who carried over into the rest of his life."

"Who were the acquaintances?" Jolley's pen hovered over paper again.

"Mrs. Purley. Mike Munroe, his co-driver."

"I understood Mrs. Purley was more than an acquaintance."

Tom shot me a look. "I guess so, though I never saw any inappropriate activity."

"Who else?"

"Jack, I guess. But that was more about sponsor dinners than choosing to hang out. Marcus Trimble. I saw him and Wade together at most races."

I asked the question before Jolley could. "Who's Marcus Trimble?"

Stuart sat up straighter. "Marcus is the son of Paul Trimble, who's with True Color Paint, a major sponsor of the American Le Mans Series and the main sponsor of the Number 12 car in the LMP2 class. True Color is an automotive paint company, and their involvement with ALMS represents a significant portion of their marketing efforts."

Jolley scratched his nose. "That's the father. What about the son?"

Stuart hesitated. Tom looked at him before responding. "Marcus hangs out. Helps his father entertain guests. He's trying to be a driver, and I think Wade was the latest of his mentors."

"What do you mean," Jolley asked, "trying to be a driver?"

"He's gone to a few racing schools. He was running a car in a regional series in the Southeastern U.S. somewhere, and he asked Wade lots of questions. I think he was working on a deal to pay for a seat in a car here next year. But I don't think his dad was too excited about it."

"Age?"

Stuart answered. "I believe he's twenty-six."

I nodded, and Jolley noticed. "What?"

"He wasn't likely to become a professional driver if he's twenty-six, been doing this a while, and paying for rides. He probably wasn't good enough in his driving courses or the local series to attract any notice. But he'd have been able to race if he paid for the rides—it's just expensive."

"How expensive?"

I let Stuart field that one. "Upwards of a quarter of a million dollars and more like half a million if you're talking about a full season."

Jolley whistled again. "For one season? That's pricey. Will he have a chance at winning?"

Tom, Stuart, and I shared a look. I said what we were all thinking. "It would be a longshot."

"That's a lot of money to spend on losing races."

"That's not how we prefer to think of it." Stuart frowned.

Jolley appeared to smother a laugh. "I'm sure not."

"I know Paul Trimble didn't want his son to race. He couldn't stop him, as Marcus has control of a large trust fund that Paul set up long ago. But he held Wade responsible for encouraging his son to—as Paul said—'waste money on losing efforts.'"

"Daddy didn't like Wade?"

"No, in fact, Paul and Wade came to blows at the end of last season."

"Really?" Jolley leaned forward. So did I.

"It was last September, at Petit Le Mans—that's the ten-hour race in Atlanta," Stuart added, for Jolley's benefit. "Paul confronted Wade about Wade's encouragement of Marcus. Paul told me he thought he could appeal to Wade's better nature."

Jolley looked up from his notes. "Did Mr. Becker have one?"

"The confrontation didn't go well. Paul didn't tell me what was said, but he and Wade each got in a couple punches before we separated them."

"You witnessed it?"

"Yes. I was speaking with someone nearby—out of earshot, until they started yelling. I pulled Paul away and brought him here to cool off."

"What was his state of mind after this incident?"

"Paul was furious." Stuart paused, obviously troubled. "He ranted briefly about Wade being evil, and then he became calm. Relaxed even. At the time, I was relieved he'd calmed down. He said all the right things: apologizing to me and the Series, saying he'd deal with his family problems away from the racetrack. But looking back, I'm not sure I believe him."

"Why do you say that?"

"In retrospect, he calmed down too quickly. He was too angry—red-faced, raving mad—to have let it go entirely."

"Do you feel he's capable of murder?" Jolley's tone was quiet. I glanced at Tom and saw him sitting still, eyes wide.

Chapter Twenty-six

"It pains me greatly to say this about one of our loyal sponsors—and I trust you will keep this absolutely confidential." At nods from Tom and me, Stuart continued. "If you'd asked me before last September, I would have said Paul Trimble is absolutely not capable of violence of any kind. Now, I'd have to admit I'm not sure."

Stuart seemed as chilled to make that statement as I was to hear it. I had a follow-up question. "How was Wade after this?"

Tom jumped in. "I remember. He was pissed. That was a terrible weekend for him."

"Why?" Jolley asked.

"First there was that fight. If I remember right, he came back to our garage and yelled at the crew for making the wrong changes to the car. But I think that was the first time Alex stood up to him—Alex Hanley, our brake guy?"

"Kate indicated he didn't like Wade either."

"Right, so Alex yells back. I was surprised Wade didn't punch him. Then the car's setup was terrible, and he had a couple awful practices." Tom was holding up his hand, ticking fingers with every item on the list. "Then his qualifying run was for crap—eighth or ninth. Terrible for this team. The race was rotten, too. Finished sixth. Finally, he's passed over for media interviews."

"I heard about that," I interrupted. "He was furious he wasn't sent to do the typical driver-represent-the-Series interviews. He'd gone for years, and then wasn't asked."

"That's right," Stuart confirmed. "We'd been discussing a change, and after he got into it with Paul Trimble, we turned to other drivers."

Jolley turned to me. "Where'd you hear about it, Kate?"

"From Mrs. Purley, who had to soothe Wade's ruffled feathers. But she couldn't remember if it happened this past March or last fall."

Stuart rubbed the back of his neck. "It was both. We didn't ask him to do the interviews at Petit, in September, or in Monterey, at the last race of the season. At Sebring, this March, Wade asked our PR person about it. She reported that he was angry when she told him we had all the drivers we needed."

"His world was falling apart," Jolley mused. "But that was months ago. Why is he dead now?"

We considered the question, and Tom spoke. "It's months later, but only a couple races. Petit and Monterey, at the end of last season. This season: Sebring, Mid-Ohio, then here. There may be a gap in calendar months, but the politics and the relationships are pretty much the same from race to race—some things shake up in the off months, people move around, but our team and sponsor roster has been stable. Everything goes into hibernation between races."

"Mr. Trimble could have held on to his mad?"

Stuart agreed, but reluctantly.

Jolley turned to a blank page. "Since I have you all here. Anything else to tell me? Anyone else have it in for Wade? Benefit by his death? Acting oddly?"

"Someone's acting oddly, but I can't think how it relates to Wade." I looked from Jolley to Stuart and Tom.

"Let's hear it."

"Jim Siddons, the Porsche driver. He's been so rude—which I don't understand, because I've never had a problem with him. Hardly know him. But he bumped into me walking down pit row and bumped me on the track with his car."

Jolley looked to Tom. "Mr. Sandham explained it. Apparently Siddons and Becker had it in for each other."

"Jim got rough whenever he and Wade were near each other on the track," Tom affirmed.

I felt another pang of guilt for spreading gossip, then quashed it. "There are the other drivers—the guys Wade had threatened, not the other way around."

"What happened?" Jolley was writing again.

I told him what I'd told the others the night before about Indiana Dave. "A few others also had run-ins with Wade on the track. Marco, Eddie, Torsten. They wondered if his death had to do with him getting slower. Or...."

"Or what?"

I shot a quick glance at Stuart. "There are rumors flying around about the problems cars have been having, that it's Delray ECUs. The rumors are wild."

Stuart bit out his words. "That's enough, Kate, the detective is aware of that situation."

"I'm sorry to bring it up. But everyone is talking about it and speculating. I don't know what's related or not, but I've heard words like cheating, blackmail, sabotage—and talked to people who have gut feelings that Wade was connected to some bad stuff. Put all that together and I have to at least ask the question: is it a problem with a supplier's part or is there real cheating going on? And how much did Wade know?"

Stuart looked stony, but Jolley was nodding and writing in his notebook.

"Anyway, I can't figure out how this helps you."

Jolley looked up and flipped his notebook closed. "You just have to look at who benefits by Becker's death and why. As an example, you benefit by getting his job. If Becker was really slowing down, Jack Sandham, every member of the crew, and Mike Munroe benefit—though death is more drastic than firing him. If he was a blackmailer or a cheater, his victims benefit by being free of him. Other drivers aren't being threatened or run off the track. Mr. Trimble and Mr. Purley don't have their loved ones involved with him. The ALMS doesn't have a loose cannon around."

He glanced at Stuart. "Your job is easier."

Stuart looked weary. "Only in some ways. Have you located a family member who will come to collect his belongings?"

"He didn't seem to have much family. We're in contact with a sister in Wisconsin, but I don't expect her to come here. They weren't close. Do any of you know anything about Wade outside of the racing series?"

No one spoke.

"We're here to do a job, and we're focused on it," I finally explained. "There's not much idle chit-chat. And Wade wasn't one for talking about himself."

"I don't think he had much going on outside of racing," Stuart commented. "Most of us in the Series tend to hear what the next step or the side projects are for drivers—whether another career entirely, broadcasting, or team ownership. But I've never heard anything about Wade."

Tom piped up. "Jack, Mike, or Marcus Trimble might know more."

Jolley nodded. "Stuart, I'll need to find Paul and Marcus Trimble. I assume you can help me with that?"

"Of course."

"And you two," Jolley turned to Tom and me. "Watch your backs, keep your ears open and your mouths shut. There's every reason to expect that Wade Becker's killer came from the racing world. Don't poke at snakes. You might get bitten, too."

He was deadly serious, and he scared me.

We emerged from the trailer to find overcast skies. Within seconds, fat, sporadic raindrops started to fall. Tom dashed off, back to the team paddock. Stuart escorted Detective Jolley in a different direction. I sat down at a table under the awning with a bottle of water and tried to empty my mind.

I was identifying the ALMS staff and VIPs seated at the other tables—Victor Delray was talking earnestly with the ALMS media relations guy, Michelin reps were pitching something to a team owner, and excited-looking people in Porsche shirts were listening to a Porsche executive—when I saw my father entering the tent.

He soon approached. "How are you today, Katherine?"

"Emotionally drained," was the true answer I wouldn't give him. "I've had better, and I've had worse."

"The item I gave you last night. Did you have any questions about it?" He shifted his weight from one foot to the other.

"I haven't had a chance to open it yet."

He spoke stiffly. "Please do so as soon as you can. You could be courte—"

I stood, tired of the martyr act. "Look. You've given me nothing. Not once. And now you're looking for courtesy. I'm fresh out this weekend."

"Katherine." He stopped me from storming away with a hand on my arm. I turned, but shook off his touch.

"I understand you're angry. I accept that. But please—even if you never change your mind about me—please give me the opportunity to explain some things about our families and your childhood. I'm going to keep talking to you until you agree."

I sighed. "Maybe you will wear me down someday. But not this weekend. I've got enough to deal with already—a new ride, a new track, finding a body, dealing with the police, ignoring rumors that I'm a homicidal maniac. The list goes on." I looked at my watch. "And now I need to go."

His eyes got big, and he grabbed my arm again. "You found Wade Becker?"

I looked at his hand on my arm. "Please let me go," I said quietly and forcefully, and he did. "Yes, I found him yesterday. Now if you'll excuse me—"

"But Katherine, if you're dealing with the police, does that mean you're a suspect? And what are these rumors?"

"I'm not a suspect—not really. There are still rumors that I did it, which I'm ignoring, because I didn't."

"But Katherine, you need to be careful. I mean, if there's been one murder—"

"Stop it! I race cars for a living, what makes you think I can't handle rumors? Good bye." I could feel him watching me as I left.

Chapter Twenty-seven

I got wet walking from the Series trailer to the Sandham Swift paddock, but I didn't care. I was thinking about my investigation. Who had the opportunity to commit the murder was important, but that was simple information to gather—for the police, if not for me. What made the opportunity mean anything was motive: why Wade was killed, what had driven someone to murder. I needed to find Wade's notebook and gather more information from people in the paddock—but carefully.

A fat raindrop landed on my nose. The showers made the paddock area smell fresh again—a break from the exhaust- and fuel-laden air I hadn't really noticed. Connecticut was green for a reason, and showers were probably part of any week's forecast. Rain. Race. I'd have to hope for the best.

Aunt Tee was standing under the team awning, looking at the rain with disapproval. "Kate! Get in here and get dry!" She tugged me under cover.

"Any idea of tomorrow's forecast, Aunt Tee?"

"They're all saying no rain until next Thursday. A dry spell, it's supposed to be." We turned to look at the rain and laughed together.

I pushed my damp hair away from my face. "I'm just hoping for the best tomorrow. Do you have an umbrella I can borrow?"

"Sure. Where are you going now?"

"Torsten and Andy are leading a track walk for fans in a few minutes. I'm going to tag along and see if I can learn anything."

Seth, the 29-car driver, approached from the garage area. "Kate, do you have a minute?"

Aunt Tee waved her hands at us. "You two talk. Kate, I'll dig up an umbrella and a jacket for you. Come get them when you're done." She went into the motorhome.

"What can I do for you, Seth?"

He crooked a finger and led me to the chairs. "It's what I can do for you."

I studied him, a short, stocky, mid-fifties corporate executive who kept himself in good shape and raced cars for fun. I wasn't surprised he'd made a fortune in the hotel business, if he applied the same focus and determination I saw him apply to his racecraft. "I'm all ears."

"You may know, I own a resort up the road in the Berkshires. My head of security, Dennis Weston, apparently moonlights as a guard for this track—I ran into him last night as I was leaving. Turns out, he was working Friday night."

He saw my interest. "Exactly. I know he's spoken with the police about the cars he saw leaving. But you might want to talk to him—since you have a vested interest in the outcome of this investigation."

"Making sure I'm not arrested?"

He laughed at my dry tone. "In a nutshell."

"Yes, I'd like that. Is he here today? Tonight?"

"He's not working until 9:00 tomorrow morning. But he's happy to talk to you."

I stifled my impatience at the delay. "Thanks, Seth. I appreciate the help. Did he tell you anything?"

"I don't remember all the details, but there were four cars leaving the track in the timeframe the police were interested in: two silver Ford Tauruses, a red rental Chevy, and a red Ferrari. The Ferrari had...an amorous couple in it."

"A busy place for that hour. Listen, thank you. I know I shouldn't be asking questions at all—"

He pointed a finger directly at my nose. "In my book—and the business world—if you're not looking out for number one, you'll be trampled. Just do it intelligently. And watch your back."

While he returned to the garage, I spent a minute considering his information. The Ferrari might be easy to track down, if it was someone involved in the ALMS, but three generic rentals didn't narrow the field—silver Tauruses were as common in race parking lots as straw in a haystack.

Aunt Tee's hands were full with a mixing bowl and spoon when I entered the motorhome. I sat on one of the sofas while she worked on cookie batter and told me about another dinner I needed to attend that night. She was listing who'd be in attendance and their importance to the team when I lost track of her words, struck by a memory of sitting on the couch the day before. That's where I'd found Wade's notebook! Then what?

"Kate?" Aunt Tee was standing in front of me with a jacket and a Racegear.com umbrella in her hands.

"I'm sorry, I was remembering something that happened yesterday."

"What was that?"

I slipped on the Sandham Swift–logoed windbreaker. "Fits great, thanks. I found a notebook in the couch. I think it was Wade's."

"A small, black one?"

"You've seen it?"

"Not recently. But I've seen Wade writing in it. Is it important?"

"I don't know. The police want it. I just remembered I found it between the couch cushions when I was changing for practice. I stuffed it into my firesuit pocket—where is my suit, by the way?"

"Hanging in the back." She led me into the bedroom and opened a clothes closet.

I reached past her and rummaged in the pockets. "Nothing."

"I'll keep an eye out for it. You'd better get going to the track walk. You've only got a couple minutes."

She followed me out of the motorhome, and I waved goodbye with the umbrella. "Thanks again. I'll check in later."

I joined the group of about fifty fans standing on the racetrack at Pit Out, and glanced back down pit road, picking out the Sandham Swift setup. That's when it hit me: I'd moved Wade's notebook from my suit into my pit cart locker along with my own. With the ensuing activity, I'd forgotten them both.

I darted to the pits, even as I heard a voice behind me introducing Torsten and Andy, LinkTime Corvette drivers, as the leaders of the tour. A minute later, notebook secured, I rejoined the group just as it started moving. I was out of breath, my heart thumping.

I knew that Detective Jolley would want me to call him and hand over the notebook immediately. And I imagined the notebook as a beacon in my zippered jacket pocket, broadcasting an alert to him that I'd found it. But my first concern was racing, and I needed this track walk. I'd hand over the notebook later—after I had a look at it myself.

Chapter Twenty-eight

I stood near the edge of the group, warding off the light rain with my umbrella and trying to be inconspicuous. Half the people carried umbrellas, including Torsten. Others wore hats or hoods. Andy wore nothing to stay dry. He just grinned at the crowd and rubbed his bald head, explaining he needed another shower anyway.

As we approached the first turn, Big Bend, the walkers had split in two, one group following Andy, and the one I was in following Torsten. He was giving a running commentary on how to handle the track and answering questions fans asked.

The wife of a married couple sporting his-and-hers fanny packs and car-themed Hawaiian shirts asked the next question. "What do all the flags mean?"

Torsten stopped walking and faced the group. "The flags. There are a lot of them, aren't there? Part of the corner worker's job is to communicate to drivers, and they do that through the flags. You'll know some of them. How about green?"

"Go racing," a male voice from the crowd called out.

"Correct. How about white? And checkered?"

"Last lap and race over," said the Hawaiian-shirted husband.

"Right." Torsten waved his arms to keep the crowd walking down the track as he walked backwards, facing us. "Yellows you probably know about; that means caution and no passing. But there's also a distinction: you might get a local yellow at a corner, or double-yellow from the start/finish line that means full course caution and lining up behind the pace car. A variation on the yellow is a yellow with red stripes, which tells me there's a slippery surface or debris on track. And a red flag means stop in place because the track is closed. Now, what am I forgetting?"

"Black?" came a voice from the crowd.

"What's the blue one?" shouted a female voice at the same time.

Torsten nodded. "Of course, one flag you never want to see and the other that we see all the time. Black first: that's telling you to leave the track immediately, either because of a mechanical problem or a rule infraction. It usually spells trouble. And the blue, with a yellow diagonal line, tells me faster traffic is coming behind me. That one's rarely out of corner workers' hands in the ALMS."

Flags took us all the way through Big Bend, and Torsten stopped to tell the group about apexes. Someone asked him what he'd thought the first time he'd driven the track, and with a wink at me, he blew my cover.

"It's been too many years to remember what it was like, except for being tight and bumpy, like I've told you. But we've got a new driver here—stealing my precious secrets. She just drove it yesterday, and she'll be racing tomorrow, in another Corvette. Kate, why don't you tell everyone what it's like to drive this beast for the first time?"

Two dozen pairs of eyes followed his gaze to me, and two dozen brains clicked, "She's that one."

I put on my best public smile. "I second everything Torsten said. It was shocking to drive the first time. Bumpy. My insides felt carbonated by the end of the first lap, and by the end of the tenth? My body still feels pounded on today from twenty minutes in the car yesterday."

The faces still looked interested, so I kept going. "You also never get a break here. Every second of every lap, you're thinking about what you're doing now and what you'll do next. A shift of the wheel, a tap of the brake, the line for the next turn or straight. There isn't a single second when you can drop your shoulders and take a breath—which usually we can do on a long straight. This track is so short and narrow that you're mentally on every fraction of every second. You have to drive very technically—being very aware of your hands and your approach to turns, that sort of thing."

Torsten winked at me again when I'd finished. He continued leading the group through the Esses, pointing out the large concrete patch in the left-hander. A couple people attached themselves to me—staying near as the group ebbed and flowed around Torsten's stops and starts. They didn't ask questions until we stopped at the top of the chicane—What was it like to be a racecar driver? Was it hard to be a woman and be a driver? What did I think my chances were in the race?—but I was frustrated at missing Torsten's information. He got people moving again as Andy joined us, and I ditched my questioners to slip into the fringe of Andy's followers. One man followed me, but he didn't say anything until we were walking down the Back Straight and Andy was answering questions.

He flipped back the hood of his light jacket and spoke in a light English accent. "You're driving for Sandham Swift now, is that correct?" When I turned to him to respond, I tripped over my own feet. He was my gorgeous mystery-man, and he was even more beautiful up close. I couldn't see his eyes behind his aviator glasses, but the rest of him was straight out of Vogue or the Abercrombie catalog, all six-feet, sculpted cheekbones, and perfect, wavy, sun-kissed brown hair of him. He didn't seem real, because he was just too beautiful.

I gathered my wits. "Yes. The 28 car."

"I thought so." He straightened, took a deep breath, and stared ahead down the track.

"Are you a fan of the team? A friend?"

"Yes, Wade's—Wade was a friend. I'm Marcus Trimble." He held out a hand and gave a sad smile—one potent enough to make me weak in the knees.

We shook. "Kate Reilly. Obviously, I'm driving for Wade."

"Yes, and I wish you all the best luck."

"Thank you." The impression of Marcus I'd gotten from Stuart was of an aimless, unfocused, and irresponsible boy. He wasn't any of that in person.

"Where did you race before this, Kate? How did you get here? I'd really like to know how someone just breaking in actually makes it." He took his glasses off, revealing an intent look. Mother of God. His eyes were light green, rimmed with the longest dark brown lashes I'd ever seen.

I had to concentrate on my breathing before I could give him a short version of my background. When he appeared ready to ask more questions, I suggested we talk later—hard as it was to shut down his attentions—in order to listen to Andy now. But Marcus was eager for Andy's pearls of wisdom also, and we finished the track walk in harmony, attentive to Andy's every word—which wasn't lost on Andy.

"So, you've got Trimble Junior now," he whispered, when I went to thank him at the end. "Just watch yourself."

"What's the problem?"

"Nice guy, crazy about racing, always around. Really terrible driver, though. He's a leech—latches onto people to suck up their time and energy. Yet everyone likes him." Andy rubbed his goateed chin.

"I thought Wade had been his mentor."

"Sure, and before that, Eddie. Before that, Dane. Before that, someone else. You get the picture. Just don't get too involved." He elbowed me and leered. "Have a one-night stand, but not a full relationship, get me?"

Did I ever.

I started to leave, then turned back. "Andy, have you seen anyone around the paddock driving a Ferrari street car this weekend?"

"Sure, Marco. He's always borrowing one from a local dealer—ever since his F1 days."

I'd forgotten Marco did a stint in Formula 1 with the Ferrari team. "But, his wife's not with him this weekend, is she? I heard it was a man and a woman in the car."

Andy spoke as if to a first-grader. "No, his wife's not with him this weekend."

"Of course. Marco. A girl in every port?"

"Something like that. See you, Kate."

I found Marcus waiting for me a few steps away. The rain had stopped partway through the track walk, and the sun was coming out, shining on the front straight, warming us, and making a halo around Marcus' light brown locks. Breathe, Kate. He didn't look unstable to me. I took off my jacket and slung it over my arm as I reached him, feeling to make sure the notebook was still safe in my pocket. I really wanted a chance to look at it.

"Kate, do you mind if I ask you a few more questions? I'm very interested in your opinions."

"My opinions?" You sound like an idiot, Kate.

"Yes, on racing, this track, this Series and others."

"I don't have much experience with this track or series yet."

"I'd still like your take on things." He launched into a conversation that was equal parts interrogation and bragging. He asked about my personal progression, what series I'd run in, and how I liked each kind of vehicle I'd driven. Then told me all about his own opinions. By the fifteen-minute mark of the same questions I'd already answered interwoven with his success stories, I was impatient. I wouldn't have minded staring at Marcus for hours on end, but I had things to do that day. I checked my watch, and he took the hint, breaking off a recital of how his racing accomplishments corresponded to mine. "I'm so sorry. I'm taking up too much of your time."

"I'm afraid I have some things to take care of. But I enjoyed—"

He took my hand in both of his. "I can't thank you enough for talking with me. I hope we can continue this—maybe next time over coffee?"

This guy knew charm would get him anywhere. "Sure."

Even while I watched Marcus as if spellbound, a voice in my head was telling me I'd met his breed of fan before: someone with a little experience or knowledge who wants his idols to see him as a peer. I came across the type most often in middle-aged fathers of young boys who needed to demonstrate greater skill and knowledge than "the girl driver." Regardless of Marcus' glamorous exterior, I recognized the pattern. But the packaging…I looked into his green eyes again and ignored the warnings. We were just talking about coffee.

I gave his hands a final shake. "Sometime soon. Nice to meet you."

"And you too, Kate. Best of luck tomorrow."

I turned to leave and found Detective Jolley, Stuart, and an unhappy-looking man a few feet away. Jolley. The flash of guilt I felt about not handing over the notebook that minute was followed by the rationalization that I shouldn't do so in front of other people anyway.

Stuart gestured to the man I didn't know. "Kate, may I introduce you? Paul, I don't believe you've met our newest ALMS driver, Kate Reilly. Kate, Paul Trimble, one of our best sponsors."

That explained a lot. I shook his hand. "Nice to meet you, Paul. I've just been chatting with your son." I gestured to Marcus, who was now talking with Jolley and looking downcast.

Stuart turned to Paul again. "Kate is replacing Wade in the Corvette."

"Oh, I see." Paul was distracted by the conversation between Jolley and Marcus.

I saw my opening in the ensuing pause. "If you'll excuse me, I need to be off. It was nice to meet you, Paul."

"Yes, you too."

"Sure, Kate. I'll see you later." Stuart was becoming downright pleasant. Something must be wrong.

Chapter Twenty-nine

Walking from the track to the paddock, I had a moment to unzip my jacket pocket and flip through the notebook—keeping it shielded in the folds of cloth. I didn't see anything I recognized, just columns of numbers and letters, and only about a dozen pages of writing at the front of book. Then I saw Zeke in the lane ahead, chatting with a woman wearing team gear for one of the larger prototype cars. I zipped the notebook away as I heard him deliver a familiar line: "Just remember, Zeke Andrews, Z-A—like A to Z, but in reverse. I'm just a little bit backwards." He waved goodbye to her and turned to me.

"Flirting, Zeke? I'll tell your wife."

"You know me, trying to soften up a new source."

I did know him, and I knew his wife had nothing to worry about. "All right, your secret's safe."

"Katie, I've, well…I've been hearing some bad things." He was uncharacteristically tentative. "I mean, don't listen to what anyone's saying. In case you have been."

"Zeke, spill it."

"OK. Some small-minded and nasty people are saying rotten things about you. And about Wade's death."

"I've heard."

"Has someone said something to you?!" He clenched his fists.

"Easy, big guy. I overheard someone in the public bathroom."

"What did you hear?"

"You want specifics?" When he nodded, I went on. "I'm not really qualified, everyone thinks I killed Wade to take his place. And I've slept my way to my success. Such as it is. Have you heard something different?"

"That about covers it, except you were stalking Wade, setting him up to fail—or to be killed."

"Who've you heard saying it?"

"I'm sorry to say from a bit of everyone. Teams, fans, a driver here and there."

"I'm pretty talented, aren't I? I get around."

He sighed. "Listen, Katie, no one worth knowing believes this crap. You know you've always had to fight an uphill battle."

"Always had to prove myself when boys and men didn't have to, yes. But this is bigger and scarier."

He put his hands on my shoulders. "I know you, and you'll get through it with your head high."

"Anyone I should watch out for?"

He gave me a quick hug. "Don't go out of your way for Nations Team, that new group running yellow Porsches. They're new and ignorant—jumping on the gossip bandwagon."

"Jim Siddons."

"What did you do to him anyway?"

"Nothing besides existing."

"He used to be a third for your new team sometimes, didn't he? Probably thinks you took his spot. The muck he's raking is extreme, but you ignore those idiots and concentrate on yourself. Remember, like I taught you?"

I'd been twelve, about to run a go-kart in my first big race with a real sponsor—and I was terrified. Zeke, the pro sportscar driver, had taken the time to hold my hand and talk me through the process of shutting out the outside world and concentrating on the job I had to do inside the vehicle. He'd introduced me to the bubble that a good driver—or athlete in any sport—had to operate in. "Yeah, Zeke, I remember. Spread the word I didn't kill Wade, would you?"

He gave me a double thumbs-up. "Already on it. Will you give me a quote on camera for the show?"

"I can't give you much more on Wade."

"Different topic. Why drivers do or don't like this track—just a quick answer."

"Yes, if you promise to be nice to me this time. Just come by the paddock. Oh, and Zeke? What kind of car did you rent this weekend?"

"White Taurus, maybe silver, why?"

"Never mind."

We separated, and I surreptitiously opened Wade's notebook again. The pages contained six columns of figures, broken up by dates, which I now recognized as ALMS races over the past four or five years. Under each were lists of varying lengths—shorter ones farther back, longer ones for more recent races. One column looked like lap times, one column contained check marks on selected lines, and two looked like initials.

"Kate! There you are!" I was standing in front of the Sandham Swift paddock, and Tom was relieved to see me.

I folded up the notebook again. "What's up?"

"Some details for the rest of the weekend to give you and a couple interview requests." Tom made notes on a clipboard as he spoke.

"But you didn't—" I took a breath and started again. "Of course, Tom, I'm delighted to talk to anyone you want. Sorry, it's been a busy morning already."

"How'd it go with Detective Jolley before I got there?"

"You were there for the most interesting stuff. But there's something—Jack?" I waved him over as he exited the motorhome.

I took a deep breath and addressed them both. "It's come to my attention there are some awful rumors about me. I thought you should know."

Jack waved a hand in the air. "No need, Kate. We've heard."

"Oh. Is there anything I can do, anyone I can talk to?"

Jack shook his head. "Since it's all untrue—I'm assuming you didn't sleep with past team owners to get a spot. You didn't sleep with me or kill Wade to get this one—so we're going to ignore it and carry on. We'll respond on the track. And that means I need 110 percent of your concentration and effort tomorrow. That'll be your proof you got here on talent alone." He looked me in the eye, and his voice went from stern to kind. "As we know you did."

He made a good point: don't focus on—or even think about—anything but the job I had to do tomorrow. But it added to the pressure.

He patted my shoulder. "Ease up, Kate. That's what we call a pep talk. I don't expect you to be faster than everyone else tomorrow—just faster than a few others in our class. Don't worry. See you at dinner." He was chuckling as he crossed to the garage.

"You OK, Kate?" Tom inquired.

I rolled my shoulders twice. "Adjusting to that added weight. All right, what have you got for me?"

Tom consulted his clipboard. "Tonight: dinner at 7:00 again, at The Boathouse this time, with sponsors again—different ones. Tomorrow: team meeting here at 8:00 a.m. Mandatory Series drivers' meeting at 9:30. Warm-up at 10:45. Skipping the autograph session. Race at 3:00."

"7:00 at The Boathouse tonight. 8:00 here tomorrow. Check. Interviews?"

"Yes, two magazines. One—and this is great—is *Road & Track*, which, as you know, is one of the top two consumer car magazines." Tom almost jumped up and down.

"That's great. I hope they don't ask me about Wade."

"No. Stuart cleared these, and they're not asking about him. *Road & Track's* topic is 'breaking into the big leagues'—coming up through the ranks as a professional. The other is about being a female driver. And that's for *Seventeen* magazine." He looked uncomfortable.

I laughed. "Tom, it's OK. It's a magazine for girls—probably the top one in the country. I'm a girl. Maybe we'll generate more teenaged girls who are fans or drivers. I wouldn't mind that."

"OK, and I'll sit in on them with you. Can we go now?"

Zeke appeared with his cameraman as we were leaving the team's area, and I recorded a quick response to Zeke's question: "I haven't had much time on the track, but so far I like it because it's so challenging—you're dealing with different surfaces, off-camber turns, and blind hills, all while you're constantly tossed around by the bumps. But ask me again after the race!"

Zeke winked and took off, and Tom and I made our way to the media center at the end of pit row next to the track. Right next to where I'd found Wade. I tried not to look.

I sat at a picnic table outside—the gray, rainy skies had given way to puffy white clouds—while Tom retrieved the *Road & Track* reporter. Fifteen minutes of questions later, he was done with me, and Tom brought the other journalist out. She'd have fit in on the streets of Manhattan, with her tailored blazer, designer jeans, and high-heeled, pointy-toed shoes, but she had to tiptoe across the dirt and grass to the table. I ignored my grandmother's voice in my head telling me I should be more ladylike and style-conscious, like her. I drive racecars for a living. Tomboyish goes with the territory.

I stood to shake her hand. "Hi. I'm Kate Reilly."

"Brandy Hutchins, freelancer, *Seventeen* magazine." Her voice was low and gravelly.

"Brandi? With an 'i'?" I studied the masterful blond highlights in her shoulder-length, wavy hair.

She curled her lip and took a pack of cigarettes out of her miniscule handbag. "No. Specifically not with an 'i'; with a 'y.' I can't stand that shit." She retrieved a lighter.

"Oops. Sorry." I sensed Tom stifling a giggle next to me.

"No problem, girlfriend." She pulled a microcassette recorder from her bag. "How about we start?"

She began with more basic questions than most—where was I from, how did I get into this in the first place, what made me think I could make it as a racecar driver. She disclaimed the last one. "Not that I think you can't or shouldn't, but let's face it, it's one of the last bastions of machismo. Am I right?"

I laughed and told her the story of racing go-karts at the age of ten. "In a regional championship race for my age group, it was all boys and me—and one was my 'boyfriend.' But when it was over, I'd won, and he'd thrown a screaming tantrum because a 'stupid girl' had beaten him. That's when I learned boys don't have special equipment that means they can drive cars better. Cars don't care if you're male or female. The strength you need most isn't physical—it's mental. Competing, thinking ahead down the racetrack, and concentrating on just one thing for a couple hours at a time."

She tapped a manicured fingernail on the table and chuckled. "That's perfect. I can just picture the little whiner." She pulled out another cigarette. "How's everyone treating you now that you're climbing up the ladder? This is climbing the ladder, right?"

"Yes, it is." I chose my words carefully. "I haven't been treated any differently because I'm a woman."

She heard what I wasn't saying. She lit her cigarette, looked at Tom, and turned off her tape recorder. "How about this? Off the record. How's everyone treating you this weekend?"

Tom bristled. "Hey, we were very clear we weren't going to talk about—"

I stopped him. "Off the record? Why do you want to know if you can't use it?"

"I'm all for a woman getting ahead in a man's world. I free-lance for lots of magazines, so I'm thinking of future stories. You know, female driver made the scapegoat, woman falsely accused, driver rising from the ashes of scandal." She took a drag. "Besides, word around the media room is the guy was a dick."

Tom was shaking his head, but I loved it. "Off the record, that's what I hear too. I knew him, but not enough to say. As for a story, we can talk when this is all over and see what you're interested in—but I don't think I'm much of a suspect anymore."

"What kind of treatment are you getting here?"

I crossed my arms. "I've had better. I've gotten great support from the ALMS, my team, and my friends. But there's some of what you might expect from other people."

"You slept or killed your way to the top?" She sounded bored.

"Yeah."

"Fucking typical jealous bullshit."

I smiled. Tom's mouth popped open.

"I've heard that crap everywhere there's a successful woman. Don't let it get to you. That just means you're getting somewhere."

She stubbed out her cigarette, stuffed her recorder back in her bag, and stood to leave. "By the way, there was a video tech in there," she pointed to the media center. "He was mumbling about looking through some tape from the night before last, because he thought he had shots of the dead dude. You should check it out."

"Me?"

She raised an eyebrow. "Sure, bring one home for women everywhere: win the race and solve the damn crime. Ta-ta." She pressed a business card into my hand and strolled off.

"What was that?" asked a bewildered Tom.

I started laughing.

Chapter Thirty

I sent Tom back to the paddock and entered the Media Center. No one paid attention to me when I walked in, so I headed for the photocopy machine. What I was doing was doubly unauthorized and potentially dangerous: I shouldn't be using the copier and shouldn't have the notebook in my hands; more, if Stuart or Jolley were to be believed, having it could get me killed. My heart was in my throat, and I jumped a foot when someone spoke behind me.

"It's Kate, the senseless murderer. Any quotes for us?"

I whirled around, breathless. The five reporters sitting at their computers had turned around to face me, one of them wearing a cheeky expression. I recognized him as Mitch Fletcher, the guy from *Racer* who'd asked me a question in the press conference the day before.

My voice cracked the first time I tried to speak. I cleared my throat. "'No comment' is probably safest." I smiled and stepped forward to shake Mitch's hand and introduce myself to the other four men.

Mitch spoke again. "How's it all going?"

"Is this for publication?"

"I wouldn't mind a quote or two, but it doesn't have to be."

"On the record: I'm settling in, looking forward to the race tomorrow, and everyone I work with has been extremely supportive. I'm very sorry for the loss of a great driver, and my condolences to his friends and family. I'm going to do my best in his seat in the car." A couple guys swung back around and typed into computers as I spoke.

"Have you heard about the buzz out there in the paddock that you had something to do with Wade's death?"

"That's off the record." I eyed each reporter in turn and got nods of agreement. "I've heard. I found him, but that's it. I didn't have anything to do with it. I wasn't plotting against him. Sure, I was trying to pick up a ride in the ALMS...but I'm not desperate enough to hurt someone to get it. I don't understand how people can say that kind of thing about me."

"Jealous and spiteful types," Mitch responded. "Rise above it and wait them out. They'll change their tune."

"Yes. Just trying to focus on the driving." I got butterflies in my stomach as I realized I'd be suited up for the race by this time tomorrow. "Maybe you can help me. I heard a video tech had some footage from Friday night with shots of Wade. Know anything about that?"

Mitch shook his head, as did two others. The guy at the end turned. "I heard someone with the SPEED crew talking about that. Didn't catch his name. Tall and skinny. Black, spiky hair. Goatee."

Mitch scented a story. "What're you looking for, Kate?"

"Anything that might clear me. By the way, what kind of rental cars did you all end up with this weekend?"

My survey netted three Ford Tauruses—two silver, one bronze—and two Chevys: a red Impala and a white Malibu. Obviously, without more detail, a list of possible Friday night drivers would include the whole paddock.

I returned to the copy machine to finish. I flipped through the pages of the notebook one last time before leaving the building and was surprised to find two more pages with writing, near the back, buried in the middle of blank sheets. One was a list of initials and codes, and the other was a half-dozen initials with cryptic notes. I didn't read them, just made copies and took off. I knew the perfect person to help me track down the tape the reporter had mentioned, and I ran him to ground at Holly's team paddock.

Zeke had his microphone in hand, interviewing one of the Western Racing drivers. I paused a few feet to the side, waiting for them to finish.

Holly sauntered over. "How's today treating you, sugar? Better than yesterday?"

"It would have to be, wouldn't it?"

She turned back to watch Zeke and her driver. "It sure would. And what are you pokin' around in?"

"Me?"

"I know you. You're as nosy as a cat."

"Isn't that 'curious as a cat'?"

She slid her sunglasses down her nose and looked over them. "I wasn't going to go there, because we know what happened to the cat."

"Good point."

"So, tell me."

I recapped my conversations with Jolley and Stuart, the comments I'd overheard in the bathroom stall, my chat with Jack and Tom, Seth's information about cars on Friday night, finding Wade's notebook, and the interviews I'd had. Then there was Marcus Trimble.

"Yeah, Marcus Trimble. Hubba, frickin' hubba. Ye-ow." She fanned herself with a hand.

"What's his deal?"

"I don't know. I've seen him attached to drivers like he's trying to absorb their mojo. I've seen grown women forget their children and smack into poles when he walks by. He's had a girlfriend around before, so he's not gay. But I don't know much else."

"Potent. Andy thinks he's trouble."

"I wouldn't mind trouble that potent. But you're here to ask Zeke for help finding that video footage…and what's in that notebook?"

"Why do you think I—" I saw her look. She knew me too well. I lowered my voice and spoke close to her ear. "I photocopied the pages, because I've got to give it to Detective Jolley."

"Why are you whispering? What's he got in there, a map to buried treasure?"

"I'm whispering because Jolley wanted this as soon as I found it, and I haven't given it to him yet. Plus, I don't want anyone to know I'm holding on to anything that belonged to Wade. I'm not sure what's in the book, because it's weird lists of numbers and initials and codes."

I saw Zeke finishing his interview and made arrangements to meet Holly later to look at the notebook. Zeke walked partway back to my team area with me as I explained what I'd heard about video footage, and he promised to investigate with Tony, the SPEED video tech. I arrived at the Sandham Swift paddock, needing to check in with the team, have lunch, and find Jolley. Tom stood outside the motorhome, eating a chocolate chip cookie and watching a swarm of crew members working on the 28 car. My car.

"What's going on over there?"

He held up a finger as he swallowed, then pointed at different groups of crew as he explained. "One of the guys didn't like the way the clutch and transmission felt—maybe a spun bearing. A couple others are helping him rebuild that. Some other guys are doing cleanup with the tranny out. The ECU engineer is inside running through the ECU code or something for the ninth time. And Alex wanted to go through the brakes again."

"Didn't he go through them yesterday after qualifying?"

"That's Alex. He'll do this now and again tomorrow morning. I can just about guarantee you won't have brake problems in the race."

"That's good. They're working on the other car too?" I spotted several guys under the hood of the 29 car.

Tom reached for another cookie. "They figured they'd check out the 29's clutch, transmission, and so on while they had the time."

I was looking for more substantial food than cookies—as delicious as they seemed—when the Purleys appeared. I stifled my apprehension.

We exchanged greetings, and Charles gestured to the crew. "Is it OK to make all of these changes? Don't they have to keep it the same from qualifying to the race?"

Susanah responded first. "Only the tires have to be the same, right, Tom?"

Tom agreed. "We have to start the race on the same tires we qualified on—so we run as few qualifying laps as possible. Once we're done qualifying, we jack the car up right there in the pits and take those tires off. They're marked by ALMS officials, and we store them in the pit until we roll out for the race tomorrow. We'll even run the thirty minute warm-up tomorrow on different tires. But we can work on and change anything else on the car at any time—as long as the end result passes tech inspection. It's pretty routine that a crew will rebuild brakes, a clutch, wiring systems, even an entire engine during a race weekend. Also, major portions of the body and frame if someone crashes in practice."

"What is it they're doing?" Charles wanted to know.

Tom led them closer and kept explaining. I slipped away to find Aunt Tee and some lunch, and I was back outside working on a large ham and cheese sandwich when they returned. Aunt Tee popped out of the motorhome and asked if she could get them food or drink as they joined me in the grouping of plastic chairs.

"Will you get the car reinspected?" Charles asked. I thought Susanah looked bored and sad. She wasn't speaking, just closely attending to her husband.

Tom handed around bottles of water. "I don't expect so. They're rebuilding exactly what was there before. If they want to go for another inspection, they can. But we have to pass inspection after the end of the race if we make the podium, or get chosen randomly."

"That's what keeps the cheaters honest."

"Something like that." Tom helped himself to one of the sandwiches Aunt Tee had brought out.

There was a lull in the conversation as Tom and I ate and as Charles turned to Susanah and said something to her in a low voice. She responded with a murmur and a shake of her head, then opened her handbag and pulled out a cigarette. The role of the perfectly submissive wife, whether fact or fiction, was making my skin crawl.

Chapter Thirty-one

We were making small talk when Paul and Marcus Trimble arrived, looking for Jack, and sat down with us. Tom made sure the Purleys knew Trimble father and son, and Paul chatted with Charles about their companies and sponsorship efforts. Marcus listened without joining in. I tried not to stare at him and ate my sandwich.

Charles was absorbed in Paul's description of True Color Paint. I'd always thought it fitting that the car sponsored by an automotive paint company had the most interesting color treatment in the Series. Photographers and journalists both praised it and complained that it never looked the same twice because its paint shifted color from brown to purple, orange, and green.

"True Color is national?" Charles confirmed. "Who would I talk to about a possible marketing partnership?"

Paul pointed to himself. "Me. Vice President of Marketing. What do you have in mind?"

"Not sure yet. Thinking of the possibilities. Racegear. com is national too—international, really. We're not a bricks-and-mortar concern like you are...but together we might be able to delve into some exciting multi-channel marketing opportunities."

I tuned out. Tom started a conversation with Marcus, and I took a pass on talking to Susanah, heading into the motorhome instead to return my plate to Aunt Tee. When I peeked through the window five minutes later, Jack had arrived and joined the business conversation. Susanah had moved closer to Tom and was also talking to Marcus. I wondered if Susanah and Marcus had met before, and if so, how well they'd known each other—since they were the only ones who seemed sorry Wade was dead. Susanah was acting more like the woman I'd seen yesterday, animated, gesturing with her hands—and missing the sharp looks her husband was throwing her.

Add one married woman with a penchant for racecar drivers to one gorgeous young wannabe…I'd bet Charles was annoyed.

Jack and Paul's conversation must have shifted to whatever brought Paul to the paddock, because they crossed to the garage. As Paul exchanged a few words and a handshake with the Michelin rep, I saw Nadia, our ECU engineer, come out of the transporter with Victor Delray and head toward the paddock lane through the garage. Charles joined Tom, Marcus, and Susanah, placing a possessive arm around her shoulders.

"What are you looking at, Kate?" Aunt Tee's voice startled me.

I was kneeling on the couch, and at her words, I turned around. "The people out there."

"Hiding, are you?"

"There are some interesting dynamics."

"Yes, I've always found the Purleys' relationship a strange one. But I know better than to comment—so you didn't hear that."

"Sure. But it is odd. And Marcus Trimble…I can't figure him out either. He seems nice. Gorgeous. But over-eager."

Aunt Tee sniffed. "Too much money and not enough responsibility, that's what I think."

"You know him? And his dad?"

Aunt Tee nodded, picking up a washcloth and wiping down the countertops. "You didn't hear this either. A nice man, Paul Trimble, who didn't come from much in his life, but made something of himself. He helped start that company."

"But he's only VP of marketing?"

"He and his partner sold it and took the jobs they wanted in the company. Made a pile of money. Now he spends his time coordinating their sponsorship activities and prize giveaways to customers."

"And his son is racing cars."

"If that."

I raised my eyebrows at her.

"It's really none of my business, after all."

"Come on, Aunt Tee. You know I won't spread anything around."

"True, unlike others I could mention." She shook her head. "Marcus grew up good looking, wealthy, and spoiled—and mostly away from home. He expects to get everything he wants, but I don't think he's worked a day in his life. He's been chasing this idea of racing cars for years now, spending his father's money—with nothing to show for it. I think his father's finding it's too late to teach his son to be responsible. But he keeps trying."

"Why doesn't he just cut Marcus off? Wait, I heard Marcus has his own bank account. I wonder why Paul doesn't take the money back. Can't give up on him?"

Aunt Tee leaned back against the sink. "I remember hearing Paul's wife died of cancer when Marcus was just a boy—and Marcus is an only child. I guess those are good enough reasons for why he loves that boy so much—why he's holding on instead of cutting him loose."

"And Marcus' accent? His father doesn't have one."

"Marcus was sent to England for almost all of his schooling."

"I thought I heard that Paul Trimble and Wade got into it last year—fighting. Do you know about that?"

"Oh, yes. Nasty business."

"What started it all?"

"That danged Wade. He'd been ornery the last couple years! I swear he got people riled up just for fun. There he was, encouraging that boy—"

"Marcus?"

"Yep, Marcus." She shook her head. "Poor boy doesn't have a lick of natural talent. But listen to Wade, and you'd have thought he was a lost Earnhardt son."

"Why would Wade do that?"

"I always thought it was for power."

"Over Marcus?"

Aunt Tee shrugged. "Over him. His father. How money was spent."

Money was a new angle. "Was Wade getting money from Marcus?"

"I don't know. I mean, I wouldn't have been surprised to find True Color coming on as a sponsor to this team, but it hadn't happened yet. I think it was more that Wade was controlling Marcus—telling him where he should race, what he should drive, how much he had to pay to get into those seats and races."

"Maybe Wade was getting a kickback for those deals."

"I think it was more about Wade having a protégé."

"OK, he liked having someone do what he said. He liked the power, you said. The control…if he had control over Marcus, he had some control over his father."

"Sure." Aunt Tee sat down in a chair at the table.

"Would he have done that just for spite? I've heard from some drivers that Wade was holding a lot of grudges lately—some of them really unreasonable, offenses he imagined. He was also making threats of payback. I don't know if he followed through with anything, but what if he was encouraging Marcus so much—controlling him—because of the fight he had with Paul?"

"But that's what the fight was about. Paul confronted Wade about giving Marcus false encouragement. When they were yelling, but not yet fighting, I remember hearing Paul say, 'Why are you lying to my son? Tell him the truth. You know he'll never make it as a professional.'"

"How many people heard it?"

"A handful of us. But Marcus walked up and heard, too."

"That's horrible. What did Wade say?"

"I was too far away to hear, because he said it quietly. But it set Paul off. That's when he hit Wade the first time."

"This manipulation was going on before the fight, which was last September." I stood up and got a bottle of water from the refrigerator. "Maybe Paul did something before then—or didn't, but Wade thought he did—that made Wade angry. I wonder who'd know."

"Marcus, maybe? Mike? I don't know if Wade talked to Mike much, but he could have overheard something. Jack—" As if summoned, Jack climbed the stairs into the motorhome. "Hi, Jack."

He nodded at us, standing slightly hunched over to avoid bumping the ceiling with his head.

I jumped in before he could speak. "Do you know of any grudge Wade might have had against Paul Trimble?"

"Other than Paul punching him?" The side of his mouth quirked up in a half grin.

"Before that."

Jack shrugged out of his jacket. "Nope. Can't think of a thing. Now, did you hear about the repairs going on out there?"

I let it go. "Yeah, Tom gave me the basics. Anything to be concerned about?"

Jack sat on one of the sofas. "You shouldn't notice a thing. I just wanted you to know what had been worked on. Tom gave you the times for tonight and tomorrow, right?"

"7:00 tonight and 8:00 in the morning. Got it." I looked at my watch and jumped to my feet. "It's 3:30 already? I was going to nap before dinner, and I've got to run by Holly's before I leave. And find Detective Jolley."

"About Jolley."

"Yes?"

"Everything OK? You're not still a suspect, right?"

"I think everything's fine. I've got to give him something, if he hasn't left yet."

"Did you ever find Wade's notebook?"

"That's what I've got to give him."

"If he's not here now, I'm sure we'll all see him again tomorrow, like a bad penny that always turns up." Jack kept muttering as he stood and moved to the back of the motorhome.

I chuckled and exited the coach. I was looking down, tying my jacket around my waist, when I turned the corner into the paddock lane and ran smack into someone.

"Sorry!" My words died on my lips as I saw Jim Siddons.

His face contorted into a snarl, and he stepped forward, too close to me. "Stay the hell out of my way, you little bitch!" Spit flew as he spoke.

I flinched and took a half step back. "Jim, please. I don't understand what you're upset about."

He moved forward again, erasing the tiny space I'd put between us. "You little priss. Don't pull that innocent shit with me. It might work for team owners and sponsors, but I see through your act. Women don't belong on the track—you're in the way of real drivers. You hear me?!" He was starting to yell.

I clamped down on my fear and anger and remained calm. "I belong here every bit as much as anyone else." I tried a diversion. "By the way, Jim, what kind of rental car do you have this weekend?"

That stopped him flat. "What? Why?"

"I've…got a bet with someone that more people get silver Tauruses than anything else."

"You're wrong again. Blue Dodge." He switched the fury back on. "It proves my point: you don't belong here."

"I'm not leaving." I locked my knees against their trembling.

He snarled again. "Just stay out of my way, and keep your nose out of my business." With a final shake of his fist in my face, he thundered off.

I braced myself on the front of our motorhome. Outstanding.

A quiet voice spoke beside me. "Are you all right, Miss Kate?"

I turned to see Alex Hanley, the diminutive brake specialist. "I think so. I wish I knew how I made him so upset. What he thinks I did." My heart was still pounding.

He wiped his hands with the red shop rag he was holding. "Well, I betcha' it's not something you did. That Jim is an odd duck."

"You know him?"

"Worked with him a couple years on a team a while back. Even then he had his moods. Like a spoiled three-year-old? Throwing a fit when he doesn't get what he wants. Kind of like that."

He patted my shoulder. "You watch yourself with him, now." He gestured to the paddock. "We'll keep an eye on you too, but you just watch yourself."

Chapter Thirty-two

I looked for Detective Jolley halfheartedly as I hurried to Holly's team paddock, but didn't see him.

Holly was sitting in a chair under the awning, sipping a soda and fanning herself with a folded piece of paper. Her contentment became indignation as I related my encounter with Jim Siddons.

"How dare he?" She sat bolt upright and banged her Diet Coke on the table next to her with a splash. "I'll have a word with that misguided boy."

"Please. Just skip it."

"He needs some facts explained—and an attitude adjustment."

"What's he going to do? Run me off the road? He's not short-sighted enough to damage hundreds of thousands of dollars of machinery, just because he's pissed at me." Then I recalled how he'd brushed my car during practice.

Holly raised an eyebrow. "No?"

"No, I still can't believe he'd risk damaging his car and others to get back at me. For what?"

"You stole his ride, remember?"

I threw up my hands and shouted, "I didn't steal anything. It obviously wasn't his to begin with!"

"He's confused."

"He's like a child throwing a tantrum because he didn't get what he wanted. Except…the look in his eyes was creepy."

"Children don't always know right from wrong—they only know what they want."

"Too damn bad for him."

"You hold onto that attitude. But also watch your back." She wagged a finger at me.

"Everyone keeps saying that. If Jim's really driving a blue car, he couldn't have killed Wade."

"If he drove it here, if he didn't leave later, if he didn't come in another way. You can't be sure."

"You really think he'd do something?"

"Sugar, what part of 'there was a murder here two nights ago' don't you understand?"

"I found the body, remember?"

"What don't you get about the idea that someone here did it?"

"But…not Jim."

"Because you know him? Because he's a driver?"

I didn't have a response for her, and she swept on. "It's going to be someone we've met. Someone we know. Maybe someone we like. I asked Detective Jolley, and he said Wade didn't have much outside of racing."

"He told me that, too."

"There you go, it's someone here. Though probably not Marco in his Ferrari."

"You knew it was Marco?"

"Every race, Kate: a Ferrari and a groupie. I hear he likes to parade around naked to dry off after a stint in the car—with a female fan in the trailer."

"Thanks for that visual." I rubbed my temples. "I get that we're not looking for a stranger. I just don't want to face it."

"Work on that. And tell the detective about Jim's latest threats—tell Jack, too."

"Yes, ma'am."

She smirked at me. "That's better."

I pulled Wade's notebook out of my pocket and handed it to her. "Look at this."

She opened it, and I thought about what she was seeing. Precise, cramped writing. Dates heading six columns of numbers, check marks, and letters.

"What the hell?" Holly read one line aloud, "DH, 2:13:63, 8, HT, check mark, 9-26-09."

"The dates that break up the columns look like ALMS race dates." I pointed to one as she turned the page.

"I think you're right. Under that you've got columns...the first is letters—initials maybe. The second looks like lap times. When was Sebring in 2009?"

"March 21."

"This list is Sebring. You were driving with Mike and Wade that race. What was your fastest lap time?"

I thought back. "I was barely slower than Wade who was just slower than Mike. I did a 1:40:50, I think."

Holly looked at me with wide eyes. "That's here, Kate. He was tracking fastest lap times—that means this first column is driver initials. See, here are yours with that time."

I scooted my chair next to hers and looked where she indicated. Sure enough, the first two columns of initials showed "WB 1:40:30," "MM 1:39:50," and "KR 1:40:50."

Holly ran her finger down the list for that race, and we identified initials for other drivers, including Lars and Seth, the drivers of the 29 Corvette, and Jim Siddons, who'd been their third driver for that race.

I stopped her as she reached the bottom of the list of drivers. "That's not all drivers in the race."

"He only tracked some of them?"

"Also, there's Jim Siddons twice—but the second instance has no lap time." "JS" was one of four sets of initials at the bottom of the list with no times.

"I can find the entry list for Sebring 2009 somewhere, and we could figure out the others."

I was remembering the race. "There was a Brian someone— that's the BS? Pablo Trujillo was a third driver for one of the prototypes, so that's PT. But I don't know who the WB was, besides Wade. Or why they have no lap times."

"We know the first two columns anyway. Here's your whole line, Kate," Holly read, "KR, 1:40:50, 4, TF, then blank and blank."

"The third column, that's how we finished. See, me, Mike, and Wade were all fourth. Lars, Seth, and Jim were sixth."

The next five minutes brought us no closer to solutions. Holly sighed. "It gets hard. Who are HT, RJ, AT, and TF in the fourth column?"

"And why do some entries have check marks and dates—that's got to be the column, some kind of date. But why do some have another person's initials, checks, and dates, but not all of them? Oh—and Holly, flip to the back of the book, there are a couple pages there."

She found the page of initials and notes first and read them aloud. "MO, crossed out, with the words 'wife plus girlfriends plus children.' Well, that's Marco, everyone knows about that."

"Marco said he wouldn't pay Wade. Think this is Wade's blackmail list?"

"Could be. The way this is crossed out looks angry." She held it up to the light. "He almost poked a hole in the page. Next, PT and MT on one line, also crossed out."

"Paul Trimble and Wade trying to control Marcus, I bet. Which didn't work the way he wanted."

"Then we've got EMA—got to be Eddie—with 'Suz' and 'Crystal.'"

"Eddie and Susanah Purley? I'd heard she had more affairs than just Wade. And Crystal must be another one."

"Never heard of a Crystal here. But the next line confirms Eddie and Susanah: SP with EMA and TU. Torsten Uhlgren?"

"I guess so."

"People make interesting choices." She shook her head and continued. "TA with question marks. Guess he couldn't come up with anything on Tom. That'll be easy for you to check. And finally, JS and TM with the words 'scam' and 'my choices too.'"

"Jack Sandham, Jim Siddons? Scam?"

"I surely don't know a TM."

"Wade wasn't much of a blackmailer yet, if he only had Eddie, Susanah, and JS/TM on his active list."

"A blackmail starter kit?"

"Detective Jolley said blackmail victims were suspects because they benefited from Wade's death. I just can't believe Susanah Purley did it. Or Jim, because of the blue rental car."

"Maybe Eddie or the mysterious TM?"

"Flip back a page, Holly, there's more." I leaned over and we studied the list together. Unlike the other pages, I didn't think the initials in the column on the left were people.

SJT	sjtadmin/yK39juP5
TRG	buddy47/leave12
BR	bradmin/don'tchangeme
RSI	32netRSI/pat19johnk
WR	admin/western2001
TWE	tweadmin2/us99richmond
SSR	jsesboss/7uj8ik9ol
DRW	drwadmin/31flavicecream
ES	esespania/fromSeville
CR	admincr/zjY741tj
NNR	teamNNR/niner93UK
RRR	tripleR42/notAbrand42

Holly confirmed my suspicions. "Looks like teams with usernames and passwords, don't they? That 'WR' could be my Western Racing."

"And SSR, that's Sandham Swift. But what are the logins for?"

"I know each team has its own radio frequencies, more or less. And I know we do our own…."

"What?"

"Hang on, Kate, let me check something." She crossed the garage and ducked into the team's transport trailer.

She reappeared a minute later, fuming. "Our IT guy says that's Western Racing's login information for our wireless network, which is how we receive car data when it's on the track and transmit it between team engineers in the paddock, pits, and wherever. Seriously? A username of 'admin' and our team name and year founded as the password? A monkey could guess that! He's changing it now."

"There's something else. Aren't all the teams who've had cornering or spinning problems on this list?"

She studied it again, tapping her finger against various rows. "You might be on to something. I think this list is Delray customers."

We digested that idea.

"Holly, what was Wade doing with this? Listening to team info? This is scary stuff to have."

"You could gather a lot of information about a whole lot of cars if you used this. But I'd never have pegged Wade as a computer or data whiz."

"It sure connects him to the car problems. Was he cheating? Sabotaging others? Or was this just for blackmail?" I looked at Holly in shock. "Did I say 'just for blackmail'? How has the racing world come to this? Maybe Zeke's right, maybe the noble sportsman is only a fairy tale."

"Being involved in racing doesn't make anyone a better person, Kate. We get all types here, too."

"Logically, I know that."

We puzzled over the list another minute, then returned to the race data at the front of the book. We brainstormed, but generated no solutions. Holly was starting to crack jokes— "These are nicknames, Kate! You're Too Fast Reilly, and Pablo was Rotten Job Trujillo"—when my cell phone rang with Jolley on the other end.

"Detective!" I heard the guilt in my voice. "I was looking for you. I found that notebook."

"I'm on my way back in the direction of the track—when did you find it?"

"I remembered where it was a couple hours ago, but I was in the middle of something, and…it took me some time to get ahold of it."

He sighed. "I'm almost to the track. Where are you? I'll meet you there."

"I'll meet you at the entrance."

"Fine. Five minutes." He clicked off.

Holly raised an eyebrow at me. "Trouble?"

"I should have called him the minute I found this. Oops. Thanks for the help."

"It was kind of fun. But next time, I'll hunt up my secret decoder ring. We could use it."

Chapter Thirty-three

Jolley made no secret of his annoyance. I explained where I'd first found the notebook the day before, what I'd done with it, and what Holly and I had figured out about its contents.

That's when he scowled. "I asked you to turn this over to me as soon as possible. You withheld potentially valuable evidence in the murder of Wade Becker."

"I didn't mean—"

"I understand, but in addition to not giving us all the facts, you may have put yourself in danger. How many people knew you had this today?"

"I was careful. I kept it hidden."

"But some people knew. And now more people know. Just be careful."

I didn't mention the photocopies. "Detective?"

"Yes?" I heard "now what" in his tone.

"Other things have come up." I told him about the video Zeke was tracking down, and he immediately radioed to get someone official involved in the search. I also related my run-in with Jim Siddons and Holly's assessment of Jim's capabilities.

"We're looking at him, as well as others. But he obviously doesn't like you. I agree with your friend: he may not have much impulse control. Again, be careful."

I was more worried now than before.

"Where will you be tonight, Kate?"

"I'm going back to the Inn now for some downtime, then I've got another team dinner, at The Boathouse. Early to sleep to prepare for tomorrow."

"You're here when tomorrow?"

"8:00. The race isn't until 3:00, but it's a full day."

"I'll see you sometime tomorrow. Thanks for the notebook, and call me immediately if there's anything else I should know."

We drove off in opposite directions: him into the track, and me to the Inn.

Once in my room, I pulled the curtains closed against the remaining sunlight, changed into sweats, and dropped face-down on the bed. The noise of my next door neighbor going into his room fifty minutes later woke me up. I'd hoped to sleep longer, but I already felt more rested. I stretched and yawned, feeling a spurt of irritation when I caught sight of the box from my father. I got up and took another shower.

By the time I'd cleaned up and changed into dinner attire— more black pants and a white, long-sleeve, button-down team shirt—I'd become resigned. I marched over to the box, moved it to the bed, and sat down next to it. I took a deep breath, surprised that my heart was thumping. Under the lid and a dozen layers of tissue paper was a silver, five-by-seven frame holding an old photo of a man and a baby.

I blinked. Looked closer. It was me as a newborn. I'd seen plenty of photos of my grandmother in the same hospital room, with baby Kate wrapped in the same baby blanket. But the man. It wasn't my father. It had to be my grandfather, my father's father who had just passed away. I was stunned.

What I'd been told—and had accepted as fact—was that my parents were young when they married without their parents' consent. Both had been students at Boston University, my mother there on an academic scholarship, my father a third-generation BU legacy from old Massachusetts money. I'd come along five months into the hasty and ill-conceived marriage— my grandmother's description—and my mother had died in the hospital just days after giving birth to me. At that point, I understood, my father and his family had abandoned me. My mother's parents—Grandmother and Gramps—had raised me in New Mexico. Grandmother told me many times that my father and his parents had never had the "decency or respect" to visit me or my mother.

But I was holding proof the opposite was true—at least of my paternal grandfather. Had she not known? Not told me? Grandmother and I were going to have a talk soon, I thought, as I replaced the photo in its tissue nest.

It was six o'clock. I wanted to be out of the room and not thinking about my family problems. I gathered up the photocopied pages of Wade's notebook. The pages of login information and miscellaneous notes—blackmail efforts?—I left behind, face down in the top drawer of the desk. I didn't want those anywhere near me. The pages listing race dates and records I carried to the hotel porch.

Fifteen minutes after I'd set myself up with mineral water and a dish of pretzels from the bar, and five minutes after I'd given up staring at the notebook pages hoping for inspiration to strike, Mike ambled up the walk.

"Hello, stranger." I saluted him with my glass.

"Hello yourself, partner." He climbed the stairs and sat in the chair next to the loveseat I was occupying. He dropped the day's paper on the table in front of us and scooped up a handful of pretzels.

"Help yourself."

"Fanks." He spoke through a mouthful.

"What have you been doing all day? I didn't see you at the track."

He brushed salt from his hands. "Worked out, golfed, napped. A little R&R."

"Sounds nice. I wanted to ask you something. When you said that Wade wasn't the only one who had an affair with Mrs. Purley...who else did?"

"Two that I know of: Torsten and Eddie."

The notebook had been right. "Aren't they all married, Mike?"

He shrugged. "Now they are. Torsten wasn't at the time. Eddie might have been engaged. You know racing though."

"Its own little world. Let me ask you something else. Zeke told me Wade's attitude changed from one race to the next three years ago. Did you notice that, too? Did something happen at a race?"

Mike considered. "I've never told anyone about this, and I wouldn't if Wade were still alive. But Zeke's right, and I think I know why."

"Really?"

"Yeah. It was one night a couple days before a race, Mid-Ohio, I think. We didn't have a team dinner, for once, so I went to the hotel bar for a beer. Wade was there, drunk. I'd never seen him even the slightest bit tipsy. But this...."

Mike shook his head and toyed with a pretzel. "He told me his father had just died. I expressed sympathy, and I'll never forget his response. He said, 'My father didn't give a shit about me—but I didn't care about him either. About the only thing that son of a bitch ever gave me was Huntington's disease, which killed him and will kill me too someday. He always told me if I went into racing I'd never be great, and it dawned on me today, the asshole might have been right. This is as far as I'll go, and I've got nothing else. Some success I am.'"

I blinked. "That's so sad. What was the disease?"

"Huntington's. I looked it up later. It's a hereditary disease—incurable. The nerve cells in your brain waste away, and you have problems with motor skills, like walking or swallowing. Maybe end up with dementia. But get this, it can start with personality changes, like aggression or irritability. Even antisocial behaviors."

"Makes you wonder if he'd gotten it already."

"Exactly. And I wouldn't have said anything, but I guess Wade needed to be sure, because the next day he threatened to ruin me in racing if I ever talked about it."

"I don't think he expected to be treated well. Though he didn't treat others well, either."

Mike threw the pretzel he'd been playing with on the table. "That's when Wade got mean."

"It sounds like the turning point. You'd never heard he had another career or backup plan to racing, right?"

"Nope."

"He had to be scared and angry about the disease. Combine that with thinking he'd only met his father's low expectations, and maybe that's why he turned power-hungry and reckless on the track. Even vicious."

"Was he all of that? I guess he was."

A few silent moments later, Mike physically shook himself. "Enough of that, Kate! What's new at the track today?" He reached for another handful of pretzels.

"They're rebuilding our clutch and transmission. And brakes. Checking the ECU, again. Detective Jolley is still asking questions. Most of the paddock thinks I killed Wade to get his job. Those were the highlights."

He started laughing.

"That's funny, Mike?"

"Sure. You wouldn't do that."

"Maybe you can spread that around, because there's a different opinion out there. It's unnerving."

"Ignore it. It'll go away."

"I hope so."

He examined my face. "Rough for you?"

"I'm handling it."

For the next few minutes, I entertained him with stories of Torsten and Andy's track walk, the Purleys and Trimbles at the Sandham Swift paddock, and my interview with the *Seventeen* magazine dragon lady—particularly her effect on Tom. I was relaxed when Stuart appeared and for once I didn't react to him by tensing up or anticipating his disapproval.

Mike hailed him. "Join us!"

I waved at an empty chair. "I was just filling Mike in on the scene at our paddock today: cars torn apart, the Purleys and the Trimbles all there at once."

"Good evening, Mike, Kate." Stuart sat and adjusted the knife-sharp creases in his trousers.

I turned to Mike. "What was it with the Trimbles and Wade, anyway? What started everything?"

Mike scratched his head. "The first thing I remember was Wade bringing Paul around a lot. Paul was already sponsoring the Series, but I think Wade wanted Paul to sponsor him individually—or our team? No, Wade wanted to run other races under the True Color banner, as well as in the ALMS."

Stuart was frowning. I turned back to Mike. "But what happened?"

"Paul turned him down flat at the beginning of last season. Pissed Wade off something fierce. He badmouthed that guy for days."

With that, Mike announced it was time to clean up for dinner. "Drive together, Kate? Stuart, you with us for dinner?" Since Stuart was at the Inn for another dinner, not with us, Mike and I agreed to meet in the car park at ten to seven.

I was turning to Stuart with a comment on the weather when it hit me—that's what Paul had done to Wade. I realized my mouth was hanging open, and Stuart was looking at me oddly.

"Yes, Kate?"

"Aunt Tee and I were discussing Wade and Paul and Marcus Trimble earlier, how Wade's behavior was about controlling Marcus to get back at Paul. But we couldn't figure out what Paul had done—or what Wade thought he'd done—to make Wade angry enough to do that. It must have been Paul not sponsoring Wade."

Stuart looked sour. That hadn't taken long. "I can't believe you're asking questions about this."

"Why?"

"Didn't you hear Detective Jolley and me telling you to leave it alone? To stop asking questions?"

"He said to be careful—"

"What did you think that meant?!" Stuart shouted, his face red. He lowered the volume. "That meant stay out of it."

I matched his glare. "Don't even think about trying to tell me what to do. I'm not trying to piss you off, but give me a little credit. I'm doing this for a reason. I'm not an idiot."

He settled back into his chair, spine rigid as always. He muttered something that sounded like, "Could've fooled me."

"Excuse me?"

"You're doing a damn good imitation of one."

"Shall we just get this out?"

He sat forward again. "Here's the problem: you're poking your nose into something you should stay out of. It's murder, and someone out there is a murderer. You want to get in the middle of that? Some of us are trying to keep you safe, despite your asinine attempts to put yourself in danger."

"Are you done?" I snarled. "Then listen up, you insufferable, patronizing ass. I get that it's murder. I also know Jolley can't get half the information from this carnival that an insider can. So I'm telling him what I know. And more than that...."

The fight left me, and I felt more tired than mad. "I'm trying to find the truth. To make sure being an innocent bystander doesn't ruin my racing career. I've worked too hard to let that happen."

Stuart took my hand, surprising me equally with the gesture and the kindness in his voice. "I'm sorry. You're not an idiot. Just maybe too trusting. Be careful who you talk to and who you place your trust in." He released my hand, cleared his throat, and sat back. "Many people care about you and don't want to see you hurt. That's not meant to be patronizing."

I studied him: the small smile, the hands together, fingers steepled in front of his chest. No BS there. I grimaced at the taste of the apology I owed him. "Sorry about what I said."

He waved a hand in the air. "I'm sure I can be insufferable and patronizing. Maybe it goes with the job."

"And the 'ass' part?"

"Maybe that, too, but don't push it."

I laughed and felt lighter. "I'm sorry anyway."

"Maybe now you can get past the antagonism?"

"We probably both can."

"Friends?"

"Friends."

We sat for a minute or two in silence. "Kate, I don't mean to pry, but I wanted to ask about something."

"I may not answer."

"Fair enough. James Reilly, our Frame Savings and Loan sponsor. Is he your father?"

I froze. That wasn't what I'd expected at all.

"Never mind. Forget I said anything."

I took a deep breath. "No. It's OK. I will ask you to keep this to yourself."

"Of course. I don't idly gossip, Kate."

"I know that. Did he—" I had to clear my throat. "Did he say something to you about me? To someone else?" I was in no mood to be claimed publicly by a long-lost deadbeat dad.

"Nothing like that. And I apologize for upsetting you. I saw him watching you on the television feed while you were driving and in the pits and paddock. Then I thought about your coloring and your names. I just wondered."

"Between you, me, and the lamppost there, yes, he's my father. But I'd never seen him before last year on the ALMS circuit. We'd never spoken until last year at the Road America weekend in Wisconsin." I gave him the abbreviated story of my birth and explained that I'd been raised by my maternal grandparents.

"I know of Hank Patterson."

I smiled. "Gramps."

"A master of wiring, I hear."

"You've never met him?"

"No. I've heard about him and his products from everyone, but he'd stopped traveling by the time I got involved with racing in the U.S."

"Gramps is the greatest. He and my grandmother were all I knew until just recently." I grimaced. "But just this evening I discovered several things I'd been told all my life were one way, are, in fact, the other."

I answered the question on his face. "I'd always known—been told—that my father and his family wanted nothing to do with me, from day one. But that's wrong. My father just gave me a photo of his father holding me as a newborn in the hospital. It's hard to argue with a photo proving my grandfather was there—that he wanted to see me at least once."

Stuart didn't try to fill the silence with empty platitudes, which I appreciated. After a long pause, he asked, "What will you do next?"

"Ignore it and get through the weekend. Then talk to Grandmother about it. Ask her what she knows."

"Will you talk to your father or his father about it?"

"His father just died. That's why he gave me the photo. I suppose I'll have to talk to my father eventually. But I can't handle it now. Not this weekend."

"I'm sorry for the family trouble, Kate. It sounds inadequate or useless, but if I can help at all, say the word."

"Keeping my father out of my hair would be great."

He smiled. "I'll see what I can do."

I cleared my throat. "In the spirit of friendship, I should tell you something."

Stuart raised an eyebrow.

"Oh, stop that. It's something in Wade's notebook."

"You don't have it, right?" Stuart went from calm to agitated in no time at all.

I held up a hand. "The police have it. I just…looked at it." Once again, I didn't mention the photocopies.

"You shouldn't even be talking about it. This is a matter for only the police."

I looked at him steadily until he fell silent. "I don't have to tell you about this, Stuart. Now be quiet if you want to hear."

He clamped his lips shut and sat back.

"One of the pages in Wade's notebook had a list of team initials and what looks like username and password information.

Holly and I—don't give me that look. Holly double-checked what was listed for her team, and we think the list is login information for wireless networks. For all the teams using Delray ECUs."

Stuart's mouth made a perfect "o" of surprise. I drank down the last of my mineral water while his mental wheels turned.

I spoke again. "I can't figure out why Wade had the information. We found other evidence of him blackmailing people—or trying to."

"Hmmm," Stuart murmured.

"Was he snooping on teams? So he could blackmail them with that data? But what else would he have done with it? I wish it all made sense."

"Mmm, hmmm."

"I guess I'll see you later—"

Stuart held up a hand. "Kate, I'm going to share something with you, but I have to ask you to not say a word to anyone."

"Sure."

"It could be critical that you don't, because your information may help us lay a trap for the person responsible for the problems the cars have had."

"If he's still alive?"

"Let me explain. We've narrowed down the problems to Delray ECUs. But the ECUs aren't defective. They're being actively interfered with from somewhere on the ground, in order to briefly disrupt engine power."

"Which wouldn't be a big deal on the straight, but in a turn...."

"Right. At the limit of adhesion, as in a corner, it can act like a brake on the rear wheels. As we've seen, it's enough to break cars loose."

I sifted through the little I knew about how ECUs collected car data for use by the team. "But the ALMS technical regulations—we can't transmit to the cars, just receive."

"By regulation, correct. But nothing in the technology itself prevents an unscrupulous team from transmitting to their car.

Except if someone was cheating, we'd see their improvement and likely figure it out. But in the case of sabotage? There's been no clear beneficiary so far. Until now, we couldn't determine how our mystery saboteur connected to the ECU system. The existence of the list you're describing tells me he's connecting to the separate systems run by each team. I also believe the list you saw must have come from Delray Electronics itself."

"But how? Who? Wade?"

Stuart shook his head. "What I know from Victor Delray is that their engineers never have access to information for all networks. I don't think Victor was the leak. He seems too genuinely distressed at the blow to his company. For that matter, so does Trent."

"Who's Trent?"

"Trent Maeda, Victor's number two at Delray. He's been around this weekend—you've probably seen or met him? An Asian man, the only one here in an official capacity besides our two Japanese drivers."

"I haven't met him—wait! I forgot. I did see him. Yesterday morning, talking with Jim Siddons and a shaggy young guy in a SPEED shirt."

Another "o" with his mouth. "Really?"

"Come to think of it, they looked upset to have been seen."

Stuart looked at his watch, then tapped it with a finger. "I need to confer with Victor this evening. And Detective Jolley. Perhaps we can set a trap tomorrow."

"Stuart? Do you think Wade was part of it?"

"Hard to tell. You say he had incriminating information, but I agree with you, I'm not sure what he would have done with it. His car and team haven't obviously benefited recently."

"Mostly he wanted power. Stuart! The next page in Wade's notebook had a list of names and initials—we think it was his blackmail list. On it were the words 'JS/TM scam, my choices too.' It must be Jim Siddons and Trent Maeda."

"If Wade's notes can be believed, that's incriminating."

"What do you think 'my choices too' means?"

"He was in on it? Choosing cars to be interfered with? I'm not sure, but Kate, this makes it even more imperative: don't say anything. And steer clear of those men."

"Trust me on that." I looked at my watch. Time to meet Mike. I stood up and offered Stuart my hand. "I'm glad we've reached a truce."

He stood also, took my hand, and kissed my cheek. "It was past time for that."

"Wait, Stuart? I heard Jim wasn't here, but do you think Trent killed Wade? Because he had this information?"

"I expect Detective Jolley would tell us to leave the questions to the police."

"I know. But if not him…who?"

"I don't know, Kate. I wish I did."

Chapter Thirty-four

Dinner that evening represented Jack's efforts to strengthen relationships: we were wooing reps from two potential sponsors and making nice with our GM liaison, who supplied us with factory parts and support. The Purleys were also there, joining Jack, Tom, Mike, and me as the faces of the team. I sat between Mike and Tom.

Talk around the table centered on Jack's thoughts for our chances in the race. After morning showers and afternoon sun, the evening had turned windy, with dramatic clouds scudding across the sky. We speculated on the possibility of rain the next day, and Mike offered input on handling. I kept quiet and listened.

The slowest eaters were finishing their main courses, and the conversation had fractured into pairs and trios talking, when Tom leaned close to me, resting his arm on the back of my chair and curving his body toward mine.

"I discovered something." His voice was just above a whisper.

I spoke quietly as well. "About what?"

"Our main sponsors here." He gave the slightest head twitch in the direction of the Purleys, seated at the end of the table.

"Really?"

"Jack pulled me aside this afternoon, and laid down the law. We get continued sponsorship if we make sure word goes no further about a relationship with Wade."

"Hers?"

"Right. Hubby was irate that police questioned them—livid at the situation and at someone giving the cops the info."

"Does he know it was us? Besides, you're supposed to tell the cops the truth."

"I didn't say he was reasonable. I don't think he knows who talked. But we're starting fresh now. Jack assured him no gossip, no comment, no judging. What's in the past is over and done with. We go on from here."

"I wonder if that kind of cover-up will work—especially in this industry."

"Jack says we'll damn well make it work, because they're important to us."

"Lips sealed. Do you have to deliver this message to the whole team?"

"Yeah. Don't you think this could be how he's 'fixing things' for her?"

"I guess so." I was reluctant to give up my favorite villain.

Tom tapped my shoulder with the hand resting on my chair. "Don't you think that clears him?"

"Maybe?" I leaned forward to peer around Tom at Mr. Purley.

"Do you want him to be the one, Kate?"

"It wouldn't break my heart."

"Think what it would do to the team!"

I shook my head at Tom. "You're as bad as me. I don't like him, so he should be guilty. You think we need him, so he can't be."

"We do need him."

"OK, OK."

Mike leaned in from my other side. "What are you two whispering about?"

I felt hemmed in. "The old zip-lips treatment we'll give our favorite sponsors."

Mike nodded. "Yes, deluxe service at Sandham Swift."

Two waiters arrived to remove our dinner plates and distribute dessert menus, causing them both to move away. I struck up a conversation with the GM guy across the table.

The rest of the evening passed without incident—at least until I returned to my room.

I drove Mike away from The Boathouse around nine. We'd pled a need for sleep before the race and left everyone else with coffee and cognac. On the way home we saw fireworks and heard muffled pops and bangs from backyard enthusiasts.

I said goodbye to Mike in the parking lot and walked to my room, unlocking it and going in. I flipped the light switch and shut the door, then felt a chill that had nothing to do with temperature. The room felt wrong. The bathroom door was closed, and I was sure I'd left it open. Swallowing hard, I tiptoed over and shoved the door open. Nothing. Blood roaring in my ears, I turned on the light and batted the shower curtain out of the way. Empty.

My heart pounded and my knees felt weak as I returned to the middle of the room and surveyed the scene. Nowhere else for anyone to hide. Nothing seemed to be missing. The only item out of place was the box from my father, sitting crooked on top of the TV cabinet, when I thought I'd left it straight. But given my muddled state of mind over its contents, I couldn't be sure.

I jumped, hearing a smattering of distant pops outside. More fireworks. I looked around the room again, conjuring an image of how it looked before dinner. I shook my head. I just couldn't tell. Aside from my mother's diamond jewelry, which I wore, and my wallet, which I had carried in my purse to dinner, I owned nothing of value.

I double-checked the locks on the front door and the connector to the next room, letting out a breath and rolling my shoulders a few times to release tension. I told myself I was imagining things, but I still felt jittery as I brushed my teeth and got ready for bed. That's when I thought of the photocopied pages of Wade's notebook, still tucked in my handbag. Was someone looking for those or the notebook itself? I retrieved them, smoothing out the folds, and opened the desk drawer to put them with the other pages.

I'd discovered what was missing.

Sixty dollars in cash I'd stupidly left in the drawer and the other notebook pages. But my thief had left something as well: a piece of notepaper from the Inn with "STAY OUT OF IT" written in large block letters. I reached out a trembling hand, then changed my mind and closed the drawer. The remaining photocopies went back in my purse.

It took me forty-five minutes, some yoga poses, and a desk chair wedged under the doorknob to feel secure enough to go to sleep.

I woke later with a start. The green numbers on the clock read 11:50, and I wondered why my heart was racing again. Fireworks popped in the distance, and I relaxed, assuming that's what had woken me. Then I heard a quiet tapping on my door. I'd pulled back the covers and started toward it when the doorknob rattled. I froze, my heart in my throat, arms and legs trembling.

Was it Jim? Trent? Wade's ghost? I was scared enough to believe anything.

The knob rattled again as I crept to the desk and picked up the receiver. I spoke in a whisper to the sleepy-sounding desk clerk, who woke up fast and promised to walk around the building and check things out, offering also to call the police, if I preferred. Whoever was outside must have heard my voice, because as soon as I started speaking, the noise stopped.

I told the clerk no police if he'd walk around. Then I hung up and remained rooted in place for five minutes—long enough to hear the slap-slap of the desk clerk's feet outside, walking back and forth in front of my door. I took my shaking limbs back to bed and sat there for an hour, my knees pulled up to my chest and my heart rate in the stratosphere. I alternately wondered what the hell was going on in my life and worried about not sleeping the night before my make-or-break race. A long time later, I stretched out and concentrated on soothing thoughts and deep breathing. Eventually, I slept.

Chapter Thirty-five

I woke up just after six in the morning, well before my alarm was set to ring. Once on my feet, I took stock: I felt good, ready for the day ahead, full of energy and excitement. No ill effects from a poor night's sleep.

When I'd showered and dressed—in jeans and a black team polo shirt—I peeked out the window, took the chair from under the doorknob, and opened the door. I examined the ground, the door, and its exterior knob. I didn't know what I was looking for, but I didn't see anything. I picked up my notebook with data I'd recorded about the track and left for the dining room and breakfast. Five steps later, I turned back and retrieved my purse as well.

I saw other racing people at breakfast, including Tom and Jack, who were signing their bill. I sat alone at a small table in a corner of the garden room—where we'd eaten dinner two nights before—and plowed through scrambled eggs, ham, potatoes, fruit, and coffee, loading up on protein and carbs for the day ahead. While I ate, I went through my notes on the track and thought my way around it over and over. I also reviewed the process for changing drivers. With so little practice, I'd be slow getting in and out of the car, but I rehearsed mentally as much as possible.

I tried to use the drive to the track to relax, but instead kept wondering if the person who broke into my room found what he was looking for or if he'd be back. I also wondered if Jim Siddons and Trent Maeda were really saboteurs. If they were also murderers.

If Jim and Trent were responsible for cheating, one or both of them had to be responsible for killing Wade too...didn't they? How many people that evil did we have in the ALMS? In racing? But it was a big step from cheating to murder.

Besides, plenty of other people had motives. Did we know everyone who'd wanted Wade stopped? I didn't think so. Stuart would set his trap for Jim and Trent. I would follow up on other clues and suspects—specifically, who drove the three mystery cars out of the track Friday night and what the remaining pages in the notebook meant. Plus why my initials were in there.

"Was there an Andy someone driving last year?" I mumbled, as I cruised along. That was Randy someone—was he the "RJ?" No, that was Randy Williams, an occasional driver in the Star Mazda series last year.

"Rotten Job Trujillo," I recalled Holly's jokes. "And Too Fast Reilly—I wish."

I turned off the highway down the small road leading to the track entrance, marveling again at the fact of a racetrack tucked away behind the tall trees and sporadic houses of northwestern Connecticut. I bypassed the six cars waiting to pay for parking by zipping through the "Credentials Only" line and eyed the guard shack on the right. In an hour, I'd be back to talk to Dennis Weston about cars he'd seen. Later in the morning, cars would clog the track entry, as tens of thousands of fans converged to watch us race. Those thoughts got my heart rate up as I crossed the wooden bridge.

Lime Rock Park was more alive today than previous days— more cars and people, but also more gussied up, as Gramps would say. New flags were out, delineating parking lots and the Corvette Corral, where Corvette owners could see and be seen. More banners had been hung, advertising the ALMS, SPEED Channel, and Series and track sponsors. Booths were set up in the midway, from which merchandise would be hawked all day. The palpable energy in the air originated from more than my revving nerves.

As I got closer to the paddock, the energy kicked up a notch. Racecars were still tucked in their garages, but crowds of wandering, pointing, picture-taking fans had started to form. Series staff, race officials, and team members were out in force, scurrying around in preparation for the day. Those who stayed in the paddock area or worked hospitality all wore crisply pressed team shirts, embroidered with sponsor logos up one sleeve and down the other. Pit crews wore fire suits and hustled back and forth from paddock to pit with tools, racks of tires, and cans of race fuel—often with a cigarette dangling out of their mouths.

Everyone was getting ready for something. Mechanics, track staff, and ALMS officials to solve problems with a car, the racetrack, or the race. Team and Series hospitality types to entertain hundreds of sponsors and guests. Drivers to drive as fast as possible. We were all putting on a show for the audience at the track and around the country—a show that happened at over a hundred miles per hour. Everything was a rush to curtain time: when the green flag dropped for the start of the two hour, forty-five minute race.

At 8:00, we hadn't reached panic stage yet, though the blood was already fizzing in my veins. I hopped out of my Cherokee and fought the urge to pump my fists in the air and jump up and down. Race day! I had a ride! I contented myself with a huge smile at the sunny day and the sparkling track as I collected my bag and jacket and headed for the paddock.

Aunt Tee greeted me with a knowing look. "Excited this morning, Kate?"

"You bet."

"I'm sure you'll do well, channeling that energy into your driving."

"That's the plan."

"You go on and stow your things inside. Mike and Seth are there, just waiting on Lars and Jack for your meeting. Did you eat some breakfast?" At my assent, she went on. "Well, help yourself to anything. Plenty of water and snacks whenever you want."

"Got it, thanks." I opened the motorhome door and climbed inside.

Chapter Thirty-six

We started our meeting just after eight o'clock. Seth and I sat on the couch along one wall; Mike and Lars sat on the other. Jack pulled up a chair from the table, and the two crew chiefs—Bruce Kunze from my car and Walter Bryant from the 29 car—sat in the motorhome's driver and passenger seats, which turned around to face the interior of the vehicle.

Jack leaned forward, elbows on knees. "OK. Our cars. The 28 should run in the fifty-three to fifty-four second range. The 29 should run solid fifty-fours. We've got no major handling problems remaining with either car. Right?"

We all shook our heads.

Jack went on. "Mike, the understeer you were feeling Friday. That's completely taken care of, right?"

"It was good on Saturday."

Jack looked at Bruce, who shrugged. "Should be OK, boss."

"Good." Jack made a note on his clipboard. "If anyone feels something this morning in the warm-up, get on the radio fast, so we can fix it. I think we can make the podium—or be damn close. The factory Corvettes will have a couple tenths of a second each lap on us. But anything can happen—just look at qualifying. And remember: one of them is starting from the back of the grid. They've got to catch us first to beat us. We know they can do it, but we'll make them work for it.

"Other cars: the Saleen and the Ferraris also look strong this weekend. The Saleen's been getting stronger each race. They'll be a big challenge. The two Ferraris weren't as good in qualifying and practice here as I thought they'd be. But they might find the speed they're missing and be a threat. Possible. The Maserati's getting better each race, but they're still a few tenths behind us. And the Viper's a few tenths behind them.

"What you all need to do is stay in front of the Saleen and the Ferraris—and the Number 64 factory Corvette coming from the back of the pack. Make them work for it—but don't hurt the car! Gamesmanship time."

Jack wasn't telling us, "Don't worry, take it easy, we don't expect to win." He'd gone into normal race mode: "Go balls-out for everything we can get." That upped the pressure on all of us, particularly me, but it also meant Jack felt confident in my driving and good about Mike and me as a driving team. That was great. And it gave me butterflies for the forty-seventh time that morning.

"Pit stops." Jack leaned back in his chair and flipped a page on his clipboard. "Mike and Kate. If there were no yellows in the entire race—"

Mike snorted, and Lars started laughing.

Jack held up a hand. "I know, unlikely. This race, Mike's going to start and finish. Kate in the middle. Changing drivers twice instead of just once could cost us time, but I think it'll happen under yellows. If there's a yellow before minute thirty, we don't stop. Any yellow between thirty and one-fifteen: we stop to change drivers. If we haven't seen any cautions up to one-fifteen, we come in anyway. Once Kate's in the car, we don't stop until she's been there forty-five minutes or more, to meet the regulations and score points. Unless, God forbid, there's a mechanical or tire problem."

He lowered his notes and stared first at Mike, then at me. "Because there will not be a problem of a car damaged by driver error."

I shook my head. Mike just laughed. Jack's mantra was "Don't hit shit," because damage to the car cost him money. All team owners wanted their drivers to be as aggressive and fast as possible without ever touching another car, curb, gravel trap, grass shoulder, guardrail, or anything that might scuff a sideskirt and cost money to fix. They didn't care that those were incompatible goals. When you spent hour after hour pushing a car and balancing it on the knife-edge of speed and control, sometimes you hit shit.

Jack nodded. "Right, you'll bring the cars back in perfect shape."

Mike snorted again, but Jack ignored him. "Now, the weather. The forecast is for clouds and possible showers. That could mean we'll get them or not. Hard to tell with summer in Connecticut. But I've got a secret weapon this year." He looked around expectantly.

Lars gave him what he wanted. "What is it, Jack?"

"I found a local. The volunteer doing security at the pit entry near us has lived a half-mile away for fifty years. We'll ask him what the weather will do. He'll know." Jack looked pleased with himself.

Seth spoke for the first time. "Just don't leave us hanging out there on slicks when it starts coming down. That track's slippery enough in the dry."

Jack made a tick on his notes. "Don't worry. We'll go to the grooved rain tires sooner here than other tracks. I know those concrete patches are slippery. Just not until I check in with our local weatherman."

I saw the dismay I felt reflected on the other drivers' faces.

"Cheer up, maybe it won't rain at all. Anyway, those are the plans. Not a single thing ever works to plan, but we'll try our best once again."

We laughed at that. He was right. Nothing ever happened as expected, but we had to start with something.

"One last thought. Remember: keep it clean and—"

Mike, Seth, and Lars chorused with him: "Don't hit shit."

I laughed at them but choked to a stop when Jack scowled at me. "That means you too, rookie."

"Sure thing, Jack."

He checked the time. "Series drivers' meeting in forty-five. I'll see you all there." With final nods to us, he left the motorhome.

Mike rolled his eyes with a smile. "Our Jack sings the same tune every race. Come on, Kate, I'll buy you a bottle of water." He slung an arm around my shoulder, and we went outside.

I left Mike fishing water bottles out of the cooler to cross to Jack in the garage. I spoke quietly. "Jack, I need you to do something, but I can't tell you why. I swore to Stuart I wouldn't tell anyone. Just trust me, OK?"

His eyes searched mine. "OK. What is it?"

"Make whoever's responsible change the password—maybe the username too—to the team's wireless network. Right now."

He stopped himself from speaking twice, then nodded and walked directly to the transporter.

I steadied my breathing and realized it was time to hunt down the guard at the front gate. Mike wanted a lift to the media compound near the paddock entrance, so we commandeered the team golf cart and rolled out. I dropped him off and continued toward the entry, dodging a steady stream of oncoming cars.

Fifteen minutes later I drove back through the infield, riding half on the right shoulder to allow cars to pass. My exchange with Dennis Weston, the guard, had been brief. He'd written down the four-car information for me—though he'd explained he was relying on memory, since the guards kept no log. Between roughly 9:00 and 10:00 Friday night, four cars left the track in this order: a silver Ford Taurus with a Georgia plate, a brick-red or maroon Chevy Malibu with the letters "BOY" on the plate, another silver Taurus with an unmemorable plate, and a red Ferrari convertible. He thought all but the Ferrari contained the driver only, all male, though he wasn't positive. My tentative questions yielded no more data, so I'd left him to his work.

Now all I had to do was stake out three parking areas or ask everyone for the color, make, and license plate of their rentals. No problem.

I spotted Eddie as I entered the paddock lane and pulled up next to him.

"Hiya, Kate."

"Tell me, Eddie, what kind of rental do you have this weekend?"

"Something red? Dunno. Why?"

"Just curious. I wanted to ask something else—and I swear it'll never go any further. Did you have an affair with Susanah Purley?"

Eddie frowned. "Don't publish it, but yes, I did, some years back. You can talk to Torsten, too. He was seeing her before I was."

"Did Wade know about that? And is Crystal your wife's name?"

I saw a flash of fear, before Eddie's eyes and face displayed his anger. His voice rose as he spoke. "Yes, Wade knew—but why are you asking? Are you trying to blame me for something? You've got no right. I advise leaving that for the police." With a disgusted look, he took off.

I hadn't expected such a vehement response. He'd rented a red car…did he have something to hide?

I spent a few minutes back at the paddock sipping water and mulling over the information I'd received, before Mike and I headed for the mandatory Series drivers' meeting at the ALMS trailer. Halfway there, James Hightower Reilly, III, appeared in front of me. I saw Stuart waiting nearby, and I waved Mike on.

"Good morning, Katherine."

"Good morning." I looked at my father, struck for the first time by how much we looked alike. No wonder Stuart asked if we were related. He was a slightly larger size of me, which meant he was short for a man and slight. Straight, black hair, fair skin, and blue eyes, all like mine. I couldn't pinpoint the facial characteristics we shared, but his face was familiar. I wasn't sure I liked the resemblance.

He cleared his throat. "I know you have a meeting. But I wanted to wish you the very best of luck today in the race."

"Thank you." I relented, adding, "We expect it to be a decent race for the whole team."

"And you? Are you feeling comfortable in the car yet?"

"In the car, sure. On the track? We'll see. I haven't had much time on it. But I'll learn fast." I stopped. I hadn't meant to have a conversation with him.

"Katherine, did you have a chance to open the package I gave you?"

The conversation was officially over. "Yes. I did. But I'm not interested in talking about that with you. At least, not yet."

He looked disappointed, but he reached into his inner suit pocket and came out with a business card. I accepted, holding it between my thumb and index finger. He stared at me in silence for a few more seconds, then turned and walked back to Stuart.

I debated chucking his card into the nearest trash can, but decided I was more mature than that. Barely. I sighed and tucked it into my back pocket, noticing Stuart watching me across the road. He flashed me a smile that felt like support, and I ran for the meeting.

Chapter Thirty-seven

The race director gave us the same message a dozen ways in twenty minutes: don't screw around. "No unnecessary hitting, aggression, or bad behavior—hear me? Don't go bangin' into each other—because we'll penalize you." The official, Guy, was liked by everyone at the track. He was a big, physically intimidating man, with a sharp mind, a great sense of humor, and an infectious slow, bass chuckle. You couldn't get much by him. His job during the race was to supervise details, settle disputes, and make final decisions. His job at this meeting was to lay down the law. And he did.

I daydreamed as Guy fielded questions, remembering the other drivers' meeting I'd attended with this series, at Sebring last year when I'd raced the first time with Sandham Swift. I thought about that room full of drivers and tried to fit names to the initials from the second column of letters in Wade's notebook: HT, RJ, AT, and TF. Looking around the room I was in, I drew a blank again. No one. Damn.

"One more thing, please, and I'll let you go." Guy surveyed the group as we quieted. "There's going to be a modification of the schedule today, by one minute. The ALMS has arranged that while we're on the grid, we will have one minute of silence in tribute to Wade Becker." Quiet murmurs ran through the group, and I wondered if anyone in the room actively missed Wade.

"Right. Keep it clean, and have a great race."

Mike promised to meet me at the paddock in fifteen minutes to prep for the warm-up session at 10:45, and he took off. I thought about finding Eddie again to apologize or ask what he was hiding, but only caught a glimpse of him as he slipped out of the meeting through an opening that didn't look like an exit. I was following the last group of drivers out to the paddock lane, when a voice stopped me.

"So, Kate." A small Italian driver named Piero, who drove one of the bigger prototypes for a Delray team and had a reputation for aggression and flamboyance, stood with his arms crossed over his chest. "Why do I hear you have the codes and passwords to access ECU data for Delray teams?"

I stopped walking and saw a dozen other drivers watching the two of us with interest. "I don't—Wade. Wade had them. How do you know?"

"Didn't you find them? You have them."

"I found them, yes. But I don't have them. I turned them over to the Series and the police. I swear I didn't look at them."

I felt the atmosphere shift. Two drivers nearby looked less bemused and more annoyed. Some drifted away, but not before shaking their heads or giving me dark looks. I shouted, in anger and to reach the ears of the retreating drivers, "I don't have them! I don't want them!"

Piero narrowed his eyes. "It could have been you. You've been at all the races, right there at the track, not doing anything else."

I was silent, bound by my promise to Stuart, unable to clear myself. "I...no. I haven't done anything."

Piero wasn't impressed. "Make sure you don't."

I found no sympathy on the faces around me. *You can't change their minds now, Kate,* I told myself as I walked back to the garage. *That will only happen when everyone knows who committed the sabotage—and murder. What you can do is think hard about that notebook. I'd go back to the basics. Why did Wade keep the notebook in the first place? Because he kept a list of people who'd made him mad.*

Stuart pissed Wade off at Petit Le Mans last year and Sebring this year, and Paul Trimble made Wade mad at the beginning of last year. But they're not drivers.

I reached the Sandham Swift paddock and waved to Tom and Jack, who were standing in the garage area. I headed straight for the motorhome and the remaining photocopies from Wade's notebook. I flipped the pages.

Last year, Sebring: PT, with no lap time.

Last year, Petit Le Mans: ST, no lap time. Just "AT" in the fourth column and everything else blank.

Sebring, this year: ST again, this time with blanks and "RJ."

I sank down on the bed, reorganizing my thoughts. I picked up the papers again to fit names to the other non-driver initials, and the door to the motorhome opened with a bang.

"Damn door!" It was Mike's voice. "Kate? You in there?"

I jumped up. "Yeah, Mike. What's up?"

"That little warm-up thing—you remember?"

"Of course. Just about to suit up." I poked my head out and saw Mike in his suit already. "Just give me five."

He popped a grape in his mouth from the bowl on the table. "Sure. Then let's talk." He sat down on the couch to wait for me.

I shut the door and yanked my duffle bag and firesuit out of the closet, taking a deep breath to stop my panic and my fumbling. I collected and straightened the photocopies I'd just crumpled and started to fold them neatly—when the top page caught my eye. Last year, Sebring. My initials there, Mike's too, among the drivers. At the bottom, with no lap times: BS, WB, PT, and JS. Benny Stephens, the SPEED Channel announcer; Walter Bryant, the 29 car crew chief; Paul Trimble, Series sponsor; and Jack Sandham, my boss.

I put the papers away. Time to prepare body and mind to drive.

Chapter Thirty-eight

It wasn't easy to focus on suiting up and driving. Nomex under-wear on, check. Whose initials were in there a lot? Firesuit on, arms through sleeves. Sit down on the bed. Fire-retardant socks, check. Driving shoes, check. Still don't know what those other initials mean—HT, RJ, AT, and TF. Earplugs around my neck. Earrings, necklace, and watch into baggie, check. Pack up street clothes and put them in duffle. My notebook and pen out of my bag, into my pocket. I've got to tell Holly what I figured out. And Detective Jolley. Grab sunglasses, and join Mike.

We walked to the pits as Mike coached me on driver behav-ior—so I'd know what they'd do when I saw them in my rearview screen.

"Heinrich, easy. He acts like he owns the whole goddamn road. He nearly does. He's looking for the first fraction of an inch to pass. Just make it easy on him and his co-driver. And the purple prototype, you seen it?"

At my nod, he went on. "One of its drivers is as aggressive as Heinrich, but his co-driver isn't. You won't recognize who's who by their helmets yet, so give the purple car some room, too. The rest of the prototypes are more patient. And we're faster than most in the sportscar classes, so no worries!" My nerves kept me from returning his grin.

Unlike the closed-cockpit sportscars, the prototypes were open-top, and you could see the driver's helmet as he went around the track. Knowing who was coming up behind you made it easier to anticipate their movements and avoid tangling with them. I'd just have to be careful with all other cars until I learned who was who.

I was putting my notebook and chapstick in my pit locker and pulling out my gear, when I saw Dave Hacker entering the pits a few stalls away, headed the other direction. "Be right back," I called to Mike, then ran after Dave.

He and I reached his pit at the same time.

"Dave."

"Hey, Kate, what's going on?"

"Quick question." I spoke in a low voice.

"Shoot."

"When did Wade think you did something to him? And when did he threaten you about it?"

"This isn't a great time."

"I know, but please tell me?"

He scowled and pulled me two steps away from his pit area. "The first time he got mad at me—for no reason at all—was last year at Sebring. He said I hit him, but that's complete crap, because he hit me!"

"What?"

"Even that was nothing! It was during a yellow. I was fourth or fifth behind the pace car, and Wade was behind me. Something happened to the line of cars in a corner, and I had to stop short. He wasn't fast enough and bumped me from behind. Just a tap. There wasn't any damage on the car, but he yelled at me, saying I was a crappy driver and it was my fault we hit because I didn't have the sense to drive right."

"That's ridiculous."

Dave grimaced. "I know. Then nothing, for months. We're at Sonoma in mid-July, and I'm walking down the empty pit row after practice—had to get something from my locker—when he comes up behind me, puts his hands around my neck, and scares the life out of me. Telling me I'd better not get in his way again or he'll fix me, fix my car, fix my team. I'd better not mess with him—not so much as look at him wrong, or he'd make sure I went out to race someday and never made it back in."

"That's horrible."

"No kidding. And then two races later, Road America last year, someone misses a turn, spins, whams into me, spins me around, and I punch the left rear panel of Wade's car. Couldn't have been when Mike was in the car, could it? No, it had to be Wade. Nothing I could have done about it."

"And?"

"He didn't say a word to me there. But once we got to Petit in September? If looks could kill, I'd have been dead forty times over. He shoved my car around once or twice during the race, and he sent me a message."

"What did he say?"

"Nothing, but in my pit locker, I found a toy car painted to look like ours. About this big." He held his thumb and index finger two inches apart. "Run over by a car. Crushed."

"He did that?"

"I can't prove it. There was no note, and it was just left in my locker. Had to be him, though. But the weirdest thing? Since then, nothing. I approached him at the first race this year, tried to straighten things out. He told me to get lost, that he had bigger fish to fry. He just dropped it."

"Thanks, Dave. Say, what kind of car did you rent this weekend?"

He looked confused at the change of topic, then wounded. "Be honest, Kate. You're asking if I was here Friday night. The police asked about my car and whereabouts already."

I fumbled, then looked him in the eye. "Yes, I'm asking you. I'm sorry."

"It's a silver Mazda. Our team had a big banquet up in the Berkshires, in Massachusetts. The police know." He returned to his pit.

I fought guilt as I ran back to my team space, where I found Mike and Jack looking for me.

Jack looked at his watch. "Ten minutes to warm-up start. Now that you've got the bathroom out of the way, let's get you ready and in the car."

I didn't correct him. Instead, I went to retrieve my gear and stood for a moment with my head resting against the pit cart. Eyes closed. Three deep breaths. Concentrate on the car, Kate. I shoved everything about Wade out of the way, breathed deeply again, and imagined being in the C6.R. Driving around the track. Getting out of the car fast. To my relief, I felt calm and confident. I straightened up and opened my eyes. Ready.

Chapter Thirty-nine

I was buckled into the Corvette by 10:40, waiting for the 10:45 start to the thirty-minute warm-up session. I'd take twenty of the minutes, leaving Mike time for about eight laps. I sat in the quiet car, waiting for the signal, and concentrated on keeping my heart rate and breathing steady.

I was first out of the pits, and for three turns, I had a rarity ahead of me: completely open track. But it lasted only that long, as one of the fastest prototypes whizzed by me when I entered No Name Straight. I swept up the hill to the chicane, remembering just in time to check my speed, and hit the perfect line through the quick turns. No punting cones today—or ever again, I vowed. However, the corner worker had been waving a blue flag, and I looked in my mirrors to see a prototype coming fast. I moved left, giving up the racing line to the faster car, and as it blew past me on the Back Straight, I recognized Heinrich. Then the track was clear, and I made the turn into West Bend.

I was just starting to feel good when I almost blew the Diving Turn. It was that damned bump! It shouldn't be affecting me, but I always hit it just as I was allowing myself a second of relaxation. Kate, you don't get to relax! Lap two. Go!

I found my rhythm again on the second lap. Lap four, a voice on the radio: Bruce. "Kate, you doing OK?"

Push radio button. "Fine. Car's great." Keep concentrating. Brake for the chicane.

"Good. Times look good. Used six minutes."

"Tell me at fifteen. Thanks," I transmitted, as I barreled down the Back Straight. I started to feel good, more comfortable. Faster. Relieved. Confident in the speed and my ability to coax it out of the car. I took a sip of water.

I'd done eighteen laps in twenty minutes and change when I hit the entrance to the pits, headed for a full-speed, racing driver change to give me the practice. On the last lap, I'd unplugged my air hose and drink tube to save time. I pressed the speed limiter button right before crossing the pit entry line, then loosened my belts and unplugged the radio cable while steering the car into our box. Crew members crouched on the low wall, ready to hop out and do anything that needed to be done. I brought the car to a stop, killed the engine, twisted my seatbelt release, and removed the steering wheel and hung it on its hook.

A fully-suited crew member, whose name I learned later was Bubs, had already opened the door and let down the safety net. I twisted, pulled, heaved, and got myself out, remembering to reach back in for my seat insert. I hopped over the wall and turned back to watch Mike get in. The crew had topped off the fuel, inspected the tires, and moved out of the way. Bubs got Mike settled quickly, and he roared off. Aunt Tee and Jack stood nearby, Jack examining his stopwatch.

I pulled my helmet and balaclava off my sweaty head and unstuck the tape holding the earplugs in my ears.

"Thanks." I draped the chilled, wet towel Aunt Tee handed me over my face and hair.

"That was good, Kate." I heard Jack's voice, and I uncovered my face to look at him. "Driver change was quick, and your lap times were a few tenths faster than yesterday. We'll be in good shape today."

"Great."

"Car felt fine?"

"Yeah. Track's bumpy, but the car is great."

"Good." Jack thumped me on the shoulder and climbed back up onto the control panel to monitor his track feeds and car data.

I walked around the back of the cart and stood watching the duplicate monitors as I sucked down a bottle of water.

Two screens showed tables of official timing and scoring data. Seven others picked up live feeds from different cameras around the track, and the eighth showed what would be live SPEED Channel coverage. The monitors were arranged roughly in order of the turns on the track, so I could follow car 28 around the track by looking from one screen to another.

Mike was the third-to-last car back in the pits, and we returned to the paddock for a debrief. By the time I'd changed out of my suit, tried to fluff my hopelessly flat hair, and emerged from the motorhome, Jack, Bruce, and Mike were sitting in chairs outside. Aunt Tee took the damp firesuit from my hand and hung it to dry next to Mike's at the far end of the awning. For all the sweaty suits that dried in the wind, I could never smell sweat or body odor emanating from them. Aunt Tee also pointed to my helmet, which was shaking gently next to Mike's on a special drying rack that blasted air at the helmet's lining.

I smiled my thanks and pulled up a chair with the others.

Jack spoke first. "Just wanted to touch base quickly. First, Mike, Kate, any issues with the car—speed, handling, anything you could tell?"

I looked at Mike and Jack. "Nothing."

Mike looked thoughtful, then shook his head. "No. It's actually really great. I thought there might have been the slightest oversteer in one corner, but I think it was just the bumps. I wouldn't want you to try to fix it at this point. Not with both of us comfortable with it."

"Great. Bruce, anything you want to bring up?"

"Kate, tell me what you want during the race. Talk to you a lot? Don't talk to you at all? What do you prefer?"

"Ask any questions you need answers to. I'll ask any I've got. Otherwise, why don't you check in with me every ten laps or so. Tell me how my lap times are doing."

Bruce made a note on a folded piece of paper in his hand. "Sure. Anything else? This guy doesn't want any of that stuff." He jerked a thumb at Mike.

"Really? I like to hear it. I'd also like any change in our class position and how much faster the cars ahead are running than I am."

"Can do."

Jack leaned forward, hands on his knees, ready to stand up. "Then we're all set? I'll go talk to the other guys. Oh, timing. No autograph session. We'll need to stay around here but mostly out of sight from noon to one. Cars and teams go to the grid at two. Be here and ready before then. Let me know if you need anything else." He levered himself up and headed over to the garage, where I saw Lars, Seth, and Walter waiting for him.

Bruce got up and followed Jack, and Mike didn't move at all. He looked a question at me when I stood up.

I gestured to the motorhome. "I want to look at a couple notes and straighten things."

"OK. I'll be here if anyone needs me. We'll have sponsors arriving soon we'll need to suck up to—I mean, entertain." He winked.

I nodded, only then realizing how I was going to spend the next few hours. So much for quiet time to prepare.

Inside the motorhome, I fended off Aunt Tee's invitations to eat the sandwiches she was readying for lunch and shut myself in the back room. I pulled out the photocopies.

I mumbled to myself as I read. "DH at Sebring last year. Shows lap time, ninth place, then HT, a check mark, and a date in July." I scanned the pages and found the same date in July listed with more initials and lap times.

"Dave at Sebring last year. Wade said Dave hit him. 'HT'… must mean 'hit.' Maybe the check marks are when he settled the score." Sure enough, the July date was the Sonoma race, when Dave said Wade threatened him.

I was shocked by the complexity of Wade's record-keeping and the anger behind it. I found the race at Road America last August. That row confirmed what Dave had said: "HT," a checkmark, and a September date. September meant Petit Le Mans, when Dave reported receiving the next threat.

That meant the column with HT, RJ, AT, and TF didn't contain a person's initials, but what the initials at the beginning of the line had done to Wade. A check mark was Wade's revenge, and a date, when he took it. I leafed through the pages again. Not every entry was tagged for offenses against him. But at each race, four to six people managed to piss Wade off enough to make it into his black book.

I returned to the page with last year's Sebring race and my initials. The other night, Wade had raved at me in the bar about stealing his ride. I laughed out loud. Holly's "Too Fast Reilly" might be on the money.

An entry for the same race listed PT, for Paul Trimble; RJ, for I didn't know what; a check mark; and a date—the date of Petit Le Mans last year. Sebring was when Paul had turned Wade down for sponsorship, and Petit was when Wade and Paul had fought. The one piece that didn't fit was that Stuart had said Paul approached Wade in that instance. I wondered if a few punches would have been payback enough for Wade.

Back to RJ. The other three RJs I'd seen had followed Stuart's initials for last year's Petit Le Mans and Monterey races and this year's Sebring...and that was when Stuart stopped using Wade as a press representative for the Series. I put all of the "RJs" together: rejection.

One more: AT, most often next to the initials MM, JS, WB, BK, and AH. I thought those were members of our team: Mike, Jack, Walter, Bruce, and Alex Hanley. Sure enough, AH showed up under Petit last year, when Alex and Wade had gotten into a shouting match. People telling Wade things he didn't want to hear would probably seem like attitude.

"Kate?" I heard Aunt Tee's voice from the front room. I discovered I'd been absent nearly half an hour. Too long.

"One more sec, Aunt Tee." I returned, then scrambled for my cell phone. Detective Jolley didn't pick up, but I left a message telling him I'd cracked the code. I made sure my belongings were put away and rejoined the racing world.

Chapter Forty

Outside I found a good looking lunch spread and most of our sponsors. Filling a plate with a sandwich, fruit, and chips—I'd return later for the cookies—I sat down on top of a cooler and dug in.

"Were you napping in there, Kate?" Mike popped the last bite of a peanut butter cookie into his mouth.

"Looking over some notes. Getting things straight in my head."

"Enough of that," Jack commanded. "You're prepared enough. Stick around here until the race."

"You got it, boss." Part of what sponsors got for their money was access to the team, especially the drivers, and I'd fallen down on the job. I didn't mind hanging around the paddock, though I was on pins and needles waiting to hear if Stuart had caught Jim and Trent in the act.

While I speculated on Stuart's trap, I smiled and chatted with Mr. and Mrs. Active-Fit and the tan guy from Leninger's Enduro Shine. After a while, I pulled up a chair next to the Purleys. I still had my doubts about Charles Purley. I didn't trust him, and I wanted to know more.

"Mr. and Mrs. Purley, how are you both today?"

"Please, Kate," the woman looked to her husband for confirmation. "It's Susanah and Charles."

I smiled, and it was Charles who answered the question. "We're just fine. Enjoying ourselves at the races here. It's been a lovely day so far." He was right. After the dark clouds of previous days, we'd seen nothing but blue skies and white, puffy clouds.

"Let's hope it holds for the race." I squinted up at the sky, which, come to think of it, showed more cloud build-up.

Susanah leaned forward and spoke in a breathy voice. "Have you raced much in the rain, Kate?"

I felt nerves tickle my stomach. "Sure. Most series run their events rain or shine. But I haven't driven this car in the rain. I'm focused on getting in tune with the car in dry conditions. If it rains, it's all different, we're all slower, and I'll have another learning curve."

Charles was nodding, and a slight frown marred Susanah's forehead.

I summoned another smile. "I was wondering how long Racegear.com has been around. And how long you've sponsored the team here."

Charles propped a foot on the opposite knee and put his arm on the back of his wife's chair. "Some of the basics, sure. We founded Racegear.com about fifteen years ago, out of our garage, didn't we Suz?" He looked to her.

"Yes. We were both working full-time jobs then—Charlie as an engineer and me as an office assistant. But we had this idea."

Charles put his foot back down on the ground and leaned forward. "We were race crazy. Some people go for football. We went for racing. But there was nowhere to buy fan gear for all kinds of racing—let alone the basic clothing and accessories a novice racer needs. So we put one together."

"The Internet was just becoming big," put in Susanah.

"Right. It didn't start as Racegear.com, just Race Gear. It started small, us buying t-shirts and ball caps, storing them in our basement, and shipping them off. Then we realized what the Internet could do—and never looked back. Quit our jobs a couple years later, expanded to real race-ready equipment, and here we are."

"And when did you get involved with Sandham Swift?" I asked.

The muscles around Charles' mouth tightened. "About five years ago."

Susanah fluttered. "We were looking to get involved in some series or other, and we'd gone to see the race at Road America, in Wisconsin. Charlie got to talking with Wade at that race, and that's how we met Jack. We started sponsoring the team in a small way at the next race, and as the major sponsor the next season. We've really enjoyed the Sandham Swift team and the ALMS."

Charles watched her as she spoke, his face only relaxing when she finished.

"It must be a great relationship, to have lasted this long. Do you get to attend races together often?"

Charles chuckled. "There's the irony. The company has become so successful we can't get to as many races as we'd like. Susanah gets to more than I do. But we manage to both be at a race, oh, three or four times a year. Right, dear?"

Susanah bobbed her head at him.

"I'm glad this is one of them, so I have a chance to meet you both." I felt like a fraud. "But you weren't able to travel here together, were you?"

Charles looked puzzled. "No."

"This is one of the tougher tracks to get to, by air at least. You know, far away from all airports, you've got to rent a car once you land, then drive a couple hours. Kind of a pain. Even driving in, like I did, is a challenge. You get through the metropolitan areas, which take all kinds of concentration, and then you just keep going out into the boonies for ages!" I was babbling, but they both had relaxed.

Susanah smiled. "You're right, it would have been nicer to share the journey. But I came in on Wednesday and had to rent a car and drive myself out here. Thank goodness I got here in the daylight!"

"I know what you mean. I got here just at dusk on Wednesday myself, and I was worried I was going to miss any number of back road turns. When did you come in, Charles?" This was my point. I kept a phony smile on my face and tried not to vibrate with tension.

"Me?" He looked suspicious, and I felt someone move to stand beside me. Jack. Charles glanced at him and looked back at me. "I didn't arrive until late Friday night—but fortunately, I had a driver, so I didn't worry about losing my way."

"How late does our reception area stay open, anyway? I always wonder about these small places. I mean, are you getting someone out of bed if you roll up at three in the morning?" I could tell this was the bridge too far, and I cringed inside.

Jack put a hand on my shoulder. Charles spoke through gritted teeth. "I'm not sure I can answer that, Kate. There was someone at the desk when I arrived at midnight, after my plane landed in Hartford at ten. Is that what you wanted to know?"

I forced a chuckle. "Oh, I was just—"

"Kate, can I speak with you a moment? Over here?" Jack issued another command.

I excused myself and followed him to the rear of the garage behind some tire racks. He clutched my upper arm with one big hand and spoke quietly, which was worse than yelling. "What in God's name are you doing, Kate? What explanation can you possibly have?"

"I was curious."

He shook me. "You're as good as accusing our main sponsor—with whom we've had a long, valuable, and trusted relationship—of murder. What are you thinking? Why aren't you thinking about the race? Damn you! I hope your driving isn't as clumsy as your snooping!"

My whole body tingled. I felt shame down to my toes. And fear. Not of Jack, not of Mr. Purley, but of screwing up my chance. I'd looked at the ground as he spoke, but now I stood straight and squared my shoulders. Looked Jack in the eye. "I apologize to you, and I'll apologize to Mr. Purley, if you feel that's appropriate. I didn't mean to endanger the relationship. But I'm fighting for my life here, as much as I will be on the track."

Jack snorted and rolled his eyes. His grip didn't slacken.

"Jack, really. Have you heard the rumors? I've heard them. People think I did this to get ahead. Killed Wade, slept with you—and now, cheated by accessing Delray team info. That I've been causing the car problems around here lately. And who knows what else they think I did, all so I could get a seat in a car. If I can help figure out who really did it, maybe I'll get a fair shake. Maybe I won't be the scapegoat for everything. That's all I'm looking for."

Jack narrowed his eyes at me, but the anger in them had died down. He let go of my arm, and I spoke again. "I overheard Charles saying some pretty awful and suspicious stuff to his wife the other day. So I tried to ask some questions. Badly." I shook my head. "I really am sorry. I didn't mean to cause the team problems."

Jack's face was still grim, his voice still harsh. "Next time, ask me first. I'd have told you I saw Charles pull up in his chauffeured towncar around midnight. We sat on the porch, had a drink together, and talked for an hour. That's when we settled the business Tom talked to you about. Since you're so curious, here's the back-story, but you are not to share this with anyone."

He shoved his hands in his pockets. "Charles was here early this weekend to surprise his wife. He was going to put his foot down and ensure she wouldn't, ah, associate with Wade any longer. We agreed the Sandham Swift team would not discuss anything about the relationship. Wade was going to have to live with both decisions. We're doing this out of kindness for a valued sponsor and for a continued racing partnership in the Series. Now, do you understand? Is that what you wanted to know?" His voice was heavy with sarcasm.

I felt awful, even though I'd gotten my answers. "I understand. Again, I'm very sorry to have let you down—and perhaps offended Mr. Purley. I'll stay out of their way from now on."

"No, you won't. You'll go back over there and make nice. Maybe apologize. Face them and deal with it, like I'll have to."

I agreed, miserable and certain I'd lost any chance at a permanent job with the Sandham Swift team.

Jack read me perfectly. "Kate, I'm pissed as hell at you. But unless we lose that sponsor entirely, I'm not going to fire you. I'm just going to watch to make sure you behave."

My shoulders slumped in relief, and I offered him a tentative smile. "I can deal with that. I'll probably deserve it, too."

"Let's go make sure this team is in one piece and that our sponsors are happy." He pushed me ahead of him back to the sitting area.

Chapter Forty-one

Over the next couple hours, my interaction with the Purleys, especially Charles, was stilted. At the first opportunity, I'd apologized for sounding accusatory, assuring them it hadn't been my intent. I joked that I'd been questioned so many times by the police myself that weekend that I'd picked up a bad habit. They didn't laugh, just accepted my apology and drifted away.

Jack was too busy smiling at sponsors to focus disapproval on me. That was a relief, too. He smoothed things over with the Purleys by giving Charles the opportunity to "be the dead man" in the pits during the race. That's the person—usually a crew member, but sometimes a VIP guest—who holds open the dead man switch on the fueling rig that allows racing fuel to flow during a pit stop. The switch is a basic safety mechanism, because when released, it springs closed, cutting off the fuel. It's also an easy, non-critical job to hand over to a guest. Charles beamed with pleasure. and I swallowed my chagrin that he'd be in the pits for the entire race. He might not be a murderer, but I still didn't care for him much.

But I behaved. I ate a cookie and chatted with other sponsors and guests. I tried not to stare when Victor Delray and Trent Maeda arrived in the garage to talk with Jack. I was even glad to see Stuart show up, Paul and Marcus Trimble in tow. They represented fresh conversational blood. And appealing scenery.

Stuart approached me right away. "How are you doing today, Kate?"

"OK, thanks. How are you? How's everything?" I flicked my eyes to the garage and back to Stuart.

"Fine." He leaned over and breathed into my ear—barely audible, even that close. "Everything's set for a trap. Just keep it to yourself. Regarding Wade, the police are checking on their alibis now."

I blinked, disappointed. I'd accepted Jim was clear, but I'd held out hope for Trent. Despite my efforts to investigate other clues, I really wanted to pin murder on them in addition to sabotage.

He straightened and went on in a normal tone. "I thought it was kind of you to give your—Mr. Reilly a couple minutes of your time this morning."

I frowned. I didn't want to talk about my father. Here. At all. "I didn't give him what he wants. But he has to give me time." I surprised myself with that admission, discovering cracks in my indifference. I cleared my head with a quick shake. "I can't think about that today. Too much else going on."

Stuart patted my shoulder. "Understood and agreed. But given what you shared with me, I understand what it cost you. And it was kind."

"Thanks—excuse me a moment, Stuart." I dashed into the paddock lane after Marco, who'd just walked past.

In contrast to everyone else, Marco was delighted to tell me about his activities. "But of course, bella. I was here with a very nice fan in a Ferrari. She asks me what a racecar driver's life is like, and I show her! I could show you also, but maybe you know." He winked with an expression that stopped just short of smarmy.

"I'm good, thanks, Marco. Have a good race." I felt dirty. I liked Marco—and the other drivers with similar attitudes and proclivities—and I respected them as peers, but I found their personal lives repugnant.

I returned to the paddock. Paul and Marcus Trimble had joined Stuart, and I sat down with them.

Marcus spoke first. "Are you ready for the race, Kate?"

I didn't stutter or drool, but it was close. "As ready as I'll get. How are you both?"

Marcus did the taking-off-sunglasses-and-peering-intently thing he did so effectively. "Just fine, thank you."

Paul Trimble seemed more relaxed than the day before. "Yes, just fine."

I dragged my eyes and thoughts away from Marcus and turned to Paul. "How do you think your car will do today?" Stuart glanced from Marcus to me with disapproval. That was the Stuart I was used to.

"Barring the unforeseen, we could expect a podium." Paul looked satisfied.

The LMP2 class, to which the True Color Paint car belonged, usually had five to seven entries at any given race. The car Paul sponsored was one of the better built, better driven, and more consistent smaller prototypes. The True Color team usually took a podium result in their class, if not the top spot.

I smiled at Paul's confidence as he continued. "With any luck, we'll see you on the podium for your own class."

My mouth went dry. The race. "I—thanks. I'll settle for decent lap times and just finishing."

They laughed at my nerves, and I tried not to mind.

Tom joined us in the plastic chairs under the awning. After discussing rival cars in the race, the conversation turned to the next few races on the schedule, particularly the race at the Road America track in Elkhart Lake, Wisconsin. Tom, it turned out, was obsessed with finding the best food available at every track.

"I can taste them now," he rhapsodized, eyes closed. "The bratwurst there! The best on the circuit."

Paul chuckled. "The racing's pretty good, too."

Marcus smiled and shook his head. "I don't know, are the bratwurst in Wisconsin better than the seafood in Monterey? I'd vote for the food in California."

Stuart looked up from his pocket schedule. "Mexican food in Salt Lake City or California."

Many cities, restaurants, and specialties later, I interjected a question for the group. "What about this track? Any restaurants you particularly look forward to? Any places I've missed so far?" I wanted the answer to a specific question, but after Jack's tongue-lashing, I'd be cautious.

"The food's all pretty good here, which you can't say for every track, but there's nothing that stands out," Tom offered, to general agreement.

"I love the atmosphere at The Boathouse." I got one step closer.

"True," Tom returned, "you have to get there at least once, don't you?"

"Twice for me, this time." I took the last step. "Marcus, Paul, have you made the pilgrimage yet?"

Paul answered, looking from Stuart and Marcus to me. "Not yet. Last night we were at the Interlaken Inn, where we're all staying. In fact, I had dinner with Stuart Friday night there, too. But Marcus had the car—wasn't The Boathouse where you went?"

I couldn't think of a way to interrupt and ask what kind of car he had, but I forgot the question as Marcus responded with a smile that made me lightheaded. "I went to The Boathouse for a beer, but I ate at the China Inn Restaurant, right next to The Boathouse. I wanted chow mein."

Paul nodded. "Saturday night we changed it up, going to the White Hart with some franchise owners and suppliers."

Tom laughed. "That's where we're staying, and where we ate the night before. Tell me, are franchisees your usual guests at the races, Paul?"

"Yes, we bring out franchise owners and staff and a handful of suppliers. Some for just the race, some for a big dinner the night before and an overnight stay for the race."

Tom questioned him further about marketing efforts. I wasn't paying attention anymore, because I'd gotten my answer: Paul Trimble couldn't have killed Wade.

In the next lull, Stuart excused the Trimbles and himself, saying Paul had wanted to talk with Charles Purley.

While Tom and I were alone, I remembered to ask about his presence in Wade's notebook. "He wasn't blackmailing you or anything, right?"

He looked confused. "Why would you think that?"

"Your name was in his notebook with question marks."

He started to deny it, then stopped, looking embarrassed. "Now I remember. He came to me once asking about a phone conversation he'd overheard where I said I didn't want people to know something. He made weird references to my secret getting out and wouldn't that be a shame. I ignored him."

"Really? He couldn't have figured it out and held it over your head? He seemed to make a habit of digging those things up."

He shrugged. "He might have figured it out, but it wouldn't matter. It's an inheritance from an uncle—a nice enough chunk of change that I can travel in the off-season instead of having to pick up extra work. I didn't want to have to explain it to everyone. But it's disturbing I made his blackmail list."

"No kidding."

Tom looked at his watch. "Hey, it's that time."

My co-drivers were nowhere to be found, and I checked the time myself. Time to change for the race.

The race! Bells went off in my head and every inch of me went on alert. I hurried into the motorhome, my heart beating so loudly I was sure everyone else could hear it.

Chapter Forty-two

By the time I exited the coach ten minutes later, one of the crew had already driven the 28 car to the pits. It was two in the afternoon, a little more than an hour to race start. We were about to begin the most carefully scheduled portion of the weekend. Series staff carried detailed "minute-by-minute" plans for the pre-race, on-track activities. And by God, those minute-by-minutes worked, and these races started on time. They had to, for SPEED Channel to broadcast live.

In the first twenty-five minutes of the hour, ALMS cars were moved to pit lane, usually by crew members who idled them from the paddock to the pit stall. Then drivers got in the cars to do a reconnaissance lap of the track, ending on the "grid" of the front straight. Mike would do that drive for us, since he'd be starting the race. My responsibility was to be on the grid with the rest of my team for the pre-race activities. And to get my head prepared. My emotions alternated between panic that I hadn't reviewed the racetrack nonstop for the past two hours and calm anticipation. I tried to keep all thoughts of Wade, murder, and alibis away. It was time to focus solely on the driving I had to do.

Our paddock and garage area had cleared out, everyone trailing off after the car, to the grid, pits, or a hospitality tent. I took advantage of the quiet to do some basic stretches and to stand still, eyes closed. For about a minute, I listened to my breathing.

After that, eyes still shut, I thought my way around the track twice, reminding myself of all the quick-braking, hard-turning, no-cone-hitting maneuvers I had to make. I felt comfortable. I remembered it all. Once I was racing, something would come up—gravel on track, traffic, or, God forbid, rain—but I had the basics down. I thought my way through driver changes. First, Mike out and me in, then me out and Mike in. I was ready. I opened my eyes, grabbed my helmet and gloves, and headed to the pits.

The first person I saw in the paddock lane was Detective Jolley. So much for concentrating on the job.

"Hello, Detective."

"Kate." Today's outfit was a navy sportcoat, with light khaki pants and no tie. "You have some things to tell me?"

"Did you figure out the first part of the notebook yet?"

"No."

I grinned. "Well, I did."

He just stood there looking at me.

"Don't you want to know?"

"Yes, I do. But first I want to know how you figured it out. You'd given me the notebook."

"I kept a copy."

He was angry. "You were supposed to hand over the evidence immediately and not keep anything."

I ran a hand through my hair. "Look, what time is it?"

He looked confused, but checked his watch and told me: 2:12.

"I've got three minutes to get to the grid. We can argue about this, or I can tell you what the stinking notebook means."

"Fine."

I didn't have time to care that I'd been rude. "The initials in the first column weren't all drivers. Some were team members, Series staff, that sort of thing."

"Yes, we figured that out right away."

"But I think I figured out the other initials—abbreviations, really." I told him what I thought they meant and about the specific incidents I'd cross-referenced, especially those, like Dave Hacker's, that had involved retribution.

"That is useful information. Thank you, Kate." He sounded grudging.

"I also discovered some information about Mr. and Mrs. Purley and Paul Trimble on Friday night."

I thought his eyes would pop out of his head. "You've been questioning people?"

"Just chatting. But there were interesting points in their stories."

"Kate. I appreciate the inside information you've been able to give us. But you've put yourself in danger by keeping copies of evidence and asking questions. Don't do that anymore. We can't keep you safe, do you understand?"

If he was mad at me, at least he wasn't yelling. "Don't you want to know what—"

"I've interviewed them myself. Leave it to me. Just drive the car."

He looked at his watch and showed it to me. 2:17. I was late.

He stopped me from running. "Be careful. Do you have your cell phone?"

"No, I can't carry it here—and you won't hear anything while the race is on anyway. I'll be fine."

I dashed into pit lane, stowed my helmet in my pit locker, and jumped over the wall.

Jack was looking for me as I ran the last few feet to the wall separating pit lane from the Main Straight and hopped over it.

"You're late, Reilly."

"Sorry, Jack. I got held up by Detective Jolley."

"What can he possibly have to talk to you about? And why now? You need to concentrate on the race."

"I've been preparing. I'm ready."

He studied my face, a smile tugging at the corner of his mouth. "Nervous?"

"What do you think?"

"I think you're nervous. Good. Use it."

I didn't respond, but stood next to him, looking down the track at the solid wall of people. After the racecars took their recon laps, they parked on the Main Straight in order of qualification. Drivers, owners, and pit crews came out to stand next to their cars on the pre-race grid. Then the unusual part: the grid was opened to fans. For about half an hour, thousands of people walked onto the track and got right up next to the cars and teams. Drivers answered the occasional question, but mostly kept to the background, leaning against the wall at the side of the racetrack and chatting with each other, with family and friends, or with sponsors. And we talked to the media: SPEED Channel, ALMS radio, and the track announcer were all on the scene. There was a lot going on in that thirty minutes of open-grid.

Holly swam up out of the crowd. "Got a sec, sugar?"

I let Jack know I'd just be a few steps away and followed her to a spot between our car and the Saleen in second position. We spoke quietly.

"Do I have news for you, Holly."

"Yeah? I've got some, too. But you talk first."

I outlined for her the meaning of Wade's notebook, as well as the alibis for Paul Trimble and Charles Purley.

"That leaves Susanah Purley and Marcus Trimble."

"Like they had reason to want him dead? Even though Paul Trimble has an alibi, he's got a hell of a motive, if he thought Wade was corrupting his son. They fought about it. And Charles Purley, he's just creepy. I still think one of them should have done it."

Holly tipped her sunglasses down on her nose with a red-polished fingernail and peered at me over them. "What on God's green earth do you mean by 'should' have done it? You think they hired out? Somehow those alibis are bogus?"

"It'd be simpler if it was one of them."

"Who else you got? The word's out you've been digging around."

"Great. Not much. Paul and Charles seemed the most likely. Otherwise, there's Dave Hacker. Wade got into it with him over bumping on the track. But I don't know why Dave would do it, except to get Wade to quit bothering him—and he said Wade stopped the threats this year."

"And murder would be extreme."

"There's Jim Siddons, who's just mean. At least to me. I—I know more, but I promised not to say anything. The ECU problems should be over, though. Cross your fingers. And maybe that solution will solve Wade's murder. Or not. I'm not sure."

"Must be serious." She eyed me for a minute. "OK, you keep those lips zipped. What other initials were in there a lot with the other letters, meaning they'd done something to Wade?"

"Me. Mike. Dave. Lots of other drivers—like Marco, Eddie—but no one else more than once. Stuart. Jack. Paul Trimble. Benny Stephens. Walt, the crew chief of the 29 car. Alex Hanley, our brake guy—I know the story on him. He and Wade argued all the time, and Wade talked about getting rid of Alex."

"He's possible."

"I guess. But he's been so open, and crew jump from team to team all the time. I told Detective Jolley about him, so he'll have checked. Marco and Eddie were also on Wade's blackmail list, and Marco was at the track—but I can't imagine he exposes willing fans to anything besides himself. Certainly not murder."

Holly shook her head. "I found out Eddie was part of a big dinner with the fuel supplier—lasted until eleven that night. Benny and Ian were there, too. They're all clear. But how about some of the other people? Mike, Walt, Jack, Stuart. Pick one."

My head spun. I didn't mind considering people I wasn't close to, but members of my own team? "Stuart, he's a cold enough fish, but—"

"Come on, Kate, aren't you over that yet?"

"I was going to say I can't think of a reason he'd do it. No motive. He's so straight-laced, he wouldn't do something illegal to fix a problem. Besides, he was with Paul Trimble all night. And yes, I have gotten over that. Mostly."

"Moving on."

"Walt." I thought hard. "I don't think they had enough interaction for it to be possible."

"Not the sister car's crew. What about Jack?"

"I wouldn't know why. He commented that he's glad it's me driving and not Wade, so maybe he was tired of Wade's attitude. And Wade was starting to slow down. Maybe Jack wanted to get rid of him. But murder's drastic when you could fire someone."

"Could he fire him? Wade started when the team did, right? Maybe Jack couldn't get rid of him."

"Do you know something I don't?"

"Maybe. What about Mike?"

"From everything I hear—and saw, that one race—Mike and Wade had a fine relationship. Mike doesn't get worked up about anything. Wade had some 'MM' entries in his notebook, but I haven't heard of any big problems between them."

"Hold on to your hat."

"What?" I felt butterflies that had nothing to do with the imminent race.

"I heard just the briefest whispers today that boil down to this. One, Sandham Swift was headed for a major shake-up that the team might not survive. Two, Wade said he was going to get rid of Mike. And three, there was trouble in the mentor-mentee relationship between Wade and the delicious Marcus."

"What?!"

"That's all I know. Someone saw Marcus looking angry and upset on Friday afternoon. Someone else heard Wade mumbling under his breath about kicking Mike to the curb. That's all the grapevine's got."

"I can't believe it."

"Makes you think, don't it?"

"The first thing it makes me think is this could be what Wade meant when he told Dave Hacker he had bigger targets in mind." I didn't have time to work through all the implications—as it was, we both should have been standing with our teams on the grid.

"Thanks, Holly. I'll keep an eye out for any undercurrents."

"Don't be too obvious about that, Kate. No sense in getting your own head bashed in. Now, we'd better get back."

I gave her a hug and scooted back to join my team.

Chapter Forty-three

Nonstop activity continued on the track and over the airwaves, including the musical montage of drivers' national anthems. Right after I stepped back into the middle of our team gathering, we got a walk-by from a SPEED Channel camera, led by Zeke.

To start the broadcast of every race, roving pit reporters, cameraman in tow, would review the top three qualifiers in each class—often walking past them on the grid and usually interviewing the driver on pole. I watched Zeke ask a question of the GT1 pole sitter—Andy in the factory Corvette—and then walk backwards, talking to the camera and gesturing to the Saleen that out-qualified us. He kept walking, and the camera kept scanning, stopping on our car. Zeke continued speaking into his microphone while the cameraman swooped his camera up and down the hood and sides of our racecar, giving viewers a dizzying close-up of wheels, vents, and the interior of the cockpit. Then the camera was pointed at the team, standing together at the back of the car. I knew Zeke would be talking about Wade's absence and my presence. I was glad to be wearing dark sunglasses.

Finally, the camera dropped, and Zeke stopped talking. He didn't approach, but gave me a wave and a cocky wink before he walked away.

The on-track system blared out again. "Please exit the grid. Thank you for your cooperation. All non-essential personnel must now clear the grid." Teams stayed put for a couple more rituals, but first we had to get the fans off the track.

Mike put his balaclava and helmet on, as we were five minutes from him getting in the car and fifteen minutes from the start of the race. Nerves hit my stomach again. My mouth was dry. I tethered Mike's helmet to his HANS and held out a hand. He ignored it and pulled me in for a hug. As he stepped back, I could see his eyes crinkle through his open visor, and I guessed there was a smile under his helmet. He leaned close so I could hear his muffled voice. "Have some fun out there, Kate." He straightened and gave me a thumbs up.

I smiled back, careful not to let my expression waver. I didn't like the suspicions planted in me by Holly's news—but I had to ignore them now and think only about the race. "You, too."

The fans had dispersed, and the track announcer gave a final warning to clear the grid. Seconds later, he ordered drivers into their cars, also the cue for the rest of the team to line up across the track next to the car, facing the front of the grid, where I could now see flags. The Coast Guard Auxiliary Honor Guard was introduced, along with the Reverend Coleman, who led a prayer for a safe conclusion to a great race.

I started to sweat. This was really it. What the whole weekend of activity had been leading up to. What all of my preparation was for. This was my big chance for a permanent ride. Right here. In the next three hours. I locked my knees as they started to shake. I knew these last minutes before the cars rolled off the grid would be the most stressful—except for the ones just before I got in the car to race. I concentrated on even breaths—giving up on slow ones.

The introduction of the national anthem singer was a blur, as was the music. The loud, low flyover of two military jets snapped me out of my daze. I pulled myself together and started to step away from the car, when a hush fell, and the on-track announcer spoke. "And now, ladies and gentlemen, we ask for your patience and your attention. We ask you, please, to join us in a minute of silence as we salute Wade Becker, a long-time driver in, and friend of, the American Le Mans Series, who passed away this weekend. Thank you."

The track went absolutely, stunningly silent. It was the strangest experience I'd ever had at a racetrack and perhaps the most fitting tribute from a sport that reveled in cacophonous noise. Thousands of people at the track, and tens of thousands more via live television, stood silent for that minute, as Wade had been silenced for all time. Whatever I knew or thought of him, I felt he might have liked it.

"Thank you very much, ladies and gentlemen." The announcer came back on as gently as he could, given the decibels the PA put out. "And now, for those famous words." There was a fumbling sound as the microphone was handed over to a VIP whose voice boomed out: "Drivers, start your engines!"

Thirty-one engines thundered to life, and the cars pulled out, one at a time, following the pace car. I hurried with everyone else over the wall back to the pits, where I scrambled for my earplugs.

Chapter Forty-four

Everyone in our pit crew gathered in front of the television screens to watch the start of the race. Jack, Bruce, and Walter sat on top of the box at the control panel, and fifteen more of us, including Charles Purley, stood around the back of the cart.

Everyone but me was wearing the team's firesuits: black on the bottom half, yellow on the torso, white sleeves, with embroidered sponsor names and logos everywhere—though my own black-and-white version blended in. We all wore earplugs or the headsets that were a combination of noise blockers and radios. And as one, we crowded around the screens, craning necks to watch the parade of cars on one monitor, then the next, then the next, as they swirled around the track at sixty miles an hour behind the pace car. It was the same scene at every team setup down pit row: some groups gathered around more elaborate displays than ours, some peering into only one or two monitors for a glimpse of their car.

After the first lap, the two extra cars in front of the pace car peeled off into pit lane. These were parade cars, with VIPs and sponsors in them. Though they traveled well in front of the field—a couple hundred yards in front of the racecars—the opportunity to start the race in a pace car was a sought-after perk.

At the end of the second lap, the real pace car also turned into pit lane. The field, which had run the preceding laps in a single line, straggled into pairs as they reached the Main Straight. That's when the acceleration started, the roaring that upped the volume even higher. Almost before we knew it, thirty-one cars were passing us, the green flag was waving, and a voice from the tower was on the radio saying, "Green, green, green, green!" We were off!

But the tension we all felt wasn't only for taking the green. It was also for taking the first corner. In every race, the first corner was the most treacherous, for the first racing lap and any restart after a caution. Announcers repeated endlessly the adage, "you can't win the race on the first corner, but you can lose it," as drivers unleashed their adrenaline, aggression, and cars on one small stretch of curving road.

Once again, someone lost his race there. One of the smaller prototypes went in too fast, braked too hard, got bumped, or did something else creative. It tapped another prototype, sending both of them spinning onto the grass on the outside of the track. They cleared the racing line quickly and didn't scatter debris, which was lucky for the cars behind them, including Mike, who avoided trouble and kept pressing forward. All of us in the pit released the breath we'd been holding. It was also lucky both prototypes got back on the track under their own power. That meant no yellow flag was required to rescue them.

I kept one eye on the progress of those prototypes, still watching for a yellow, in case they couldn't drive fast enough or dragged too much grass or gravel back onto the track. I kept the other on Mike. He'd been careful in the first turn and was lying right on the bumper of the Saleen, which in turn was a couple car lengths behind the Number 63 factory Corvette. Mike was keeping himself in position to pass the Saleen if he found the right opportunity or the Saleen made the slightest mistake.

I transferred my gaze from the TV screens to the straightaway in front of me to see Mike scream by. First lap down! Tension in the pit abated slightly, and over the next few laps crew members drifted away from the monitors to their positions near the fuel pump, the tires, the food. Sometime during lap three, Jack leaned down and handed me a radio and headset. With it on, I'd be able to hear communications with Mike—not that there were many.

For almost all of the first half-hour, I stood watching the monitors. I sipped water and followed Mike around the track, thinking through each shift, brake, and turn with him. I also spoke with a few guests we had in the pits: the tan Leninger's guy and four of his people, all wearing ill-fitting Sandham Swift firesuits—a requirement during the race—and observing the action with wide eyes. Tom introduced me and fed me questions about driving and race strategy. I didn't mind shouting some answers over the din of cars, but I tried not to linger. Better to be concentrating on the track.

Nothing eventful happened in the first thirty laps of the race, except that the Number 64 factory Corvette worked its way from the back of the field through the slower GT2 class and began to harass the Viper and the Maserati, running at the back of our own class. Two Porsches from different teams and one of the smaller prototypes had come in to the pit with problems—tire problems on the Porsches and something electrical for the prototype.

Now that the race we'd spent four days preparing for had begun, the crew was less tense. Everyone was alert and ready to jump into action, but there were crew members relaxing in the pits and eating a late lunch, even as they kept an eye on the car. The contradiction amused me: when the race began, some people relaxed. I wasn't one of them, with my humming nerves and inability to stand still.

I was nervous about the driving I'd do soon, but also uneasy about what Holly had told me. I knew firsthand how wrong rumors could be, yet there'd been tension in this team that had evaporated with Wade gone. Motives everywhere.

I clapped both hands to the sides of my head and ordered myself to focus on the race. It wasn't the time to think about Wade. I stepped around the cart with the monitors on it, heading for the cooler of water, and I kicked something small that went skittering under the snack table to my right. I went after it and found a set of rental car keys—labeled for a red Chevy Malibu, Connecticut plate 617 BOY.

Aunt Tee tapped me on the shoulder, pointing at the keys, then me, with a questioning look. I came out of a daze enough to respond. "I found them on the ground."

She examined them, then nodded. "Jack's always losing his keys. I'll take them." She plucked them from my unresponsive hands.

The ground fell out from under me. Jack? My boss? Was at the track Friday night when Wade was killed? He'd been glad Wade was gone from the team—maybe Holly's rumor was true, that Jack couldn't fire Wade. Had he taken matters into his own hands?

A Porsche blasted away from a nearby pit stall, snapping me back to full attention. I couldn't dwell on this now. I needed to focus on the race. I made my way back to the monitors, concentrated, and found Mike coming down the Diving Turn. We were at twenty-five minutes and thirty-six seconds, all of green-flag running. That's where it ended.

I looked at the correct monitors in time to see the end of the live incident and the first of many replays. A blue and red Porsche got sideways coming out of the left-hander in the Esses. Its rear end kicked out to the right, pulling the nose farther left than the grip of the tires could save, and started to spin. A silver LMP2, one of the smaller prototypes, was unlucky enough to be next to the Porsche, preparing to pass on the inside of the next turn, a right-hander. The back end of the Porsche punched the LMP2 in the left rear quarter panel and sent it spinning off the track as well. The prototype spun on a path that would have led to a metal guard rail and the creek beyond. But fortunately, it started at about seventy-five miles an hour, scrubbed off a lot of its speed on the surface of the track, and didn't travel far once it reached the grass. The Porsche went off the paved track almost immediately, carrying a lot more speed onto the gravel shoulder and then the grass, a surface that didn't do much to slow the car down. It ended up with its nose buried in a tire wall at the foot of a billboard covered in sponsor advertisements. The replays caught a funny sight: the determined scattering of the corner workers stationed between the tire wall and the billboard.

I eyed the clock. Under thirty minutes. In our pre-race meetings, Jack had decreed we wouldn't stop. The yellow flag was thrown about a minute after the cars came to rest, as the LMP2 drove itself off the grass and back on to the track, trailing a damaged rear deck lid and making for the pits. The Porsche was still nestled in the tires; it would need a tow truck and a rope.

The radio crackled to life: Mike asked if he was coming in, Jack told him to hold on. My heart boomed so loud I had to turn up the volume. I saw Mike go by on the Main Straight behind the pace car with the rest of the field. Once the field was collected and orderly behind the pace car, the pits, which were closed at the start of yellow flag caution periods, would be open for cars to enter.

Jack on the radio: "Mike, pit for driver change."

No sense asking why plans had changed. Just scrambling to my locker. Tearing the headset off my head, fumbling to unclip the radio from my belt. Shit. Mental checklist time: balaclava, HANS, helmet, gloves. Ready. Three quick steps to the wall, and up, crouching next to the pit crew ready with tires, air hoses, and the fuel pump. Charles Purley next to the dead man switch. Bubs, the driver change helper, next to me, handing me my seat insert. The second the car entered our pit space, we'd all leap off the wall into action.

I coached myself, visualizing the driver change process over and over in the endless sixty seconds before Mike pulled up. I was as ready as I could get.

And then it was happening. Mike stopped our Corvette with a jerk. A second later, the fueler was pumping race gas in. Bubs and I ran around behind the car, and I stood behind the door, waiting for Mike to emerge. The two guys with air guns—one for right side wheels, one for left—crouched with the guns hovering a half-inch from the single, central wheel nut of the front tires. Their partners stood poised with new tires at the ready. They couldn't touch the car while fuel was going in, per ALMS safety regulations, though we could make the driver change in that time.

One other crew member hovered over the car, also waiting for fueling to end. It was his job to plug in the air hose and deploy the air jacks that lifted the car so the tires could be changed. Fueling took about thirty seconds, and tire changes about twenty more. We'd be nearly done with the driver change by the time they started on the tires. I'd have five to ten seconds between getting set in the car and getting the signal to start the engine and go.

Mike was out. I jolted forward and shoved my insert in place, following it as quickly as possible, banging my helmet against the doorframe as I slid and twisted. I found the right-side belt and flopped it into my lap, then grabbed for the drink tube and stuffed it into the front of my helmet, trying to keep my torso back as far as possible and my hands high. Bubs was reaching in to fasten my belts, and we both rode the car up as the air jacks deployed. Shoulder straps on top of the HANS, check. Fuel done, tires started. Only a few more seconds.

I felt rather than heard the belts click into place, though the shoulder straps were still loose. Bubs moved to the air conditioning tube and the radio cable, on the left doorframe behind my helmet. A pat on the helmet to tell me he was finished, and he was gone, sliding the window net fastened and shutting the door with a thump. I'd already snapped the steering wheel into place, and I tugged down the loose ends of the shoulder straps, tightening them and locking myself in the seat.

The tire changers were on the back wheels now, and the guy in charge of the air jacks watched them carefully. I pushed the clutch pedal in and pushed forward six times on the sequential gear shift, making sure it was in first gear. My finger hovered near the ignition button.

Bruce's voice on the radio. "Kate, radio check. OK?"

I pushed the radio button on the steering wheel. "I'm set."

Two seconds later, the car bounced back onto all four new Michelins, as the air jacks were released. Service done!

"Go, go, go!" shouted Bruce.

I pushed the ignition button, and the seven-liter, 650-horse-power, small-block V-8 woke up and bellowed at me.

Chapter Forty-five

I reached the end of pit lane, moving at what felt like a snail's pace. Passing the pit exit line, I pressed the speed limiter button to turn it off, slammed my foot to the floor, and hurtled onto the track.

Bruce spoke again. "Pace car is on the Back Straight. Clean-up still happening in the Esses. Take it easy and warm up the tires."

"OK." I tried to keep my voice steady, but it shook with nerves. Hopefully the team wouldn't notice. I took as deep a breath as possible.

With the field half a lap ahead of me moving at sixty miles per hour because of the caution, I was free to catch up—and warm up—slowly. Until I caught the pace car, I didn't have to maintain sixty myself, though I shouldn't go much faster. For the first lap and a half, I eased through corners on my cold tires, tested my brakes, and reacquainted myself with the course. I reached the back of the line of cars at West Bend on my second lap, and I tucked in behind a prototype to play follow-the-leader.

As we trundled through the Diving Turn, I examined the line of cars. All four classes were jumbled in no particular order, faster prototypes sometimes behind slower GT cars. When a yellow came out, the pace car got in front of the overall leader and everyone else stayed in line where they were—unless you made a pit stop, and then you re-entered the track and went to the back of the line. Position in that line didn't mean anything about class placement. What mattered was where the other cars in our class were. I was on my fourth paced lap when Bruce told me pit stops were nearly done, as was the cleanup of the wreck—which I'd seen for myself, circling past it—and that we were P3, or third position in class.

"Don't worry about that, Kate. You just do your thing."

"Thanks."

I swerved back and forth down the Back Straight, warming the tires, as most drivers did for at least a portion of each caution lap. Our tire pressures didn't vary much—we used nitrogen instead of pressurized air in them for that reason—but the rubber itself gripped the track better when it was warm. I had a new set of rubber, and it was up to me to take care of it. Mike would get another set when he got back in to finish the race.

"They're saying two more laps to green, Kate."

"OK." I swore I heard my heart beating, even over the noise of the Corvette and the other racecars. Almost showtime.

I radioed in. "Bruce, what's the weather like?" More clouds had rolled in at the start of the race, almost as if they too had been waiting for the green flag to wave.

"Hold on."

I did another lap, trying to glimpse the sky, but seeing nothing. The windscreen on the C6.R didn't offer much view, except of the track in front of me. But a bigger issue was how much I was strapped in place. I couldn't lean forward at all, and even if I could, I wouldn't be able to twist my head to look at the sky. Knowing that didn't stop me from making an attempt. It was the kind of thing you did during a caution.

One lap to go, and the pace car turned off its flashing yellow lights. Bruce got back to me. "Radar's not looking good, Kate. Showing possible rain. But Jack's source says it won't happen."

"Got it." I really, really, really hoped it didn't rain.

I reached the Back Straight and started to gather myself. Around West Bend, I double-checked everything compulsively. We swept down the Diving Turn in a single line and turned onto the Main Straight. The restart counted once the green flag fell, so we all started accelerating even before the pace car turned off, to be at full speed as soon as possible.

Pace car into pit lane.

Bruce shouting, "Green, green, green, green!"

Green flag waving at the start/finish line. Foot to the floor, watching the cars around me. Racing!

We all entered the first turn carefully at more than 100 miles an hour. Racing was a balance between hanging your guts out and not being stupid. In the first turn after a restart, that meant not letting excitement take over and hurl me into the melee. Not giving up position, but not trying to pass five cars there either. I eased into that turn and the ones that followed, also easing open the floodgates of my adrenaline and putting it to work for me on the track.

By the time I'd made it through the Chicane—without hitting any cones—and onto the Back Straight, the prototypes behind me had gone past, and I didn't have to watch for overtaking cars so closely. Bruce would give me a heads up from the pit when more cars approached, though I'd watch my mirrors and the corner workers' flags too.

When I completed the first lap, I was breathing more normally, and time started to elongate. People often asked if it was difficult to do everything so fast in a race. The truth was, time slowed down at high speeds. Once I got in my groove in the car, everything slowed down. I had plenty of time to look down the track, check traffic around me, plan my angle of attack on a corner, apply the brake, and turn the wheel. There was plenty of time to think—especially when you had an accident. I'd had time once as I slid off a track to predict where I'd hit, evaluate two or three evasive maneuvers, and put the car into a spin that resulted in a softer impact and less damage. There would be no spinning today, however.

I swept down the front straight on my sixth or seventh lap, passing a Porsche on the right. Nearing the end of the straight, I tapped the brakes with my left foot, keeping my right planted on the throttle. At marker three, I switched from full throttle to full brakes. Downshifted twice, still braking. Glanced at mirrors to be sure no one had come up inside me. Moved right, hitting the first of Big Bend's two apexes. Drifted left in the middle of the turn. Light on the throttle, fluttering my foot, finding the edge of grip. Hit the second apex.

Throttle out of the turn. Stay in third. Brake lightly for the left-hander. Turn in. Line yourself up right. Hit the apex. Throttle out. Let off. Right-hander. Now. On the throttle. Upshift twice. Blazing through No Name Straight.

A piece of Benny's advice had returned to me that morning, and I'd incorporated it. "That left-hander," he'd proclaimed over dinner, waving his dessert spoon at me, "here's the thing: it's a throwaway corner. Oh yeah!" He'd gone on, seeing my disbelief. "You give up speed in that corner so you can hit the correct line in and out of the right-hander—all so you're going as fast as possible on the right line to carry speed into No Name. That's where you'll gain tenths."

As I'd gotten up to speed in my first racing laps, I'd remembered his words and given it a try, sacrificing speed through the first turn of the Esses to be perfectly aligned in No Name. It felt right. Felt faster. No Name was the second longest "straight" on the track, and I was hard on the throttle, going 130 by the end of it. I slowed to about 50 in as little space as possible for the Climbing Turn into the Chicane, and momentum sent the weight of the car tipping forward. I turned right and climbed simultaneously, tipping the weight left and back with a lot of force. It was the toughest corner on the track for keeping the car balanced.

Zip up the hill. Miss cones. Blue flag waving. Steer left, right. Throttle onto the Back Straight, upshifting, building speed off the last corner onto the straight. Move left on the track for the prototype coming up behind me. Aim carefully at West Bend. Tap brakes for balance. Fourth gear turn. Throttle. Speed: 112.

Upshift on the downhill. Carry the speed into the Diving Turn. Turn wheel, ready for the bump, stay on the racing line. Almost flat out. Gasping for air from compression as the car sweeps down the hill and turns at 115. Full throttle as soon as the tires can barely hold grip. Unwinding the wheel. Accelerate. Upshift to sixth. Flying down the front stretch.

Out of the next turn, Big Bend, I came up behind two Porsches running nose-to-tail. Bruce came on the radio. "Doing OK, Kate?"

"Fine. Car's great," I responded, just before braking, downshifting, turning, tapping the throttle, braking, turning, and finally accelerating out of the Esses. All the while, I was lying back behind the Porsches, trying to find an opportunity to pass.

Bruce transmitted again. "Those are the class leaders you're following. They won't give you any room."

"OK. Who's behind me?"

"Top three prototypes coming fast. You're still P3 in class. P4 is three seconds behind you."

"OK." I was through the Esses and into the Climbing Turn by that point, still behind the Porsches. Got to get past them so the car behind me doesn't catch up. Maybe I can pass on the Back Straight going into West Bend. Blue flags waving madly in the Chicane. Check mirrors. Damn. The overall race leaders, coming up fast. I wasn't obligated to move over and let them by. By some rights, I could have passed the Porsches, leaving the prototypes to lump it behind me. But I wasn't sure I'd make the pass in time, and I preferred them in front of me, instead of angry and pressuring me from behind.

Once they were past, it was my turn, though for all of my impatience to be in front of the Porsches, I remembered Benny's other lessons and hung back as we dove down the hill onto the front straight. As soon as I leveled out, I pulled right and nailed the throttle. Both Porsches obligingly stayed left, and I flew past them down the front straight.

I called Bruce. "How much did I lose?"

"A couple seconds. P4 coming up behind you."

Damn. I looked in the mirrors. Sure enough, there was the familiar bright, flag blue of one of the factory Corvettes. I pressed the radio button as I swung into the left-hander. "Sorry."

I heard Jack's voice this time in my ears. "It's OK, Kate. Just keep pushing."

And that's what I did for the next couple of laps. I held the Number 64 factory Corvette off as long as I could, but sooner than I wanted, it was on my tail.

Chapter Forty-six

I was bumping down the front straight when the 64 caught me, riding close to my bumper in an attempt at intimidation. I gritted my teeth. Not happening.

I focused on maintaining my line through Big Bend and not giving him an inch of extra room to get next to me. I pushed the radio button going into the left-hander. "Prototypes behind me?"

Bruce came back. "One coming up quick—the wild guy in the black and white LMP2. No one else for half a lap. Do what you can with Duncan."

I didn't bother responding. Only one prototype would be pressing to get past—and because I had my own problems, I wasn't getting out of its way. Bruce had told me it was Duncan Forsyth behind me in the 64, a nice, funny, and very clever Englishman. I looked ahead and spotted an opportunity. I wouldn't be an easy mark.

There was a lone Porsche in front of me, one of Holly's orange cars from Western Racing, just exiting the Esses into No Name. The driver was going to help me out. I put my foot down in No Name, but let off early for the Climbing Turn. I'd caught the Porsche in plenty of time, but I held off passing, braking late and only slipping inside him into the turn at the very last second. My car wiggled through the bends, the back end skittering, objecting to the speed at which I'd cornered. It looked like a rookie move, and I didn't care.

I'd been unkind to the Western Racing driver, by leaving my pass so late and making it harder for him to make his turn. But what I'd also done, I confirmed with a glance in my mirrors, was leave the 64 stranded behind the Porsche through the Climbing Turn, the Chicane, and the first part of the Back Straight. Meanwhile, I gained a couple seconds by blasting my way to West Bend. It wouldn't save me forever, but it bought me time.

I'd no sooner made it onto the Back Straight than a black and white prototype popped out to my left. Oops. I could have moved over for him. The driver—Piero, already suspicious of me for other reasons—was annoyed with me, as evidenced by his fist waving high in the air above the open cockpit. I chuckled to myself and looked in my mirrors to see the 64 still stuck. Sorry, Piero, but I'd do it again, given the chance.

I kept pushing, concentrating on traffic patterns ahead of and behind me to time when I passed other cars and when I was passed by prototypes. I also kept watching my mirrors for the reappearance of the blue Corvette, which wouldn't take long. I roared past the two Panoz and the smaller Ferrari on the front straight, and I was coming out of the right-hander into No Name, watching again for the blue car. What I saw was a yellow flag.

Then Bruce was in my ear. "Yellow, Kate. Double-yellow. Full course caution."

I reduced speed, wondering where the leader was and how the yellow would affect us. I'd been in the car only thirty minutes, so I knew I wouldn't be getting out.

"Where's the leader? Are we stopping?" I radioed, hearing my voice climb an octave. Already the waiting period was more stressful than the driving itself.

Bruce radioed back. "Overall leader is behind P4 in class. Repeat, pace car is picking up the leader behind the Number 64 Corvette. We gain a lap on positions five through nine. You, the Saleen, and the two factory Corvettes are all one lap up now."

As much as my belts allowed, I slumped in relief. We'd been lucky the yellow hadn't come out forty seconds or a minute later.

When a yellow came out, the pace car picked up the overall race leader, usually an LMP1, wherever he might be in the field of cars. Those behind him lined up, regardless of type of car or position in class. Those in front of the overall leader went all the way around the track and joined the back of the line, effectively gaining a lap on the other cars. A minute or so later and the overall leader would have been the car in front of me, and I'd have gone a lap down—which would have been impossible to make up in a short race like this.

I'd been lucky. The two Ferraris, Viper, and Maserati behind me in class hadn't been. I spent futile seconds wishing the leader had been between me and the 64, to have gotten that monkey off my back. I heard Gramps' voice in my head telling me beggars can't be choosers.

Bruce again. "We'll only stop if you need to, Kate."

I shook my head in reflex, then pushed the button. "No. Everything's fine."

I'd caught up with the field of cars, and we were all doing a sedate sixty miles an hour around the track in a single file. I could see now what had caused the caution: the smaller Ferrari I'd passed on the Main Straight had missed the left-hander of the Esses. Instead of turning left, he'd gone straight off track-right into swampy grass.

I swung past the incident, into No Name. All of a sudden, the unthinkable happened. It started to rain.

Chapter Forty-seven

Not rain, exactly. Heavy mist. Drizzle. Nerves jangling, I examined the drops hitting the windscreen.

I jabbed at the radio button. "Are we seeing this?!" My voice came out squeaky. No reply. "Hello?!"

Bruce replied. "Hang on, Kate. Jack's checking on it."

I continued to circle the track behind the pace car, and my anxiety leveled out, but didn't subside. The water falling out of the sky was making the edges of the track damp, but it wasn't coming down enough to pool anywhere, and I didn't yet need the single large windshield wiper. Still, what I could see of the sky was ominous: dark, dark gray.

On the Back Straight, a few quarter-sized drops spattered on my windscreen. "Am I coming in for tires? The drops are getting bigger."

"Hold on, Kate. Not yet."

We circled around to the Diving Turn, and I watched with envy as cars dove to the right into pit lane, no doubt heading for wet-weather tires. The fat drops continued to fall—maybe there were more? I was concentrating so hard on them, it was tough to be sure. I passed the pits and saw, among others, the Viper, Maserati, and the two Ferraris in my class stopped for tires. I took deep breaths and told myself Jack was the boss, not me.

Through Big Bend and into the left-hander again, and I could see the GT2 Ferrari had been pulled out of the swamp. Track workers stood next to it at the side of the pavement, directing us to stay well left of the racecar and safety crew. The car was being unhooked from its tow strap, indicating it was running and would return to the pits on its own power, making it eligible to return to the race.

I called in again. "The caution's nearly cleaned up. We're not going to have much time if we're going to stop. It's getting slick off the racing line." Where the cars drove, on the racing line, the track was still dry, from the heat of the cars and tires. Offline, however, it was wet. I shuddered. I didn't want to drive on the already slick concrete patches with the added complication of water—on tires without grooves. The sky didn't look better. Jack would have to call me in.

"Kate." Jack's voice. "You're staying out."

"What? Repeat? What?"

"No wet tires. You're staying on the slicks."

"Are you trying to make me wreck?"

There was a pause before Jack responded. "No." Another pause. "This is my call, Kate. It's not going to rain. It's going to blow over." Jack's voice radiated confidence.

I wouldn't find out until later that contrary to what Jack was telling me, the radar showed a massive storm moving in right on top of the racetrack. And that Mike, Bruce, and Walter were all holding their breath over the call. But Jack's local guy, the volunteer security guard, had assured Jack this happened all the time: a storm looked like it was headed straight for you, teased you with a few sprinkles, and veered off. Jack gambled on the local farm boy over the evidence of his own eyes and technology—he later called it "the triumph of redneck over high tech." Jack put all his energy into promoting a certainty he couldn't have felt, to make me and Lars, in the other car, feel comfortable.

All I heard that moment in the car was that the rain would stop. I worked on ignoring my fears. "OK."

In two more laps we went back to green flag racing. We took off down the front stretch, and again I was careful not to push too hard for position going into the first turn. The entire field got through it cleanly. Bruce let me know the 64 was still three seconds back, and I kept pushing—careful to stay on the dry pavement of the racing line, no matter who tried to pass. It continued to drizzle, but with smaller drops. After a few laps, I thought it might be lessening, and cars around me started driving off the racing line on purpose. Those were teams who'd put grooved, wet-pavement tires on and were now having to keep them as wet as possible. I concentrated on staying where it was dry and staying ahead of the 64.

But it wasn't too many laps before I got caught behind dueling GT2 cars—a Porsche and a Panoz this time. I wasn't confident enough in the grip at the edges of the track to be sure I could make the pass stick, and I couldn't get around them before the 64 was right behind me. Duncan came up fast, but couldn't get past me on the front straight. I did what I could to stay in front of him.

Bruce on the radio. "Keep pushing, Kate. Clear track around you."

I didn't respond, concentrating on carrying as much speed as possible through Big Bend and not breaking the back end of the car loose or running straight ahead off the track. Duncan roared up before the left-hander, poking his nose to the left side, and I cheated left to block him. In a flash, he'd swung right, going wide through the left-hander, and pulling alongside on my right. He was up far enough that I wasn't sure I could stay in front of him.

I eased right on the track as I turned into the right-hander, hoping he'd get the message and back off. He didn't. My heart rate surged. His attempt might work, but he'd have to take what he wanted. I eased right again, ready to touch. He'd have to earn it.

In the turn now. My line swings to the right. Foot hovering over the throttle. Where's his nose? Bump. There. Rub. Scrape. Damn. Shift wheel left. Can't get to the line. He's made the pass. Shit. Shit. Shit. Nail the throttle and get after him into No Name.

Jack's voice on the radio. "Careful with the car, Kate. Don't worry about the pass. You did good. Keep pressing him."

I popped out of the Chicane. "We're racing for position, I'm not going to give it away."

I started to strategize. The first step was to stay close, so I settled in to shadow him. I'd stick like glue, but stay a car length or two back. Then I'd watch for an opportunity and take my position back. I damn well wasn't going to be the one who'd lost us the third spot on the podium.

The next time into the Diving Turn, I pressed against the left side of my seat again and felt for the first time my growing bruises and muscle fatigue. I wasn't in shape for this yet, but giving everything I had was the least I could do for the team that was giving me a chance. With Wade in the car, they'd be working on second, not scrambling to stay in fourth. But I had to admit, the team hadn't been happy with Wade's attitude or his driving lately. Jack might have been very unhappy. Maybe I wasn't a step down after all. Wait a minute, I can't be thinking about this now!

I shouted at myself. "Concentrate! Kate! Your job is to drive!" Focusing now on the feel and sounds of my car, I flashed past the pits on the front straight, not understanding until I turned through Big Bend what I'd seen: the Maserati and the Ferraris in their pit stalls. I realized the track was mostly dry, and what I could see of the sky was blue. Amazing. Jack had been right. The extra stop those cars had made to put slicks back on was dropping them another lap behind the rest of us contending for a podium.

I was still sticking to the 64 Corvette. More, I was developing my plan. It hinged on what everyone thought of me. I was the rookie, the untried one, the one without much experience in the car, Series, and track. The girl. But I was a pro, and I'd been learning fast. I was learning more by following Duncan around the track—especially how to get around him.

For the fifty minutes I'd been in the car, I'd played everything cautiously. The only exception had been the blocking maneuver I pulled on Duncan with the orange Porsche in the Climbing Turn. But everyone who'd seen me do that had seen me almost lose the back end of the car and later be passed—they might think I was gun-shy now. The advantage I had was that no one would expect me to make a gutsy, aggressive move. I smiled under my helmet. They didn't know me very well. Time to show them what Kate Reilly can and will do.

It took me a dozen more laps to find the right opportunity. During that time, I watched, waited, and hung back, making sure not to get too close to Duncan, which would signal I was looking to pass. I'd keep that a surprise.

Then it happened. Coming out of West Bend behind him, I saw a Porsche ahead and realized the timing would work out perfectly. Mirrors: clear. No faster prototype to come from behind and mess this up. This was it. Time to see if I'd learned just how far I could push this car. I stepped on the throttle, zooming up behind Duncan going into the Diving Turn, carrying more speed through it than ever.

Just as I'd expected, Duncan made no move to get around the Porsche early—which he might have done if he'd thought about blocking me. Which he should have done. But he hadn't expected my move. My nose next to his rear wheels, on the right. He was turning, stuffed up against the back of the Porsche. I held on to the Corvette, turning as hard as I dared, foot hovering over the throttle, squeezing it. Hoping. Not sliding yet. Turning. Past Duncan. Turning. Not sliding yet. Next to the Porsche. Past! Past! And I'd done it!

"Whoooo hooooo!" I yelled. I was shooting down the front straight, building on the tremendous speed I'd carried through the Diving Turn. Duncan wasn't far behind me, but he'd lost speed in that last corner and lost time and momentum with it.

My radio burst to life. "Hot dang, Kate! Great move! That's our girl!" Bruce sounded almost surprised.

I pressed the radio button and treated my pit crew to another "Wooo hooo!"

Mike transmitted for the first time, laughing. "Hell of a pass, Kate. Good work."

Then Jack. "Fantastic job, Kate. That won't work too many times on these guys, but it sure as hell did this time. Keep it up."

"Whatever gets the job done," I returned, then bent my attention to staying in front of Duncan. My adrenaline was so high by that point it would have taken a miracle for anyone in our class to pass me. I was in the groove, and I stayed that way until a caution came out ten laps later.

Chapter Forty-eight

I was prepared for this caution, since I had a front row seat to its cause: a Porsche that lost an argument with the tire barrier in West Bend. From the number of body parts it shed limping back to the pits, I knew we'd see another full course caution for debris. I also knew my stint in the car was over.

I stayed on the throttle, still racing hard, until I saw the double-yellow in the Esses.

Bruce radioed. "Full course caution. Driver change, Kate. Come in when pits open."

"OK." I was already halfway around the track, and the pits weren't open the next time by. The officials displayed a red flag at the entrance, for safety and to give all drivers a chance to enter the pits at the same time. You could still enter them on a red flag, but you'd incur a penalty—you only did so if you couldn't make it around the track another lap.

The pace car was twelve or fifteen cars ahead of me—and the cars in first and second place in class were between it and me on the track. We'd gotten lucky again not to lose a lap.

I circled the track once more, sedately this time, soaking in my last lap. For the first time, I wasn't tense, panicked, or scared. I was relieved and proud. I'd pulled myself together quickly and performed well. I could only have been happier if it was a victory lap after winning the race. But I'd won my own race.

All too soon, I followed half a dozen cars into pit lane, hitting the speed limiter button, loosening belts, and yanking out cables.

I reached our pit stall and stopped the car with a jerk, pulling off the steering wheel almost before the engine died. Bubs was there to help me the second the car shut down, opening the door and taking down the net. I hauled myself out of the car as quickly as possible, directing my quivering muscles to do this one last job before they collapsed. I reached back in for my seat insert and got myself out of the pits and over the wall.

I turned to watch the crew finish the pit stop as I removed my gloves, helmet, and HANS. Aunt Tee was next to me, also watching, waiting to take my gear. Mike pulled away in the car, and we all moved forward to the wall, looking left to the blue LinkTime pits of the factory Corvette team. Seconds after Mike left, the 64 car passed us. Our crew climbed back over the wall, whooping and exchanging high fives for staying ahead with a fast pit stop. I breathed a sigh of relief at holding up my end of the bargain.

I pulled off my balaclava and moaned at the pleasure of a breeze blowing against my face. The fire-retardant layer was vitally necessary and effective, but it wasn't comfortable. My whole body and every stitch of clothing was soaking wet. I tried not to think about feeling clammy and gross.

Aunt Tee held out a wet towel and a bottle of water. I took the bottle first, drank half, then leaned back and poured the rest over my head. I handed her the empty and finger-combed my hair, noticing I had an audience: Mr. and Mrs. Purley and Mr. and Mrs. Active-Fit, suited up and watching avidly from the back of the pit.

"Thanks," I mouthed to Aunt Tee, as I slung the wet towel around my neck. I unzipped my firesuit and struggled out of the top half with her help. More relief. I pushed up the sleeves of my Nomex undershirt, and then I was ready for a second bottle of water.

She turned to go, and I put a hand on her shoulder. "Thanks for everything, Aunt Tee."

She gave me a huge smile, crinkling up the corners of her eyes. She reached out and cupped my face in both of her hands. "You're welcome, Kate. Great job."

That nearly brought tears to my eyes, as keyed up and emotional as I was now that my stint was over. Then Jack was in front of me, having climbed down from his perch at the control panel.

"Kate."

"Jack?"

His face creased into a smile. "Damn good drive, kid."

I relaxed. "Thanks, boss."

He stepped closer to me and put an arm around my shoulders. I told myself not to think about his rental car. We turned together to see the pace car lead the field down the front straight.

He waited until they'd passed and the noise had died down to speak. "You were driving great, and then you got passed, and I thought, hell, that's too bad, but I'll take fourth after this crazy weekend. It's more than I would have hoped for, to be honest. And then, damn! You got him! I'll remember that for a long time. You took everyone by surprise—what I wouldn't give to be a fly on the wall down at the 64 pit."

I must have been glowing, filled with pride and pleasure. I took a deep breath and held it, regaining control—because I'd lose all credibility if I cried in the pits. "I was so pissed when I let him by. I had to get it back."

We paused again as the noise level rose and the field passed us once more. The pace car lights were out. Last lap before green.

Jack squeezed my shoulders as he moved away. "You did good. Take a break. Or talk to the media." He jerked his head toward the pit walkway, where I saw Zeke waving at me. Tom and our sponsors were also back there, crowded against the back fence, watching my every move. I smiled and waved to them as I made my way to the SPEED crew.

"Great stint, Kate!" Zeke said when I reached him. "Can I have a word on camera?"

I nodded at him, about to respond, when he pressed his earpiece to his ear and held up a finger. "Yeah," he said into his microphone, talking to the control booth. "OK, I'll wait with her."

He turned to me. "We've just got to wait for Allen to interview Greg." He gestured at his SPEED Channel colleague, standing in the next pit with a driver whose crash had caused this caution.

We saw them start talking as the noise level ramped up and the field swept down the front straight for the green flag. Zeke's cameraman stood across the aisle in a patch of shade, and Zeke and I watched the monitors. Mike was still in third, using traffic well to stay ahead of the 64. A piece of notepaper appeared in my face, handed down by Jack. It read: "Fastest lap: 51.970. Faster than Mike so far. Consistent laps in fifty-twos and fifty-threes."

I looked up at him, but Jack was facing forward again, watching the monitors. I settled for bouncing on my toes and showing Zeke the paper.

"Looks like Katie-Q's trying to get herself a job!"

"We'll see, Zeke."

His face went blank, listening, and he gestured to the cameraman. He spoke into his microphone. "OK, we're ready." He turned to me. "Five seconds, Kate."

Then the camera was in my face, and Zeke was talking. "I'm here with Series newcomer Kate Reilly who got a late call to drive this weekend for Sandham Swift Racing. She got in the car today and delivered a great performance. How did you get up to speed so quickly, Kate?"

"You know, when you get tossed in the water, it's sink or swim. I was gonna swim!"

Zeke laughed with me. "Now that you've actually spent some time on this track, what do you think about it?"

"It's pretty interesting. There aren't as many challenges as on others, since it's short, but they come at you faster. So you're always on, always working."

"Now, Kate, tell me about that great pass you pulled off near the end of your stint. Took some people by surprise, don't you think?"

I nodded. "The Number 64 made a minor mistake, carrying a little too much speed into the corner behind another car and not being able to defend the inside. He left it too late to turn in and block me. But I was waiting for that. And I couldn't have done it without the fantastic crew here with the Sandham Swift Racegear.com Corvette, and Mike, my co-driver. They all gave me a wonderfully prepared car to drive. And thanks also to our sponsors, Racegear.com, Active-Fit Clothing, and Leninger's Enduro Shine, for welcoming me this weekend and making our effort possible."

"Thanks, Kate, and we'll hope to see you at more races in the future with this team. Benny, Ian, back to you."

Zeke slapped me on the back. "Great work, Kate. See you!" He trotted off, cameraman in tow.

Immediately, Tom, Mrs. Purley, and the Active-Fits stepped in front of me, mouthing "Congratulations," and "Great job." They patted me on the back—yuck, wet shirt—and shook my hand, wearing perma-grins that stretched from ear to ear, a typical reaction of visitors to the pits. Tom led them away, with a parting thumbs-up.

I finally stood alone—there were people around me, but no one else demanding my attention. I turned to the monitors, looking for Mike but not really seeing anything onscreen. Instead, I replayed my drive, searching for errors and areas to improve, but also exulting over what I knew had been a great job. Maybe not the best job, and maybe not the best I'd ever drive the car or the track—but a damn good showing, given the circumstances. I wanted to jump up and down, scream, and throw my arms around, but I restrained myself. I looked at Jack, running the team up on his perch, and Tom, shepherding guests through the pits, and I felt sorry for anyone who couldn't go racing for a living. I had the best job in the whole world.

A few minutes later, as I was drinking my third bottle of water and realizing how wet and clammy I still was, Zeke hurried toward me. He stuck his mouth next to my ear, to be heard over the wailing engines.

"Meant to tell you," he shouted. "Our guys found that tape with Wade on it."

I nodded my head.

"We can show you, if you want. But I saw it." He pulled back and grimaced before leaning forward again. "Wade was standing outside your team area. It's nearly dark—the time code showed 9:15."

"That's after we saw him at The Boathouse that night."

"He was arguing with someone. There was no sound on the tape, no other people—the track was basically empty, and the crew was getting shots of the sunset for background, montage stuff. They were filming from the other side of the track, zooming in. But you could see them both accusing each other. Yelling—you could read a couple swear words on Wade's lips. And once, it looked like he said 'you are done,' as he made a throat-slashing motion. They came to blows. Threw a couple punches, then stopped and went in different directions."

I nodded, waiting. Zeke didn't say anything. I pulled back and made a "come on" motion with my hands.

"Kate, it was Mike."

Chapter Forty-nine

Zeke had been gone for ten minutes before I stopped feeling numb. He'd assured me the police had their own copy of the tape. I didn't know if that reassured or upset me. Both, probably. It was hard to ignore evidence putting Mike and Jack both at the scene of Wade's murder.

The police would also have the car evidence already, I realized—and have checked it out. If they hadn't arrested Jack yet, maybe he was clear? There was still one car unaccounted for Friday night. I wanted to believe Jack wasn't involved. But what about Mike? Was he angry Wade was going to get him kicked off the team? Mike admitted arguing with Wade, but I was surprised to hear they'd come to blows, given how nonviolent Mike appeared. Then I remembered the incident Benny and Ian teased Mike about over dinner—the time he went after another driver on the track.

Still, I didn't like to think it was Mike who'd killed Wade. He was in Wade's notebook a number of times, as was Jack—but why would Mike bring up the notebook if he'd been the one to kill Wade? To find out who had it? Or to shift the blame to other people? Did he know about Jim and Trent cheating and think they'd be obvious suspects? I shook my head. It would have taken a lot of duplicity. But a video tape didn't lie: Mike had been at the track late Friday evening, exchanging punches with Wade.

I was distracted from these thoughts as a driver strolled down the pits and stopped next to me. Duncan Forsythe was expressionless as he stuck out his hand.

I warily shook.

His face broke open with an enormous smile, and he laughed—I could hear it over the car noise. He pumped my hand twice and, still holding it, leaned in. "Hell of a move. I'll never underestimate you again!" With a wink and another handshake, he ambled away.

I grinned after him and turned back to the monitors to find our car.

Mike was staying ahead of the 64, running good times. How could I face Mike when he got out of the car at the end of the race? Or Jack? At least there would be plenty of other people around, including Detective Jolley, since he must have gotten the information about the video by now. Jolley. I needed to talk to him. He didn't have the information Holly had given me—which added significantly to Mike's possible motive. And I wanted reassurance that Jack wasn't a killer.

I looked around, at the pits, at the parts of the paddock I could see through the chain link fence. I couldn't see Jolley. But I did see Eddie two pits away, and I ran down there.

Before Eddie could react, I'd pulled him to the back of the pit walkway next to a rack of tires.

"Kate, this isn't—"

"Eddie, listen. I only want to apologize and make it clear that nothing Wade knew will go any farther than me."

He hesitated, then nodded.

"Just tell me one thing. Was Crystal someone connected with Wade? Or any other driver or supplier here?" I wanted to ask about Jim or Trent, but didn't.

Eddie tilted his head back, squeezing his eyes shut. Then he heaved a big sigh, put his head close to mine, and looked me in the eye, grabbing my forearm as well. "I'm going to tell you something to get you off my back. But I never want to hear it mentioned again, to me or to anyone else. Do you understand?"

"Whoa, Eddie, forget—"

He shook my arm. "Shut up, you've asked, and you'll not let it go, I'm thinking." He looked grim and spoke in a low tone. "Years ago, I was very stupid. Very stupid indeed. I was addicted to drugs."

I stared at him, eyes wide.

"I was addicted to methamphetamines. Meth. Crystal-meth. Wade found out."

"I'm…sorry, Eddie." I gasped, horrified I'd pushed to know this.

He glanced away, licked his lips. Looked back at me. "My team owner knows. Wade found out. Now you know. That's it. I've been clean for a decade. I'll never go back. But it would ruin me."

"Wade…was Wade blackmailing you?"

"Not yet. He was toying with me. I'm glad that piece of shite is dead, but I didn't kill him over it—I can prove that. I made peace long ago with the idea that if this comes out, I'll deal with it. I'd just prefer it didn't."

I nodded. Shook my head. Babbled. "I'm so sorry, Eddie. I thought—a woman. Wade. I…I swear I will never tell a living soul. And I'm impressed you got past it and became so successful here. For what it's worth."

"Just keep quiet. I'm going back to work." He was abrupt in tone and manner, dropping my arm and striding back to his pit box.

I scurried back to my team, acutely shamed. I'd known that asking questions might turn up answers I didn't want to hear. But I expected to feel virtuous about uncovering the truth. Instead I'd forced Eddie to share his personal demons with me. For no good reason. I felt an inch tall.

I looked for our car on the monitors, and with effort, tried to remember what I was thinking about before I'd gone running to bother Eddie. Detective Jolley. Jack's car. Mike on video. I was done snooping. Over it. I wanted to dump what I knew on Jolley and abdicate all responsibility. But there was no good reason for leaving the pit. My job as a driver was to stay with the team, in case I was needed for some reason—I wasn't likely to be put back in the car, but anything was possible. Jack would have my head if I went more than a few pit spaces away.

I was watching the monitors for Mike's progress, checking the time remaining in the race, and swiveling around to look for Jolley in the paddock, when Marcus appeared next to me.

He gave me a big, warm smile and mouthed the word "Hello."

I smiled back and waved a hand.

He leaned in close to my ear, and I pulled back that side of the radio headset I wore. For heaven's sake, he even smelled delicious, too. "Great stint, Kate." He rested his hand on my shoulder. "Really, really great move you made."

I pulled back and smiled wider. "Thank you," I said, knowing he'd only see and not hear.

He leaned close again. "Did it just happen, or were you planning that move?"

"I was planning it for a long time."

He looked impressed. "But how on earth did you do that? I'd really like to understand."

I was more interested in watching our car or finding Detective Jolley than explaining, but I played nice. "Mostly I knew Duncan wouldn't expect it from me—it's something I can't do again. I thought, if I could just find the right combination of a big turn like that one or Big Bend and a slower car that Duncan would reach just at the end of the turn, he might underestimate me enough to leave me the opening. I made sure I was there on his right before he had a chance to move." I was breathing hard by the end, from the shouting it took to communicate over the race noise, through someone else's earplugs, and on my tiptoes to reach his ear.

He straightened, his head cocked to the side, eyes narrowed, lost in thought. "You're planning that far down the track? You're thinking up situations and waiting for the other cars to fill them?"

"Yes, I'm thinking about how every car I come across might move. Don't you?"

"The ones next to me, yes, but all of them?"

"All of them."

"I understand. Thank you very much."

"Anytime." I was still flush with the pride of driving well, as well as helping Marcus understand what I'd done.

"I would be very grateful for a bit of your time and some advice. Maybe some pointers. Would you be willing to share some of that with me?"

Under the influence of my racing high and the weird brand of intimacy created by admitting someone into your personal space enough to communicate in the pits, I agreed. "Sure. I'll tell you what I can."

Marcus beamed. Then he leaned down and kissed my cheek, tracing my jawline with his finger as he pulled away. "Thank you, Kate. I know I'll be able to learn a tremendous amount from you—you're such a talented driver."

I looked up at him, dazed. For ten seconds, I felt mushy and girly—once I remembered my name. Then I got a grip on myself and looked around to see who'd noticed. No one, thank God. Marcus might make me tingly, but if there was a place for that kind of sensation, the pits during a race wasn't it.

Voices came over the radio, and I turned away from Marcus to listen.

"Yellow out for debris from that Porsche, Mike," Bruce said. Paying attention to the monitors again, I saw a Porsche with a blown tire limping back to the pits, scattering rubber from West Bend to Pit In.

Bruce went on. "Shouldn't be a long one. P1 and P2 in class, the 63 Corvette and the Saleen, went up a lap here. But the Saleen has to come in for some fuel, and you don't."

"I don't? And where's P4?"

"P4 in class, 64 Corvette, thirteen seconds behind you. They'll be closer now, but may also need a splash. We think you're going to be OK on fuel, so you're staying out and going for it. It'll be close, but we'll see what happens."

"You *think* we're OK?"

Bruce laughed. "I think we'll be OK. Our engineer says it's close, but he's positive. The more caution laps we get now, running at slow speed, the better. Do what you can to short shift, coast, and save us some more."

"OK, boss, we're going for it!"

I smiled, appreciating Bruce and Mike. Then the weight of what I knew about Mike crashed onto me again, and I felt my shoulders slump.

Marcus tapped me on the arm, and I followed his pointing finger down the pits to see a flurry of motion. For at least thirty seconds, the cars on the track might not have existed, for all the attention the people in the pits paid them. Instead, everyone was transfixed at the sight of a driver being escorted out of the pits in handcuffs. It was Jim Siddons, furiously kicking any tire, hose, or piece of trash he got near. Stuart followed Jim and two police officers, who each held one of Jim's arms. I watched, open-mouthed, with everyone else. The buzz of explanation made its way to us.

"Jim Siddons and a guy from Delray—sabotage! That's what the problems were. And Jim took a swing at one of the cops!" One of the crew from the next pit box over shouted the bones of the story to Jack and our team.

Stuart saw me watching and headed my direction instead of following Jim and the officers out of the pits. I met him partway.

"We caught them, Kate. Jim and Trent and a camera guy for SPEED."

"But did they kill Wade?"

"Still not positive, but I don't think so. Trent told us that Wade was blackmailing them into sabotaging cars he chose."

"But, Stuart, they had to have killed Wade. If they didn't, then who?" I reached out to steady myself on the chain-link fence. I didn't like the answers staring me in the face. I wanted Stuart to give me a name that wasn't Jack or Mike.

He frowned and shook his head. "I'll let you know what we find out."

I returned to my spot in front of our team monitors, shrugging at Marcus and others who wanted more information. I tried to concentrate on cars, not killers, but I was shaky. The pace car brought the field around, and the cars opting to pit streamed in. Sure enough, the Saleen came in for fuel and tires. Bruce relayed that information to Mike, and we all perked up. The Saleen would be faster on fresh rubber, but Mike would get around them by not pitting, and he might have enough left in his tires to hold them off until the end of the race. Racing strategy was always a gamble—that's what made it fun.

Mike was six cars ahead of the Saleen when the field got the signal for one lap to go. We were all preparing for the fight he'd have on his hands. When we went back to green, we'd have just twenty minutes of racing left. Hectic ones.

I was listening to Bruce give Mike a pep talk when I noticed the screen showing the live SPEED Channel feed was presenting a photo and video montage of Wade's career. We couldn't hear the sound, but we got the idea: lists of his accomplishments, wins, and championships with photos of him looking racy, tough, and happy. The photo they ended with was Wade and the whole Sandham Swift team, three years ago, when Mike started with them. In contrast to my experiences with Wade, he lit up the screen, smiling and drawing the eye of others in the shot with him. He looked full of life, laughing at the world and daring it to interfere with his plans.

Jack and Mike were in the photo, too, watching Wade. I was staggered by the poignancy of that shot. Wade in his element, at the center of everything. Jack and Mike. What was I going to do?

Chapter Fifty

Movement in my peripheral vision pulled me out of my morose thoughts. I turned to find Marcus also watching the SPEED Channel feed with the most extraordinary expression on his face. Anger. Beyond that. Rage.

Marcus saw me watching him and, after a blank moment of surprise, he unclenched. He leaned forward and put his hand on my shoulder again. I moved the headset off one ear to hear him. "Kate, I am so upset."

"Angry?"

"Yes. Angry at the loss of such a wonderful man. Devastated at the loss of my friend and mentor."

That made sense. "He was a very talented driver."

Marcus nodded, and his fingers tightened on my shoulder. "He was helping me so much, guiding me. I hoped to be of use to him, too…." The field thundered past, and the green flew.

I looked at Marcus, raising my eyebrows. I darted a glance to the monitors—damn it, what was happening with Mike? I searched for our car as Marcus put his lips near my ear and spoke again. "Contacts, networking, sponsorships, that sort of thing. I've put him in touch with some interesting people."

There was Mike. The Saleen had caught up! It was right behind him, trying to make a move, but Mike made a great block down the Back Straight and into West Bend.

Marcus was still talking. "Wade always spoke of us—him and me, that is—being able to drive together someday. He was working with me, helping me improve my driving, and we were getting close."

Mike swept down the front straight, and what Marcus said registered. I turned to him. "That's great. Where were you going to race together?"

"If I worked hard enough—which I've been doing—possibly driving the Corvette here."

I forgot about Mike and the Saleen in my surprise. "Great. As a third driver sometime?" I wasn't sure his abilities were up to the task.

"Perhaps."

I pulled away to see him smiling. "What about Mike?"

"From what I understand, they weren't getting along too well."

"I didn't know," I lied.

"They'd even come to blows recently. In fact, I'm surprised the police haven't questioned him." I detected an undertone of malice in his voice—anger on his former hero's behalf?—which wasn't easy to do, since we were still yelling through earplugs and headsets.

I hadn't responded, and Marcus went on. "I'd be happy to introduce you to some of the contacts I have who are looking for good sponsorship opportunities—they'd be extremely interested to meet you. Perhaps there'd be an opportunity in the future for you and me to drive together. I think Wade would have wanted that."

That was creepy. I gave him a half-hearted smile and a small nod. "We'll see what happens. Thanks." I pressed a hand to my radio headset and pasted an intent look on my face, as if I was hearing a transmission. I needed a break from Mr. Intensity.

Marcus waved a hand and headed down pit lane. I found Mike on the monitors and lived through a few corners with him as he bobbed, weaved, and passed other cars, staying in front of the Saleen. Go Mike! Oh, Mike. I kept forgetting…maybe because my image of the big, shaggy, teddy bear of a guy was hard to reconcile with the idea of a killer.

Aunt Tee walked around the corner of the pit box and held up a bottle of water, asking if I wanted it. I shook my head. Then I went after her and spoke next to her ear. "Aunt Tee, do you know if Mike rented a silver Taurus this weekend?"

She laughed. "Actually yes, we joked about it the other day because it had a Georgia plate, and he's from Georgia."

He'd been the first to leave. Before Jack and before the other Taurus. "And does he lose his temper much? Does he ever get violent?"

She started shaking her head before I got the words out. "No, Kate. I can't say never, because I've seen it once or twice. But he's the last one to lose his temper—everyone else will go bananas before Mike will. He'll only lose it if pressed well beyond the limits of anyone's endurance—only during a race, when his blood's up. I've never seen him turn a hair during a practice or qualifying. And never to anyone on the team—with the exception of Wade, and only to him once. After that, Mike told me he knew he had to hold his temper and defer to Wade, that he'd always have to, but it wasn't too hard."

This painted a different picture. "Did he and Wade ever come to blows?"

"Never."

"You're sure?"

"Absolutely."

I returned to the pit walkway and the monitors. Mike was still holding on, outrunning and blocking the Saleen for all he was worth. A thrill fluttered through me, electrifying me—we might take second!

I stomped on the idea. Anything and everything could happen in the last ten minutes, five minutes, or thirty seconds. I'd seen leading cars break in the last two minutes of a twenty-four-hour race. Nothing was over in a race until your car took the checkered flag.

Think about what Aunt Tee had said. They'd never fought, ever. I knew they'd fought the night Wade died—that was on the SPEED Channel's video—but Aunt Tee wouldn't know it.

I froze. How did Marcus know? Did Marcus have an in with SPEED Channel, like I did? Did Mike tell him? Did Wade tell him?

My stomach dropped to the vicinity of my feet. Or was he there?

My Nomex shirt was dry, and I was standing in the sun, but I shivered violently. Did Marcus know they'd come to blows because he'd witnessed it? I started to rearrange facts, ideas, suppositions, and wild guesses.

Marcus had his father's car Friday night. He said he'd gone to the China Inn Restaurant, but no one had seen him—at least not until later that night at The Boathouse. Not much of an alibi. But motive? Aunt Tee disapproved of him and thought him spoiled. Andy thought he was unstable. I couldn't think straight around him. No one else I'd talked to really knew him.

And there was that look of rage in response to the on-screen tribute. Plus the rumor Holly had heard about trouble in his relationship with Wade. Which finally prompted a more fundamental question: Why would Wade exert himself to be a mentor to anyone? It was easier to believe there'd been trouble between them than harmony.

I ran out of time to compose my face before I saw Marcus walking back toward me along the pits. He was watching me and smiling, shoulders back, head up, exuding confidence. Arrogance, maybe? I stared at him, feeling the underlying menace I hadn't recognized before.

Chapter Fifty-one

My face must have betrayed my thoughts as I sorted through my suspicions, because as far away as he was, Marcus' stride faltered. I was still numb with shock. I couldn't believe it. If he'd walked toward me with a puzzled and calm expression, it might have all blown over. But he didn't.

Instead, his jaw tightened, and he looked angry. Murderous, even. My suspicions coalesced at that moment into certainty. He walked toward me faster—no more amiable, sauntering stride, but a determined stalking.

I came alive with a start. This was a murderer? Not Jim, not Trent—not someone already safely in custody? The voice inside me couldn't help asking. One more look at him. Yes. This was a murderer four pit stalls away from me. One who knows I recognize who and what he is. I swallowed. I needed the cops, pronto.

I fixed a fake smile on my face and waved at him. I set down my headset and radio, mouthed "bathroom" to Aunt Tee, and headed for the exit at a jog—away from Marcus and toward the Series trailer in the paddock where I knew I could find the police. I kept telling myself Marcus wouldn't do anything to me in front of everyone at the race.

I exited the pits and discovered the monumental error I'd made. At this point in the race, the paddock wasn't bustling with life. It was mostly dismantled. In heading for the Series and police, I was taking myself away from all the people. I glanced back: Marcus was closer, jogging. Worse, he was only twenty feet away, and he'd gotten between me and people in the pits, so I couldn't change course. He'd also shed his pretty-boy expression and looked pissed-off and crazy. My heart leapt into my throat, and I started running.

That's when my plan fell apart. More correctly, when I fell over some cables on the ground and went down on one knee and two palms. Scrambling, feeling the future bruise on my kneecap and the fresh, gritty scrapes on my palms. I staggered to my feet and took another step, only to be snapped back. Marcus had grabbed one of the trailing arms of my firesuit, and he was reeling me in. I shouted. I yelled my head off, knowing no one would hear me. Still, I screamed in desperation, panic, and bone-deep fear. I didn't know what Marcus might do—looking back, I still don't know what he had in mind. But I didn't want any part of it.

I made life as difficult as possible for him. Through a roaring in my head, I wriggled, twisted, bucked, flailed, and kicked. I moved everything on my body that could possibly move to make it hard for him to get a grip on me. I wasn't going to go quietly or easily. I knew it was the end of the race, but where was a nosy ALMS official when I needed one? Anyone to come to my rescue? No one. They were all focused on the track.

Despite my movements, Marcus hooked an arm around my waist. I got more frantic. I snapped my head back and to the left, in the direction of his head, hoping for a good head butt, which didn't do anything but make me dizzy. Kick, Kate. Between the legs, dammit! Fight dirty. I tried to heave and kick to get him in the groin, but I was short enough and he was tall enough that I couldn't lift my feet or knees that far. I kept twisting and waving my right arm as high as possible to keep him from grabbing it and maybe land a lucky blow to the head. A fist, Kate! Swing for the crotch!

Ignoring how he had captured my left arm and was bending it up behind my back, I started swinging low with my right. After a few useless efforts, I tried something else. Pulling forward, I slumped down and pushed my right hand out, my arm almost straight. Then with every bit of strength I could gather, I threw my elbow back—and connected with his throat.

Marcus gave a choking cry and doubled over, releasing me. I couldn't hear the track noise for the hammering of my heart and the voice in my head shrieking "Run!" I took off without a backward glance, rounding the front corner of the paddock and heading for the ALMS compound—and ran smack into someone. We both went down on the grass in front of the trailer that sold tee-shirts and hats. I was panicked, sure Marcus was still coming after me, and I scrambled to my feet, tripping over whoever it was I'd bowled over and starting to run off again.

Hands grabbed at me. Voices spoke. I batted them away to keep running—and then the fog cleared. I'd found Detective Jolley, my father, and Stuart, who was picking himself up off the ground. I was safe.

"Stuart, sorry—but we've—I've—" I was incoherent, clutching his arm to help him stand up and pulling him to stand in front of me. "I—he's coming—"

Jolley stepped closer. "Kate?"

Stuart put an arm around my shoulder. My head knew I was safe, but my body didn't. I shook, feeling weak and hating it. I could have cried from relief.

"Kate," Stuart said. "What and who?"

I pointed a trembling finger just as Marcus dashed around the corner of the sales trailer and stopped short in front of us.

Stuart shifted to stand in front of me, a physical barrier. Jolley looked stern and turned to the newcomer.

Marcus made the best of things. He smiled at me, and I was afraid I was the only one to see it was more snarl than warmth. "You're OK, Kate? You seemed so upset. I thought I'd catch up with you and see if you were all right." He looked at Jolley and my father and nodded. "Since you're in capable hands, I'll just see you later." He gave a jaunty wave and turned to leave.

Jolley stepped forward and stopped him. "Just a minute, there, son. What's this about?"

Marcus turned back, grim smile still in place. "Why, I don't know. I saw Kate take off at a dead run from her pit stall, and I wanted to see if she was feeling all right."

"I was running from you, because you killed Wade!" I ducked behind Stuart at the look I got in response.

Marcus turned the smile to Jolley again. "She's obviously hysterical. I don't understand any of this. Wade was my dear friend."

They weren't going to believe him, were they? And let him get away? I knew I sounded as unhinged as he claimed, but I couldn't stop myself. "He was your friend until he dumped you. Then you killed him because he wasn't going to give you everything he'd promised."

Marcus' color rose, and his smile started to slip, even as he denied my accusations.

I was being cruel, and I didn't like it—but I remembered the panic of him grabbing me, and I spoke again. "Driving with Wade for Sandham Swift—he didn't mean that. Telling you that you were a good driver. He was lying to you! He lied to everyone. Wade promised you the world to get back at your father. Stringing you along. You couldn't handle it, could you? Your 'dear friend' was lying to you!"

Marcus cracked. His beautiful face turned ugly as his mouth twisted into a snarl and his eyes narrowed into slits. He lunged toward me, shouting, "You bitch!"

As soon as Marcus moved, Stuart swung me out of the way. My father helped Jolley grab Marcus, and Jolley cuffed his hands behind his back. Marcus still struggled to reach me, ranting. "Just like that lying shit, Wade. Think you can all use me? Lie to my face? Well, I showed him, and I'll show you, too."

Jolley got him subdued, though Marcus was red-faced, breathing heavily. Stuart led all of us to the ALMS trailer area, where Jolley held Marcus outside, waiting for an officer and a car to come down from the track entrance. I cowered inside the tented hospitality area. The last view I had of Marcus Trimble was through the back window of the cop car. The pretty face was blank; the eyes burned with anger. I shivered again.

"Kate?" Stuart held a chair out for me. I sat, and my father handed me a bottle of Gatorade. I'd forgotten he was there, and I looked at him in surprise. His expression was somber. Worried? Disapproving? I couldn't tell, and I didn't really care. I drank some of the sugary sports drink.

Jolley sat across from me. Stuart and my father sat to my right and left.

Stuart looked at his watch. "We've only got five minutes before the race ends, then just three minutes before it's chaos here." He gestured to the Winner's Circle, adjacent to the trailer. I raised my head. The race. I wondered where Mike was. It seemed a lifetime ago I'd been concerned with a podium finish—and a lifetime before that I'd been driving.

"We'll be quick for the moment," Jolley decided. "Kate, what happened?"

As Stuart turned aside occasionally to murmur into his secret agent radio, I explained, starting with reluctantly giving up on Jim and Trent as murder suspects, gossip and a video making me think Mike was the murderer, wondering about Jack, and finally realizing it was Marcus. Then, of course, my escape.

Jolley shook his head. "You were guessing?"

"Sort of. Everything I'd learned about Wade indicated he'd never do anything nice for anyone. He was mean and nasty to everyone, in return for real or imagined insults. It didn't make sense that he was being so generous and helpful to a guy who was younger, more attractive, and had more money. Even if Wade could drive better than Marcus could."

I could still see the hate on Marcus' face. "First I saw his expression. Then he knew something only Mike and Wade and the video guy knew—that I'd only heard five minutes before. And something clicked. I didn't believe it until he started coming after me. Then I ran, and he grabbed me." I shivered again. "That sealed the deal."

I wouldn't ever forget the terror of Marcus, someone who'd taken another person's life, grabbing me. The rage and murderous intent, aimed at me. I crossed my arms on the table and dropped my head on them. Took three deep breaths, which didn't help as much as they usually did. Tried not to weep with relief at being safe.

Stuart put a hand on my shoulder.

Jolley sighed. "You really shouldn't have done any of that, you know, Kate. You could have been hurt."

I sat up. "I got that. A little late. Sorry."

"Well, you flushed him out for us, but we were on our way to ask him some questions."

"You were? You knew for sure it wasn't Jim or Trent? Jack? Or Mike?"

"Jim and Trent both had solid alibis. We'd cleared Jack, who was here at the time, but only briefly to pick something up. Mike told us he'd been here, and though the circumstances were suggestive, we didn't seriously suspect him."

"You knew about Mike? But he didn't tell me—"

Jolley raised an eyebrow.

"Right. You're the police, not me."

He nodded. "We thought Marcus or his father might have a motive, because Paul Trimble's initials were in Wade's notebook so many times, and we were checking on the cars the guard at the front gate reported seeing. One of them matched Paul Trimble's, but we didn't know yet if Marcus could have been driving it."

"The second silver Taurus? I didn't know what they were driving, but he and his father were sharing, and Marcus had it that night."

"You found out about the cars, and you spoke with them about it?"

I frowned. "I didn't know they were snakes I was poking at."

Jolley looked exasperated, then amused. "You might yet make a good detective, Kate, you just need to be more careful—and have some training, maybe."

I summoned up a smile. "You're pretty sure now I didn't do it?"

He laughed. "I think you're off the hook. And thanks." He held out his hand for me to shake. "Let's not do this again."

Extra loud voices on the PA system and cheers from the crowds signaled the end of the race. I jumped up and ran to the large television monitor in the corner. All it showed was the overall winner, the LMP1, taking its victory lap and workers at each corner waving every flag in their arsenal. Usually, I loved that about the end of races. All those flags waving, corner workers saluting the drivers and teams. But today, damn it, I just wanted to know how we'd finished.

Chapter Fifty-two

Twenty minutes later I stood at the edge of the Winner's Circle, watching the presentation for the LMP1 prototypes, the biggest and fastest class.

The race had just ended when Paul Trimble arrived. Jolley had moved to intercept him and spoken with him quietly while Paul crumbled, his face in his hands. Shortly after that, Jolley led him away, with a nod over his shoulder for us.

That was the last I'd seen of Detective not-so-Jolley, though he'd called me a week later to tell me my theory was correct. Marcus was retrieving a new helmet from his car when he saw Mike and Wade fight about Wade trying to oust Mike from the team. Marcus saw Mike storm off and pressed Wade to deliver on his promise to add Marcus to the team. Wade laughed in Marcus' face, told him he had no talent and wouldn't ever be a real driver. Then told him to get lost.

Marcus couldn't face the disintegration of his dreams. Enraged at Wade's deception, Marcus had bashed Wade over the head with his new helmet and driven away, not knowing or caring if he was leaving Wade to die—but aware of the possibility. "In the hands of fate" was how Marcus put it, according to Jolley.

Furthermore, Jolley—after reprimanding me for not telling him about the incident—said Marcus copped to searching my room for Wade's notebook, stealing the photocopies and money, and leaving the note, as well as trying to get in a second time when he thought I was asleep. All because he thought he was in the notebook. That freaked me out all over again when I heard it. Marcus Trimble: as unstable as he was attractive.

Jolley also filled in the gaps of the Jim Siddons and Trent Maeda story. The two men had bonded months prior over not getting what each felt he deserved. Trent had a gambling and cash-flow problem and felt he should be a partner in Victor Delray's ECU business. Jim had a "not winning enough" problem and felt he should be getting better rides. Trent wanted payback, plus the kickback he'd get for driving customers to a competitor. Jim wanted the field cleared so he was more likely to win.

After Trent bullied a programmer at Delray to write the code, Jim got his cousin, the SPEED cameraman who looked like my high school friend, to activate it, disrupting the ECUs, affecting the balance of a car already at the limit in a corner, and often making them spin. Not long before his death, Wade discovered their secret and demanded they sabotage cars of his choosing also.

The day of the race, Delray's engineers and Stuart's IT guru had monitored networks and found the intruder. When the cops confronted the cameraman, he pointed to Trent. When Trent was arrested, he fingered Jim. The cops, Series, and Victor Delray had all the proof they needed of Jim and Trent's cheating and sabotage, but the duo was in the clear for murder. I'd discovered that for myself.

Just after Paul and Jolley had left the ALMS area after the race, Jack stormed in, Mike, Tom, and Aunt Tee trailing behind him. He'd been breathing fire and had torn into me, the irresponsible temporary driver who'd run off and left the team. I'd taken it, feeling if I didn't deserve that dressing-down, I deserved censure for other actions throughout the weekend—like suspecting him briefly of murder. But when Stuart stepped in and explained, Jack turned off the anger in the blink of an eye and regarded me silently. Then he'd put his hands on my shoulders. "Sorry, kid. You did good." He'd given me a quick hug and yelled at us to get to the Winner's Circle, pronto.

I'd followed, but only after speaking with two people.

My father approached me as Jack left. "Katherine," he'd begun, looking at his hands. "I was worried."

I still didn't want that the responsibility or burden. But I'd looked at him and seen something of myself for the first time. I put my hand on his arm. "Call me Kate. I'm not ready just yet, but we'll talk someday."

He'd nodded at me, smiled, and walked away.

I'd stopped in front of Stuart before I left. "Stuart."

He held up a finger and spoke into his radio.

I waited.

"Sorry, Kate. A little cleanup."

"Listen, thanks. For being there."

He raised an eyebrow at me.

"Don't give me that look. Thanks for catching me and warning me and having my back."

He kept on with the look.

I threw my hands up. "Whatever. See you later."

Stuart burst out laughing and grabbed my arm, stopping me. "Sorry, Kate, it's so much fun to wind you up."

It was my turn to look at him blankly. Stuart Telarday with a sense of humor? That was proof: on this Fourth of July weekend, the entire world had officially turned on its head.

Stuart put his hands on my shoulders. "Kate. You're tough and smart. Just keep being careful." He gave me a quick, firm kiss on the lips, and I went numb.

He released me. "And you're a hell of a racecar driver."

The emcee snapped me out of my reverie when he finished with the LMP2 class presentations and started to call up the GT1s. Our class.

"In third place, after a hard fought battle: the Vance Racing Saleen!" The two drivers and team owner trooped up to the podium, accepted their trophies, posed for photos, and moved to the third step.

"In second place, after a weekend of tragedy and new beginnings: the Sandham Swift Corvette! Mike Munroe and gutsy newcomer, Kate Reilly!"

Smiling so wide my cheeks hurt, I followed Mike to the top step of the podium, waving at the cheering crowd. We accepted our trophies and held them over our heads for the photos. Then we moved to the second step as the Number 63 factory Corvette was called up for first place.

I looked at Mike beside me and smiled. Someday, I'd have to explain to him that for a few awful minutes, I'd suspected him of murder. But that would keep.

The first place presentation was done, and we each shook hands with every other driver. Then we posed for photos with trophies overhead.

Next, Jack was called up for a trophy given to the top private team. It was during those photos that Jack looked down at me. "Whadddya say, kid? Want to do this for the rest of the season with us?"

He laughed at my shock and elation. "Good. Enjoy the champagne."

It began to sink in as we took the group shot with the flying confetti. I'd done it. Proven myself. Gotten a ride. I looked at the red, white, and blue paper squares flying through the air and thought I was flying higher than any of them.

My euphoria broke loose the second Mike sprayed me with champagne. I'd been slow to grab my bottle, but I made up for it. I picked it up and chugged a few mouthfuls, shoving my arms in the air and yelling. That was my moment. My celebration. My incredible ride, my outrageous weekend, my promising season.

Then I shook the hell out of the bottle and did my best to douse the five guys there with me on the podium. I might be female, but I was no pushover.

To receive a free catalog of Poisoned Pen Press titles, please contact us in one of the following ways:

Phone: 1-800-421-3976
Facsimile: 1-480-949-1707
Email: info@poisonedpenpress.com
Website: www.poisonedpenpress.com

Poisoned Pen Press
6962 E. First Ave. Ste. 103
Scottsdale, AZ 85251